The Reluctant Debutante

Book One of the Cotillion Ball Series

Becky Lower

Heather,
Happy Reading!
Hope you enjoy the series.
Becky Lower

The Reluctant Debutante
Copyright © 2012 by Becky Louise Lower
Prairie Rose Publications Edition 2018
Cover Design Livia Reasoner
Prairie Rose Publications
www.prairierosepublications.com

Prairie Rose
Publications

This is a work of fiction. The characters, incidents, and dialogues are products of the author's imagination and are not to be construed as real.

Dedication

I'd like to thank my critique groups and all the other dedicated early readers who help me get it right.

Chapter One

New York City, February 1855

Ginger Fitzpatrick was in a pickle, that much was certain.

Her mother took her by surprise at breakfast by announcing to the family that Ginger would participate in the Cotillion ball two months hence. While her younger sisters squealed in excitement, Ginger couldn't find her voice to object to her mother's idea. She knew she must, considering that her father was known to grant every wish his wife had, but Ginger could only stare in confusion. And that wasn't the worst of it.

"George," her mother stated calmly to her father, "you must relieve Ginger of her duties at the bank so I have time to teach her the rules of etiquette she'll need for a full season of events. Dear Lord, I have only a couple months to cram in everything."

Astonished and stunned, Ginger turned to her father, hanging onto a thread of hope that her valued involvement at the bank would save her.

"Let me think about the best way to handle the shift in responsibility, darling. I'll make sure Ginger is free by the end of the week." He glanced at Ginger's stupefied expression and reached across the table for her hand. "Perhaps we could also offer a reward of some kind. Possibly a trip to St. Louis if she gets through the season without incident?"

He had actually smiled over the breakfast table at her. As if the allure of a trip would make everything all right.

Now, Ginger strode down the hallway of the bank to talk to her father before he could continue the discussion with her mother. She had always been able to convince him of anything, if she wanted it strongly enough. After all, he allowed her to work alongside him at the bank, which went against all the rules of society, and a woman's place in it. She stopped briefly at the window overlooking the street, watching the snow falling outside. It clung to the red bricks of the ornate bank building, and she longed to be as capricious as one of the snowflakes. Instead she had to present a strong argument to make her father see the folly in her mother's latest idea.

She stopped in front of his office door and smoothed her long gray skirt. Brushing her hand over her quivering stomach, she knocked.

Ginger was certain she could right this ship and make her father see things her way. At his gruff reply to enter, she inhaled deeply. She was going to have to tread softly to get out of this predicament.

"Papa, may I further discuss Mother's idea with you?"

"Yes, of course, my dear. But you know by now that once your mother makes up her mind, it's best to go along with it."

Ginger glanced at him as her voice quavered. "But, Papa..."

Her father merely raised a perfectly arched eyebrow.

Hmmm, the trembling voice trick usually worked. She'd have to try a different tactic. *Tears, maybe?* She hated resorting to something as totally feminine as sobbing.

She cleared her throat and started again. "You are aware, are you not, of my worth here at the bank?"

With a sigh her father laid down his fountain pen and began to reposition his sleeves, which had been rolled up to avoid staining them with ink. "Your mother's decision for you to participate in the Cotillion has nothing to do with your abilities at the bank. I'm well aware of your contributions. Now, do you want to talk about what's really at issue here?"

Ginger attempted to regain her calm and to remember the precise arguments she'd planned to present. "You obviously believe dangling a trip to St. Louis before me will be enough to get me through the Cotillion ball and the season Mother wants for me. And I agree with part of your logic. I should go to St. Louis, but without any strings attached. Basil has written to me, Papa, and told me about the West. Men there are more open-minded and not so stringent about what a woman can and cannot do."

She began to pace around the office as she warmed to her subject. "Basil might be able to charm little old ladies into depositing their life savings into our bank, but I can make their money work for the good of the bank—and for them—at the same time." She turned to face her father. "Please, Papa, I am begging you to let me go now before the season begins. I must get away from stuffy old New York City. Our clients in St. Louis need me now, not in the fall."

"I agree it would be a good move for you, my child, even though I have full confidence in your brother's ability to run the St. Louis branch. Your mother is the one who needs convincing. And you know what she considers important."

"The Cotillion," Ginger whispered her reply, as tears began to well up in her eyes, unbidden. She knew she was losing this argument. Nonetheless, she persevered. "Who thought up this wretched ball idea, anyway? I will feel like a piece of horseflesh at the Cotillion, being paraded about like a fine filly and up for grabs to the highest bidder." She stamped her foot in frustration.

Ginger watched her father's jaw flex. He was not an imposing man, but he had a will of iron. He needed a strong constitution to have successfully raised nine children and to have provided a privileged life for all of them. So, when she saw the movement of his jaw, she knew what it meant. Things were not going to go her way.

George Fitzpatrick stood and placed a comforting hand on her shoulder. "I know you despise the idea, but you are not the only one concerned here. You have your sisters to consider. You know how high society works in New York, especially when the Astors and Schemerhorns are involved. If a precedent is not set this year for our family, your sisters will bear the brunt of it."

"But, Papa… "

He raised a hand to silence her. "They will not be invited to any future balls and will miss their opportunities to be presented to society, all because of your selfish acts. I doubt you want to carry that mantle on your shoulders for the rest of your days, do you?" He smiled to soften his words.

"Papa, you can't be serious! My actions really won't have any impact on my sisters, will they?"

He nodded in affirmation, and his eyes flashed at her. "Should you choose not to participate, or to make life difficult for your mother, there will be no trip to St. Louis for you, now or in the future. You'll stay at our home here in New York with only your sisters for company, who will be forever known as the 'Spinster Fitzpatricks.' Won't you have a lovely existence to look forward to?"

She dropped her head and softly asked, "So exactly what do I have to do?"

George raised both hands in front of him, ticking off each item on his fingers. "You will do whatever your mother wants. Obviously, there will be fittings for new clothes between now and the ball in April, so you will be relieved of your duties here at the bank as of Friday. You will also limit the amount of time you spend with that rabble-rouser, Amelia Bloomer. Your mother will spend the next two months giving you the etiquette lessons you've been avoiding for years, in preparation for the high social season of balls, parties, plays, and operas. You will participate in each and every event, and will present yourself with dignity in accordance with our family's position in society. You will appear to have a good time, even if it means you will be putting on an act every night. All this will be over and done with by August, and if you have done everything to your mother's satisfaction, I will allow you to go to St. Louis. But only if you still want to."

"Of course I'll still want to."

Ginger gulped as a tear slid down her cheek. She turned her face away, hoping her father wouldn't notice her moist eyes. He had never been this unreasonable before. For one of only a few times in her life, she could not cajole him into doing her bidding. She brushed the tear away, smoothed her skirt, and then turned back to him, meeting his tough yet tender gaze.

"All right then. I will do what you ask, Papa, to appease Mother and for the sake of my sisters. But I want you to know I will hate every moment of it. I will be marking off the days between now and the end of August when I can escape the bonds of conventional society and move to the frontier. I will never become any man's chattel."

Her father smiled. "That's all I ask for, Ginger. Peace and harmony on the home front. Thank you for being so agreeable." His voice held more than a touch of irony.

She closed her father's door and walked slowly back to her office. Ginger stood in the middle of the small room and placed her hands on her hips. Under her breath she muttered, "Bless my bloomers, I've been outfoxed."

New York City, April 1855

Sitting astride his most stubborn horse and leading another, Joseph Lafontaine attempted to navigate both horses through the wide and bustling cobblestone streets. He had successfully managed to move four of his six horses from the railroad car to the livery already; these were the last—and most troublesome—of the group. Broadway was the main boulevard in this part of town, and Joseph kept an eye out not only for buggies and carts, but also for pedestrians crossing from one side of the street to the other—a perilous act.

His hometown of St. Louis might be raucous, especially down by the docks on the Mississippi River, but New York, and particularly this street, was beyond his wildest imagination. Now, if he could just get these last horses to the livery—only one more block—and then find his way to his hotel, he would breathe a whole lot easier.

Loud noises up ahead caught his attention. Several policemen were attempting to break up a group of people in the street. Joseph scanned the area, searching for a clear route around the chaos. Despite what his good friend Basil Fitzpatrick said about how affluent New Yorkers would accept him as a French-Canadian, the Indian half of his background was barely tolerated in St. Louis—and would be much less so in New York City. He wanted to avoid confrontation while he was here in this strange town. Staying away from the authorities was probably a wise decision, and he was not eager to test the waters on his first day here. He should have remembered to tie his shoulder-length dark straight hair back into a queue, to lessen the look of his ancestry. *Too late now,* he thought as he focused on handling the horses under his command.

"You there! Stop!" Police shouted as women scattered in different directions in front of him, some of them screaming as they rushed by.

Joseph halted his horses in the middle of the clogged street and watched. A number of ladies ran directly in front of him, but he noticed only one. Her brown hair was shot through with dark red, reminiscent of a chestnut roan. Rather than being tied up in a chignon, her hair floated around her face in glorious disarray. The waist-length locks billowed out behind her as she ran. Joseph watched as she skittered just out of reach of the approaching policemen, glancing about for a means of escape. If this was what New York women were like, Joseph was glad he had agreed to come east.

She skirted around his horses to the opposite side of the fray. *Very clever*, Joseph noted, *using my horses as a shield from the authorities.* He began walking his charges, which now included the woman, slowly forward through the chaos.

Joseph nodded to her, acknowledging her presence. "Is this street always so crowded?" he asked the woman.

"It's always busy with the open-air vendors on the sidewalks and all the street traffic, but not usually like this. My friend and I just staged a rally, which is why the police are here."

"You are safe now, with me. Just follow my lead."

The woman nodded her head in agreement, shielding her eyes from the sun as she walked beside the horses and stared up at him. Her other hand reached out to touch the withers of the horse nearest her.

"How handsome," she said, not moving her eyes from Joseph's face.

"The black?"

The woman seemed a bit startled, but continued to look at him. Joseph pointed with his chin to the dark horse nearest to her. "The black horse beside you. He is my favorite, too. I may have to keep that one. Take care, though. These horses are barely broken, and they are skittish in all this noise."

At that very moment, a dog ran into the street, startling the black horse, and he lunged. Joseph held the reins tightly in his hands, but the horse reared. Joseph concentrated on controlling his horse and lost sight of the attractive woman. When the horse finally quieted, Joseph scanned the street for her again. She had backed off from the horse's side, and was rubbing her forearm.

"Did he hurt you?"

"He only bumped me slightly. It was my fault for getting too close. I'll be fine."

Together, they made their way up the street. When they reached the livery, Joseph dropped from the horse's bare back in a fluid motion and stood in front of the woman he had shielded from the police. He noticed she had a light dusting of freckles sprinkled across the bridge of her nose. And even though she was not as small as she appeared to be when he was astride the horse, his large frame still towered over her.

"This is as far as I am going, miss. We have come a fair distance. You should be safe now."

"Thank you for helping me evade the police." The woman did not move from the livery doors as she craned her neck to look him squarely in the eyes.

"I think you would have managed quite well on your own, but I am glad I was able to help." They stood in the door of the livery, their eyes locked for another long moment until one of the horses nickered.

Joseph gathered the horses' reins again tightly in his hands. "I must take care of my horses. They will settle down once they are comfortable."

Joseph spent the next few minutes getting the two horses safely into their stalls. When he finished, he was mildly disappointed to see that the bewitching woman had vanished. In a town the size of this New York City, he doubted if their paths would ever cross again.

But a man could hope.

Chapter Two

Ginger rushed into the parlor, her hair loose around her face, still not quite able to catch her breath. She watched as her mother raised her eyes from the current edition of *Godey's Lady's Book*, which showed the latest fashions from France, and her sisters glanced up from their embroidery.

"Land's sake, child, where have you been? The twins and I have been waiting for you for nearly an hour!"

"I'm sorry I'm late, Mother. I promised Amelia Bloomer I'd join her today." Ginger decided to leave out the part about the rally and the dash away from the police. "We met Elizabeth Blackwell. Can you imagine? What an inspiration she is for young women – the first female physician in this country! How could I possibly have missed it?"

"That doesn't explain why your hairpins are missing. And what did you do to your forearm? It's all red." Charlotte Fitzpatrick stood up from her chair and moved to her daughter's side to inspect the injury more closely. "It will probably bruise. We'll need a lot of Pear's Almond Bloom to cover it up for the ball tomorrow evening. Whatever did you do?"

"I—uh, I was running back here so I wouldn't be late and I bumped into a parked carriage, that's all. It's just a small bruise, Mother, and it will be mostly covered by my gloves."

Ginger gazed down at the lower half of her arm, which still ached from the bump she'd received from the black horse. But it was the memory of the horse's owner that made her stomach flip over. She hadn't been referring to the black horse when she blurted out her outrageous comment about how handsome he was. She still could not believe she had spoken those words out loud.

"We have so much to do to get you ready for your big night, Ginger. I'll have no more of your shenanigans," Charlotte said in despair as she ran her hands lightly over her dark blonde hair. "What was Annie Schemerhorn thinking of when she came up with the idea of a fancy ball to introduce our daughters into society?"

Ginger picked up her needlework and settled into a chair opposite her sisters. Embroidery was yet another accomplishment Ginger needed to perfect in accordance with society's expectations of how well-bred ladies should spend their afternoons. From the looks of the wretched piece of cloth, her poor mother had an uphill battle on her hands if Ginger was ever to become an accomplished embroiderer. Ginger glanced at her mother in surprise and decided to take advantage of the moment to press home her objection to the ridiculous dance one last time.

"I'd be happy to bow out of the Cotillion, Mother. It's a stupid concept anyway. I know it's been a tradition in Europe for years, but this is America and we don't have any kings to whom we need an introduction! So, if it's providing a hardship for us, I don't see why we should bother."

Charlotte stared at her unruly daughter. "Sitting out the Cotillion is not an option. We both know the only way to ignore an invitation from Annie Schemerhorn is if you are in confinement while expecting a child or mourning the loss of a loved one. This is a huge event for New York society, and we will attend and claim our rightful place."

The twins, Jasmine and Heather, glanced up from their fine stitches.

Jasmine asked, "How can you not be excited about the Cotillion?"

Heather replied, "Just thinking about meeting my future

husband at the ball makes me shiver all over." She sighed dreamily.

Ginger glanced at her sisters and smiled. "I somehow doubt either of you will be looking for husbands for too long when it's your turn. You're both lovely girls."

Ginger spent a moment comparing the twins' beauty to her own appearance. Ginger's light brown hair had these damnable reddish highlights, whereas the girls' had such rich brunette coloring. Ginger's eyes were an ordinary green, but the twins had beautiful dark brown eyes. And, curse of curses, Ginger had freckles. She was afraid the twins won hands down in the comparison.

Jasmine glanced at her older sister again. "Did you say you were with Amelia Bloomer today? Isn't she the one who wears trousers in public? And holds public rallies in the streets?"

"They're called bloomers. At least they are now, since Amelia Bloomer is such an advocate of them. They are a long undergarment divided into pants and cuffed at the ankle and are usually worn under a short skirt. The feeling of freeing your legs from the layers of petticoats and fabric is absolutely exhilarating."

Ginger chose to ignore Jasmine's second question. The less said about public rallies, the better. She continued. "It's all part of the suffragette movement. Some of us want more from life than to chain ourselves to a man and do nothing more than bear and raise his progeny. We want to be on an equal footing. That's why my work at the bank is so important."

"You'll change your mind when you meet the right man," Jasmine replied, sure in her knowledge that a husband was the only goal worth achieving. "There must be no better feeling in the world than to know you will be cared for and made to feel safe from everything life throws at you."

"I won't say it's beyond the realm of possibility, but I don't think just sitting back and having children while my husband produces the income is going to be enough for me. I'm good at making money, and I want nothing more right now than to further my position at the bank."

Charlotte glanced up from her fashion book. "For now, Ginger, I want no more talk of the bank or Amelia Bloomer. You are to nap, relax, and prepare yourself for the biggest night of your life. I'll have no more of your wild ways. Tomorrow night will be monumental, and I want nothing to go wrong."

Chapter Three

The new maid Charlotte Fitzpatrick had employed for the season made a few final adjustments to Ginger's hair. Each big curl on the top of her head was anchored with a pearl pin and a trio of sausage curls draped softly over her left shoulder.

"Colleen, I love it!" Ginger took the hand mirror and studied her new up-do from a variety of angles. "Who would have ever thought my hair could behave like this? You truly have a gift."

Colleen beamed at the praise. "You have the most lovely hair to work with, my wee lass, so it's easy to create a fetching hairstyle. It's such a rich shade of brown, with these reddish highlights. I love how it gleams in the light of the candles."

"I do sometimes wish my hair was the same color as yours, though. You have the most striking, gorgeous flame-red locks. I just have a bit of red. It's like my hair couldn't make up its mind."

"'Tis the Irish in me, miss," Colleen proclaimed proudly, flashing her lively blue eyes as she gave one final touch to Ginger's hairdo. "But your hair coloring is beautiful. Now that we're done with the hair, I'll help you into your dress. Of all nights, you don't want to be late tonight."

Jasmine and Heather came flouncing into her room to examine their sister's hair.

"Oh, Ginger, you look so grown up! Colleen, I want you to attend to me and Heather next year when it's our season," Jasmine said with a touch of envy as she ran her hand over her brunette curls.

"Let's see the dress Mother has been talking about for weeks," Heather chimed in.

Together, they held their breath until Colleen stripped away the final wrappings and, with a flourish, revealed the white-and-cream gown. Jasmine and Heather sighed.

Ginger smiled at their enthusiasm. "Soon enough, it will be your turn. I'd give anything to trade places with you tonight."

They stared at her in dismay.

Heather gasped, "You truly don't want to go to the ball? Oh, Ginger, it should be the most important night of your life!"

Jasmine added. "Don't you feel like you're about to step into your adulthood? Just think, you might meet your future husband tonight. I'm so jealous."

Ginger smiled, ruefully. "It's just not that big of an event to me, for goodness' sake. It's a silly ball, and I have to get elaborately made up for it to please Mother. That's all. I have no more aspirations of meeting a husband tonight than I do when I walk down the street." Briefly, she thought again of the tall, handsome stranger who'd helped her on the street the previous afternoon. Shooing away the memory, she said to her sisters, "You're making much more of the Cotillion than you should."

"Well, I know that we can barely wait until next year. Just think, Heather, men will be anxious for our attention every night that we're out. And we will have hordes of invitations to events—not like this year, when we're not invited anywhere." Jasmine threw herself on the bed in a show of anguish.

"Hush, now, you two sprites," Colleen intervened. "Soon enough, it will be your time. Don't be upsetting Miss Ginger on her special night. You've seen the gown, now leave us be so I can finish getting her dressed. You can come back one final time to see her right before she leaves."

♦◊♦

Charlotte had tears in her eyes as she perused her daughter. "Why, Ginger, you're lovely."

"You sound so surprised, Mother." Ginger smiled at their

reflections in the mirror. "With all the money this gown and everything under it cost, I'd better look good!"

Even though her words were a bit sharp, Ginger's fingers continued to fondle the luscious silk faille of her dress. Unaccustomed as she was to using her body to attract notice, even she could appreciate how much her appearance was enhanced by the quality of the workmanship in this gown. The skirt of her dress had three tiers of flounces, each a shade darker than the one above, ending with a patterned border of light cream silk. The low décolletage allowed a glimpse of her bosom. She had lost count of the numerous crinolines holding the skirt out in a dramatic wide fashion. The petticoats and the silk created a pleasant, gentle noise as she turned to study the back of the dress in the mirror.

Charlotte watched as her daughter preened. "I see the Pear's Almond Bloom worked well enough in covering your bruise. Don't forget your gloves, dear. And your fan. Your father has the carriage waiting for us. Come now, stop fussing."

Charlotte ran a gentle hand over Ginger's gleaming hair. "Colleen did a wonderful job tonight. I've never seen your hair lovelier."

She reached for her daughter's hands. "Thank you, Ginger, for doing this. I know how much you've despised the idea of this Cotillion and the high season to come. I truly appreciate the way you have carried yourself without so much as a whimper during all the shopping trips and fittings you've been made to endure."

Ginger rested her head lightly on her mother's shoulder. "Although most of it was more tedious than I had ever imagined, I didn't really mind, because I was spending time with you. Have you heard yet from Basil? Has he made it home from St. Louis in time to attend tonight's ball?"

"Yes, he sent word yesterday afternoon that he and his friend have arrived, and will meet us tonight at the ball."

"Why on Earth did he not come over last night?" Ginger asked.

"I asked him not to disturb you until this evening. I didn't want you to get terribly excited yesterday. Tonight will be soon enough. Basil is here now, and will be in attendance at your special night. You'll see him soon enough. Besides, it's only right for your father and eldest brother to lead you down the staircase tonight at the Cotillion."

"And into the horde of men who will want to jockey for a position on my dance card."

"Oh, Ginger, don't consider it as a foot race. These young men are only interested in getting to know you better. Most of them have their mothers to blame, too, for participating in the ball. I bet they are every bit as nervous as you are."

Ginger bristled at the comment. "I am not nervous, Mother. I am merely anxious to get this over with, so I can put it behind me and move to St. Louis as Papa promised. If I could, I would fill up my dance card with the males in my family. Then, there would be no time for any of the other men at the ball."

Unless maybe I could have the good fortune of dancing with the marvelous, tall man who helped me escape the police yesterday afternoon, Ginger thought.

She glanced in the mirror one final time and smoothed her dress again, placing her fingers lightly on her stomach. Well, all right. She could admit to herself, if not to her mother, she was maybe a little nervous. Taking a deep breath, she finally exited the room.

Her anxiety mounted when her father helped her into the carriage and her mother straightened her gown. When they pulled up in front of the beautiful Metropolitan Hotel, Ginger caught sight of her best friend Elizabeth Martin and several other friends alighting from their carriages in their gorgeous gowns. Excitement finally overtook her nervousness and she began to look forward to the night ahead.

Chapter Four

Ginger watched as her father helped Halwyn straighten his white cravat, and then correct his own. He flattened the tails at the back of his long formal tailcoat and then turned back to his son.

"We resemble a couple of matching bookends with Ginger in between us." George's laughter helped dispel some of their collective nervousness before he turned to his daughter and offered her his arm.

"Are you ready?" He smiled at Ginger as she fiddled with her skirt.

"Yes, let's get this over with," she grinned up at him. "Then I can mark it off the list, and I'll be one day closer to St. Louis."

"There's my girl. Or should I say, young lady? When did you grow up, anyway, Ginger?"

"It's the dress, Papa."

"No, it's you. My little girl is all grown up and ready for a husband."

"Oh, my, not you too? Mother keeps telling me the same thing. I can find my own way in this world without dancing attendance on a husband."

"You'll change your mind when the right man comes along, believe me. But speaking of dancing, you are next in line to go down the stairs. Come along, Halwyn. Let's take our places."

Charlotte had struggled for two months to impart years of essential etiquette into a compressed amount of time. Ginger now knew how to perform a deep curtsy, how to embroider, albeit not well, and the proper way to delicately pour a cup of tea. She had a difficult time seeing the relevance of these accomplishments and she often expressed her discontent to her father, who calmly listened to her complaints. But in the end, she learned what was expected of her.

They arranged themselves at the top of the staircase. Ginger took a deep breath, threw her shoulders back, and held her head high. When her name was called and she moved forward to be introduced to New York's wealthiest families, Halwyn and her father stepped back. She bowed her head and sank into the deep curtsy she had been practicing for months. Quite unexpectedly, tears formed in her eyes as she stared out over the crowd who clapped for her. The soft light of a thousand candles made her eyes sparkle. She blinked the sudden tears away, rose from her curtsy, and stood proudly as Halwyn and George Fitzpatrick resumed their places on either side of her. As one, they descended the wide marble stairs of the grand ballroom.

Ginger's dance card filled quickly, as some of the most eligible bachelors claimed their places. The noise of the crowd intensified as more people arrived at the ball and joined in the chatter. The gentlemen surrounding Ginger and Elizabeth kept raising their voices higher and higher, adding to the din. Ginger thought these fine men looked like gnats flying around her body, getting in her face, causing her to squint at them and shoo them away.

Ginger and Elizabeth covered their ears to partially drown out the clamor. Suddenly, everything went blissfully quiet. The air stirred with excitement. The only sound came from the swishing of fabric as people turned to find out the cause of the break in their conversations.

"What is it?" Ginger whispered to Elizabeth. She grabbed the arm of a gentleman near her, who gazed down at her adoringly. She stood on tiptoe, trying to peer over the shoulders of everyone in the room. Then she found her answer. At the landing of the stairs stood two tall muscular gentlemen with broad shoulders and narrow waists, both impeccably dressed in formal attire. One of the men intently searched the room, looking for someone. As his eyes met Ginger's, he grinned and waved.

"Basil!" She swatted away the hands of the men around her and made her way through the crowded room to him.

Ginger launched herself into Basil's arms, and kissed him on both cheeks. She was aware that every eye in the ballroom watched them with interest, but she threw convention to the wind and welcomed her older brother warmly as she had always done.

"Oh, I've missed you so. When did you arrive? How handsome you are in your formal wear. Have you grown taller in the past year?"

Laughing, Basil took her hand. "One question at a time, Sis. But before we get to the answers, I must introduce you to my good friend from St. Louis." He clapped his other hand on the shoulder of the man standing next to him. "Ginger, I'd like you to meet Joseph Lafontaine."

Ginger turned her attention to her brother's friend. The dark chocolate eyes of the elegant man made her breath catch in her throat. *It was him!* The mysterious, handsome man on horseback whom she'd met on Broadway during the protest! He raised an eyebrow in recognition before he bowed low and kissed her hand.

"Enchanté, Mademoiselle."

Little pinpricks of delight raced up her arm from the spot where his lips had touched her hand. She could feel each of his fingers as they enveloped hers—even through the cloth of her glove. Her heart pounded faster, as it had the previous day when she watched him handling his horses with quiet authority. She was mesmerized then, and she was now.

She gazed up at him, noting his sculpted cheekbones, tanned skin, and hair that was black as night. The air suddenly felt as though it had been sucked from the room. She could not catch her breath, and when she opened her mouth to reply, no sound emerged. She swayed on her feet. Basil wrapped an arm around her.

"Whoa, there. I think you need some air. Come, Joseph. Let's take her out to the balcony."

Just what I need, Ginger chided herself, feeling foolish for exhibiting such a display of weakness. *To go into the semi-darkness with such a magnificent man. I've never met a man so strong, handsome, and well-muscled. He is so unlike any other man here tonight. He definitely does not remind me of a gnat!*

As they reached the balcony, Elizabeth hurried to her friend's side. "Ginger, are you all right? I saw you run up the staircase and then suddenly you were being rushed outside!"

Ginger smiled. "I just got a little emotional over the return of my favorite brother. Surely, you recognize Basil under all these fine clothes, do you not?"

Elizabeth turned toward the man standing beside Ginger, peering at him closely. "Is it truly you, Bas? You look so different from a year ago."

Basil grabbed Elizabeth in a big bear hug, sweeping her off her feet. "Lizzie-Beth! I would not have recognized you either, except for your tell-tale blonde hair. You and Ginger certainly have blossomed into beautiful young ladies. You both are lovely tonight."

When he released her from his hold and placed her feet back on the floor, she turned to the other member of the group. "You must be Basil's secret friend. He has taunted us for weeks with your promised appearance, yet we have been told nothing about your background."

Basil turned to the man beside him. "Let me make the proper introductions. This is Joseph Lafontaine. He joined me on the trip to New York because he has some horses to sell. And, because he's such a big lug, he acted as my bodyguard during the trip, as I was transporting some holdings from the bank. I could think of no better man to help me than this imposing French-Canadian."

After acknowledging Joseph briefly, Elizabeth returned her gaze to Basil, and began to bombard him with questions about life in the West.

Charlotte and George Fitzpatrick arrived on the balcony and halted the girl's deluge. They hugged and kissed Basil, whom they hadn't seen in more than a year. As they all returned to the ballroom, the orchestra struck up a waltz.

Ginger pulled on her brother's arm. "Dance with me, and tell me all about your life on the frontier."

"Ginger, dear, you already have a young man on your dance card for this number, and he's coming this way right now," Charlotte reminded her.

"Oh, bother," Ginger replied under her breath, as the gentleman who had claimed the dance appeared by her side. "Don't you dare leave, Basil. I want to talk to you some more about St. Louis." She turned to her dance partner. "Mr. Gray, I'd like to re-introduce you to my long-lost brother Basil. Bas, you remember Quentin Gray, don't you?"

The two men shook hands just as the music began.

Ginger took the hand of her suitor and glided out onto the floor with him. Her mother had pounded the rules of society into her head over the last two months so, in keeping with her etiquette training, she smiled up at her partner encouragingly. She watched Quentin Gray's Adam's apple bob before he spoke.

"So, Miss Fitzpatrick, remind me again. How long has it been since you've seen your brother?"

"He's been in the West for over a year. He looks completely different. I mean, he was always charming and handsome, but he was rather pasty-faced and not so rugged..."

Her voice tapered off when she realized she was describing

the same characteristics that Quentin possessed. She cleared her throat and decided to wait for him to ask the next question instead of digging a deeper hole for herself. She glanced around the room while waiting for Quentin to pick up the reins of the conversation, and spied Joseph standing beside Basil.

Her gaze flickered from Joseph to Quentin as she assessed the two men. Joseph had beautiful light brown skin; Quentin's pale white flesh hadn't seen sun in months. Joseph's strong black eyebrows arched above eyes that were like pools of dark chocolate; Quentin's unruly brows met in the middle over pale blue nondescript eyes. Joseph had lips she wanted to kiss; Quentin's protruding lips made her skin crawl. Joseph's touch left her weak in the knees; Quentin's sweaty palm made her want to pull back. Her head swiveled back and forth as Quentin made no further attempt at conversation and merely moved through the steps of the dance. She thought the waltz would never end. The moment the music stopped, Quentin deposited Ginger back at her mother's side and quickly walked away.

Ginger turned to her mother in exasperation. "I don't care if my dance card is filled for the night. I want to talk to Basil. It's been forever since we've seen each other. And we should welcome his friend into our midst, don't you think?"

"You will have all night to talk to your brother, not to mention the next few months during his visit here with us. It is such a coup to have your card filled so early in the evening of your first ball and you need to honor the requests of these fine gentlemen. Glance around the room and see all the women who are sitting by the walls, unable to find a partner for even one dance. You are an extremely lucky, young lady, and I won't have any of your foolishness. However, you're right. We should welcome Mr. Lafontaine. I will let you have one dance with him. He'll replace Halwyn on your dance card."

A shiver crept up Ginger's spine. A dance with Joseph! She ducked her head as she replied, not wanting her mother to see her excitement. She willed her voice to be calm as well. "As you wish, Mother. One dance with Mr. Lafontaine. Basil can wait."

Charlotte and Ginger approached the two men at the edge of the family gathering, Charlotte spoke, "Mr. Lafontaine, we wish to welcome you to our town and into our family. I told Ginger she can have one dance with you this evening."

Joseph and Basil exchanged glances before Basil smiled slyly. "You'd best do what our mother says, Joseph, if you value your life."

Joseph took Ginger's hand, and they took their place among the other couples on the ballroom floor. The crowd hushed as the strings of the violin and harp plucked out a gentle rhythm. As the dancers began moving around the floor, Joseph placed one hand on Ginger's waist. She gulped and put her hand on his shoulder. And promptly tripped over her feet.

She glanced up at him, horrified. He smiled slightly.

"Calm down, *ma petite*. I will not bite. Just follow my lead." His voice was soothing.

She took a deep breath and raised her eyes to him again. "That's exactly what you told me when we met yesterday. 'Just follow my lead.'"

"And by doing so you were spared the experience of going to jail and missing your ball. How is your arm?"

"Oh, it's fine. A little Pear's Almond Bloom was all it took to hide the bruising."

"And your friend? Have you heard of her fate?"

"No, I read in the paper that she had been arrested, but I haven't had a moment to myself to talk to her. She gets arrested frequently," Ginger said with a smile.

Ginger settled into the dance, allowing Joseph to set the pace and the steps. After a few moments, her heart stopped galloping and she risked glancing at him. He was staring straight ahead and didn't catch her gaze. She lowered her eyes again. What was it about this man that set her heart racing so wildly? Why could she not even steal a glance at him without her legs turning to jelly, making her trip foolishly all over herself? Why could she not think of one thing to say to him, whereas she could take to a soapbox in support of the rights of women and talk to anyone who happened to be willing to listen?

She'd overheard her sisters giggling to each other about how watching gentlemen made them feel, but men just didn't affect her in the same manner. She cleared her throat as her mother's rules of etiquette floated through her mind, screaming at her to say something to him, anything.

"This is quite elaborate attire you are wearing tonight."

Joseph smiled slightly. "Basil told me to pack my good suit, because we were going dancing."

"How did you and my brother meet?"

"We met in a bar on his first day in St. Louis. I will let him tell you the full story."

He gazed into her eyes, and her throat suddenly went dry. She ran her tongue lightly over her lips and watched as Joseph's eyes followed her tongue's movement. His observation rattled her even more, as she attempted conversation again.

"Did you tell Basil about our previous meeting?"

"No."

"Why not?"

"I assumed you were involved in something you were not supposed to be doing, and telling your brother about it would have tipped your hand. It will remain our secret."

"Oh." She fell quiet as she digested this information. Now they were sharing not only a dance, but a secret! She shivered in delight. "I appreciate your concern for my privacy. And, I apologize for nearly fainting when I saw you earlier. You can imagine the scenario that raced through my head. I thought for certain my involvement in the rally was about to be exposed. But, I'm puzzled at my reaction. I've never in my life fainted."

"It is a big night for you, so it is understandable." His steps were sure as he moved her around the floor.

"Are the horses I saw you with yesterday some of the ones you've brought to sell? I'd like to look at them more closely."

Joseph raised one of his magnificent eyebrows at her. "What do you know of horseflesh?"

"I know how to ride. I've been doing so my entire life."

"And that makes you a qualified expert in the field?"

"I didn't say I was an expert, for heaven's sake," she replied in exasperation. "I was merely making polite conversation."

"You know, as I was watching you on the dance floor before with your partner, I began to compare you to horseflesh myself."

Ginger bristled. "How dare you!" She tried to pull her hand away from his, but he held her tightly in place.

"Yes, I thought you were like a thoroughbred, finely boned and high-spirited, and he was a plough horse holding you back."

"Oh." Ginger inhaled sharply at his words. She was still struggling for breath as the last strains of the song ended, and he led her back to her family. When Joseph released her hand at the edge of the dance floor, her body deflated like a balloon that had suddenly lost all of its air.

The night continued with Basil and now Joseph, taking to the dance floor as a crowd of eager young ladies circled around them, all with dance cards that suddenly had empty spaces on them. Ginger performed her duty of dancing with each and every man who had claimed a place on her card. She tried to keep track of whom Joseph danced with, but even though he towered over most everyone else in the room, she still lost sight of him in the crowd frequently. She felt dizzy from all the swirling about.

♦◊♦

Several hours later, Joseph watched as the Fitzpatrick family gathered together when the party began to wind down. Basil wandered over to him as he left the dance floor.

"So what do you think of my boisterous family?"

"They are not so different from my people, Bas. A bit pale, perhaps, but nothing else."

"You've been pretty quiet all evening. I thought perhaps meeting most of my family at once was too much. They do have a tendency to overwhelm people."

"Not at all. They are enjoyable."

"Well, we have managed to keep Ginger on her best behavior for one night, anyway. I know my parents are breathing sighs of relief. Thank you, my good friend, for providing a diversion."

"Judging from the crush of people who spoke to us, I would say you are the diversion, not me. Do you know every last person in New York? They all seemed to be eager to welcome you home."

"I'm the excuse for everyone coming to greet us. You're the reason. All these young ladies wanted to dance with you—you're someone new in their midst. I can't wait to read the society pages in tomorrow's paper."

"Let us hope these young ladies never find out their dance partner was an Indian. I still think inviting me to come with you to New York was a huge mistake."

Chapter Five

Basil let himself into the family brownstone the next afternoon and followed the sounds of voices and tinkling china cups into the parlor. On every table throughout the house sat a bouquet of flowers. Their cloying scent made Basil groan inwardly. So many flowers meant one of two things: either someone had just died, or Ginger's debut into society was an overwhelming success. No one he knew had passed away; therefore, the flowers meant he would have his hands full keeping Ginger and her various suitors in check for the remainder of the season. That made his mission today even more crucial.

As he strode into the room, all conversation stopped and every pair of eyes in the parlor turned to him. He wore his usual western casual attire. His duster coat was draped over his shoulders and open in the front to reveal a pair of deerskin trousers. The pants hugged his thighs, which had turned into hard muscle during his year in the West. He spent his free time with Joseph, learning how to round up and break horses. Well-worn boots came up to his knees. His mother smiled and set down her teacup.

"Basil, you're here!" She stood and gave him a peck on the cheek. "Did you bring your things so you can move back into your room and get out of the hotel where you spent last night? And where is your friend, Mr. Lafontaine?"

Basil gave his mother a hug, lifting her off her feet. She giggled like a girl. Several of the young ladies who had been talking to Ginger sighed.

"Joseph is at the livery, taking care of his horses. Some men have already expressed interest in them, so he's adamant that he should be the only one to care for them and make certain they are in prime form."

Ginger hugged her brother too, and tugged on his sleeve. "You and Mr. Lafontaine will be moving in here for the season, though, won't you?"

"I don't know, Ginger. Joseph and I may not want Mother to know what we're doing in the evenings." Basil grinned at his mother.

The girls in the room sighed again. They were all Ginger's closest friends, along with their mothers, and were discussing last night's Cotillion in elaborate detail.

Basil asked, "Mother, may we talk privately for a moment? Is Father in his library?"

Charlotte glanced around the room at her guests, seemingly befuddled at this lapse in etiquette. "I suppose so. Ginger, please take over the hostess duties for me, if you don't mind."

"But…"

"Hush, Ginger. I'll only be a minute. Colleen can help you with the tea," Charlotte replied as the Irish maid wheeled a fresh teacart into the room.

Basil turned back to the group. "Ladies, please forgive me for interrupting your tea party." He bowed at the waist, but raised his eyes, taking in each face.

He followed his mother down the hall and into the library. George Fitzpatrick was sitting behind his large mahogany desk, smoking his pipe. His slippered feet were propped up on the desk and he was engrossed in the newspaper. He folded the paper down over his knuckles and gazed above it as Charlotte and Basil entered. His blue eyes crinkled in pleasure at seeing his son.

"To what do I owe this unexpected visit?"

"I know it's your day off from the bank, Father, but I feel I must discuss a matter of the bank's business with you most urgently. I have to be totally honest with you and Mother before another evening's entertainment begins. I may have inadvertently stirred up a potential disaster for us."

They stared at him quizzically. He cleared his throat.

"The reason I came to you today is to tell you about Joseph. I'm afraid I left out some vital information about him." Noticing that he now had both parents' rapt attention, he hurried the conversation along. "He's part Indian, common enough in St. Louis, but not on the streets of New York."

His father set the paper down on the desktop. "You mean to tell me you brought an Indian home with you? A savage?"

Basil grimaced. "Indian, yes. Savage, no." He stared at his father. "Joseph is half Indian. His father is as white as you are."

He studied his mother, whose eyes had grown enormous. She clutched her hand to her heart and collapsed in the nearest chair.

"Oh, dear. Ginger's reputation will now most certainly be ruined. For goodness' sake, I'm the one who gave her permission to dance with him last night. And, after she danced with him, so did many other young ladies. Oh, my gracious, their reputations will all be jeopardized, too!" She glared at her son. "Why did you not warn me?"

"Because I don't think of him as an Indian. At least, not most of the time. His father is a French-Canadian, his mother is an Ojibwa from Canada, and the family is a mix of both cultures. The entire family can read, write, and speak English, as well as Ojibwa and French. When I first set foot in St. Louis, I stopped into a tavern to get a meal. I must have been viewed as an easy target, being a soft young man just off the train from back East. Several men hauled me outside and began to attack me."

He listened to his mother's quick intake of breath.

"You never told us you had encountered trouble."

"Well, I was just a bit embarrassed about it, since I hadn't been in St. Louis more than a couple of hours. I felt certain if

Father discovered what had happened to me he'd force me to return without ever opening the bank."

George smiled and took up his pipe. "You were wise not to tell us, son, because I probably would have brought you back home. But, please do continue."

"They were doing a good job of pummeling me. I'm quite certain they would not have stopped until I was dead, or at least mortally wounded, and they had stolen what money I had on me. And then, suddenly, they ceased and disappeared. Joseph only had to raise his voice and they ran off. He helped me to my feet and we've become best friends. I thought bringing his horses here would open up new business for him, and I owe him that much at least for saving my life. And, I'm proud to say our bank funded his family's recent excursion into the West to capture ponies for the settlers and to purchase saddles."

His father's eyebrows shot up. "He's Tall Feather Enterprises?"

"One and the same. They named the business after his mother, Mary Tall Feather. I thought he'd be able to pass as a French-Canadian among New Yorkers, but I wasn't thinking clearly about the ramifications of bringing him to the ball last night. The situation kind of got out of control as one lady after another danced with him—I never expected so many of them to line up for a dance. So you see, I've put you into a precarious predicament. If anyone were to find out his true identity it would damage our standing in the community, for we have tattered so many ladies' reputations by allowing them to dance with him. If you want us to turn around and head back to St. Louis right now, we will."

Charlotte took a deep breath and held her hand to the side of her head. "Let me think for a moment. I know there's got to be a way to fix this." She studied the floor. Suddenly, her face brightened and she stood up. "You will not turn tail and run back to St. Louis, Basil." She tapped his arm with her fan. "Even though we have done something totally inappropriate, your retreat would only compound the problem. After all, Mr. Lafontaine is one of our bank's clients, a point we must bear in mind. But, you are correct in thinking we would be ostracized from New York society if we let his true heritage be known. What we must do is merely alter the story a bit so as not to put a blight on the reputations of all those fine young ladies. And ourselves."

She began to pace the room as her plans took shape, her small feet tapping out a quick staccato rhythm, matching her thinking.

"How many of our friends have come into contact with a true French-Canadian? I can't imagine it would be many. So, we, the Fitzpatricks, pillars of society that we are, are quite excited to have a real, live exotic French-Canadian in our midst. We'll be an even bigger hit this season. Ginger will be invited everywhere with you and Mr. Lafontaine accompanying her." She clapped her hands together in excitement.

"It would be unseemly for him to stay here in our house, of course, because we do have young women living here. So the two of you will keep your rooms at the hotel. But he will be welcome into our midst. We'll host a dinner to celebrate your return from the frontier, and Mr. Lafontaine's presence among us, here at the house, in a few days. Oh, I need to confer with Ginger on whom to invite. I'm quite certain it will be the most talked-about event of the week. Annie Schemerhorn will be so jealous. Do you suppose our cook can prepare some Chateaubriand?"

Charlotte ceased her excited ramblings as she noticed both men staring at her. "What? Is Chateaubriand not appropriate for a Frenchman? I can't very well serve bison and expect to keep his Indian identity secret, can I?"

Basil and George locked eyes, and then simultaneously broke into fits of laughter. George came around the desk to embrace his wife. "Although I'm not thrilled with having to dupe our peers for an entire season, I knew you'd figure out a way to manage it. Leave it to you to take what could have been a devastating situation and make it the most sought after social event of the week!"

Basil put his arm around her. "Thanks, Mother. I knew I could count on you."

Charlotte wrapped her arm around his waist. "You'll have dinner with the family tonight, both you and your friend. But the big affair will be the formal dinner. You do have some appropriate clothing to wear, I hope?" She ran her hand down the sleeve of his duster.

Basil's smile was easy. "Yes, Mother. I do run a bank after all, even if it is in St. Louis. I will make certain both Joseph and I are properly attired for your big event, although I'm more excited about dinner with the family tonight. Shall we say eight o'clock?"

"It will be a challenge to keep his true identity a secret from the children. You know how inquisitive they are. Jasmine and Heather are sure to pester him to death. And Ginger seemed to enjoy their dance last night. I only hope he doesn't let something slip out about his Indian mother."

"Somehow, Mother, I don't think Joseph will be the one we need to worry about. He's accustomed to keeping things to himself. It's the three of us I'm concerned about." He shifted his gaze from his mother to his father. "This will be interesting."

Chapter Six

In the livery, Joseph ran the currycomb over his spirited black steed. His soothing words and repetitive motions put the animal at ease.

"Calm down, *mon petit*. I will not bite." He realized with a start he was repeating the same words to the horse he had used the previous evening to calm Ginger on the dance floor.

In a way it made sense, because he had thought of little else since his dance with her. Joseph had not been joking when he had compared her to a fine filly. What he neglected to tell her was the horse came up short in the comparison. He ran his hand over the horse's flank, thinking of the swell of Ginger's hips as his hand had encircled her waist. He found his hands could nearly span her waist, she was so small. But not delicate. She was a spitfire, not a fragile blossom. She would do well in St. Louis should she choose to move there. Unlike New York City, his hometown had plenty of fresh air, and hard work was necessary.

He sighed as he imagined her, smiling as she turned her face up toward the sun while walking along the streets of St. Louis. With the firm resolve he had developed over the years, he called a halt to his line of thought. No, it was best she stay in the privileged atmosphere of New York's high society. It was what she was accustomed to, and he must not interfere with her parents' and Basil's wish to find her a suitable partner, despite his own feelings.

He rested his head on the horse's neck in an attempt to get his mind off the wisp of a woman he had met only two days ago—was it only two days? Basil was expecting him to help protect Ginger's reputation and to keep her focused on the goal of finding a husband during the upcoming season. Joseph did not think she needed any help in handling herself. That was part of what fascinated him. Her calm assurance and self-confidence.

Joseph remembered his conversation with Basil, when they began to talk about the trip. Basil first convinced him that he could make better money selling his horses to wealthy New Yorkers, an idea Joseph latched onto immediately. But when Basil presented his harebrained scheme that Joseph pass himself off as a French-Canadian and hide his Indian heritage from Basil's family and friends, Joseph had strongly objected.

He still did not think it wise to present himself as something other than what he was. Though equally proud of both sides of his heritage, Joseph was smart enough to know most of society did not share his feelings. He thought the better approach would be to stay in the background while Basil had his fun with his family, but Basil had insisted.

Still filled with apprehension, Joseph had agreed to the trip, hoping Basil was correct in both his assumptions—that he could sell his horses at a huge profit and that his Indian blood could be masked. Then, on his first day in New York City, he met the woman he had been dreaming about all his life and it was his hard luck to discover she was Basil's sister. He could still smell her scent. The lilac fragrance clung to his clothing. And just as her scent stayed with him, so did images of her body, and her upturned mouth.

Basil might be his best friend, but if he even guessed the path Joseph's thoughts were taking he would turn his back on Joseph and demand he leave town immediately. They might lay down their lives for each other, but Joseph knew Basil would never consider him good enough for his sister.

Even knowing where his treacherous thoughts might lead, he could not still them. He remembered again watching her tongue gliding over her lips last night. Such an innocent gesture on her part, displaying her nervousness, but it had aroused aching flames of desire in him. He was thankful she had not noticed the swelling in his dress trousers as he painfully completed the dance with her. To feel her supple body moving in time with him was almost more than he could bear. He stifled a groan at the memory.

He must contain himself. He *could* contain himself. Being part Indian and part white man, he was used to straddling both cultures and did so by keeping his thoughts to himself. The first time he had come home from town with a black eye, which he received while defending himself against the taunts of "half-breed," his mother decided to teach him everything about the Indian side of his heritage. He and his brothers spent long summers with Joseph's grandfather, who still lived in an Ojibwa settlement in Canada, and Joseph learned about their proud bloodlines and traditions. His grandfather was a wise man among his peers, able to interpret dreams and see visions of what was to come.

Joseph knew the jeers and torment his father endured over the years for taking an Indian woman as a wife. And he knew of all the people in town who had shunned him and tormented him and his brothers over the years because they were half Indian. It had made him stronger and developed his steely control over his emotions. His reputation as someone others did not want to cross grew in the town.

His father took great pains to teach his children how to speak English as well as his native French, and to read and write—all necessary tools for making a living in a changing world. Still, the white part of his heritage was always the lesser part when it came to acceptance in the community. Basil had been the only white man to show him an honest friendship. He would not let this mere slip of a girl destroy it. After all, he had not even set eyes upon her before a few days ago.

He knew Basil had gone to the Fitzpatrick home to discuss Joseph's heritage with his parents and to question if they should leave town now. After all, most of the ladies of society had performed a serious breach of etiquette by dancing with him last night, unaware of his true heritage. He shook his head, unable to understand the ways of these New Yorkers.

Neither he nor Basil had expected Joseph would be as popular on the dance floor as he had become. It was all due to Basil's mother allowing Ginger to dance the first dance with him, and having Basil's family accept him wholeheartedly. Would they tell Ginger of his background or keep it a secret? For her sake as well as his, he hoped they would tell her, so she would know to keep her distance from him.

Perhaps it would be best to leave today, and to avoid further involvement with New York's upper classes, the Fitzpatricks, and especially Ginger. He controlled the impulse to jump on his horse and run away from this danger. In his gut, he knew any rational person would do exactly that. But ever since he had agreed to this trip with Basil he had not been thinking logically.

He put away the currycomb and walked back to the hotel to find Basil. He was anxious to hear how the Fitzpatricks had reacted to the news, and if he was no longer welcome in their midst. Despite his better judgment, he hoped for one family dinner with them so he could spend the evening etching Ginger's lovely face into his memory. He'd leave town tomorrow.

Chapter Seven

With mixed feelings, Joseph looked forward anxiously to dinner at the Fitzpatrick home that evening and he could tell it was going to be a noisy and relaxed affair. As the house staff made the final preparations in the large dining room, the family gathered in the parlor.

All nine children were in attendance. One at a time, they introduced themselves to Joseph and welcomed their brother back into their midst. They each regaled Basil with tales of their accomplishments in the year since he'd seen them last. Basil was making a noisy show of measuring each of the children against himself to see how much they had grown during his absence.

Joseph removed a slim cigar from his shirt pocket, and raised a questioning eyebrow to Mr. Fitzpatrick.

"Mrs. Fitzpatrick put her foot down yesterday and has now confined my smoking to the library," he said. "You're welcome to use it, Joseph. Down the hall, first door on the right."

"Thank you, sir."

He exited the noisy parlor and took solace in a sumptuous leather chair in the quiet library. He lit his cigar and closed his eyes, enjoying the smell of the leather-bound books, the burning tobacco, and the small crackling fire.

With his senses honed from years of hunting game and horses in the West, his body tensed almost imperceptibly when the door to the library opened quietly. He did not open his eyes, but let his other senses take over. He listened to the soft rustle of fabric as the person came closer to him. When the air shifted as the person raised a hand in front of his face, his dark eyes flew open. His hand darted out and ensnared the smaller one before it could touch him.

Jasmine, or Heather—one of Basil's twin sisters—let out a small scream. "Unhand me, please, Mr. Lafontaine." She struggled against him. As he continued to hold her hand and stare at her, she opted for coyness. "But then again, if you are finding my hand hard to release, I'll have to see what else you like." Her brown eyes twinkled as she lowered her head, making her lips more accessible.

Joseph released her hand a bit roughly and stood up, towering over her. "Little girl, you do not know what you are doing. The next time you try tempting a man, he may not be as honorable."

"I am not a girl!" Her eyes flashed as she confronted him. "Heather's the one who is still holding on to her youth. I am seventeen, which qualifies me as a woman, and you are certainly the most handsome man we've had in this house in a long time."

"Respectable women do not throw themselves at a man."

"Humph. Perhaps you're not so handsome after all. I don't need to throw myself at a man to get his attention. How dare you even suggest that!"

She turned and flounced out of the room, her tattered dignity falling around her.

Joseph sighed and took his seat again. He smiled to himself at her awkward attempt at seduction. Girls, be they white, French, or Indian, all went through the same painful stages to adulthood, it seemed. He puffed on the cigar and the pleasant odors of the library once again began to relax him.

When the door opened a second time, his eyes were wide open as Jasmine, or Heather, returned to the room. She let herself in quickly, and turned, surprised to find him watching her.

"Oh, my goodness." She fluttered near the doorway.

"You are back again?" Joseph once again stood.

"What? Oh, do you mean Jasmine has been here? She said she was going to our bedroom for a new hair ribbon!"

"You are the other one, then? Why are *you* here?"

They stared at each other in confusion for several heartbeats. Then both watched the door open yet a third time. Ginger hurried through the slight opening at the doorway with a backward glance to the hall and then turned to see both of them watching her, adding to the confusion in the room.

"Heather, what are you doing here?"

"One could ask the same of you, Ginger."

"I was coming here to, ah, to tell Joseph we are ready for dinner. Stop avoiding my question. What are you doing here?"

"I...I was about to do the same thing. Tell Joseph it's time for dinner. But, doing so hasn't made me blush, as you are."

Ginger's blush became even more pronounced. She put a hand to her cheek as if to check the heat. "Go on with you, Heather. And Joseph, it is time to eat."

Heather quickly backed out of the room.

Joseph's gaze warmed as he raked his eyes over Ginger. Her color deepened, but she stood unwavering in front of him. Their eyes locked and neither spoke for a long moment. Then Ginger dropped her eyes and cleared her throat.

"I apologize for my sisters' behavior."

"You are not to blame for their silliness. They are just trying out the wings of adulthood, as all young ladies do."

"I hope they weren't too obnoxious to you. I fear there's more to come over dinner. Prepare yourself to be assaulted by questions from them."

"And you? Do you have any questions for me?"

Ginger's eyes moved back to Joseph's warm brown ones. She gazed at him for another long moment. She had a million questions for him, but nothing that was anywhere close to being appropriate. Were his lips as soft as they looked? Was his chest as hard and muscled as it appeared to be? She wracked her brain, unable to think of anything suitable to say. Then, she turned and fled the room.

♦◊♦

The roast chicken with its sage stuffing, sweet potatoes, garden vegetables, and luscious hot flaky rolls gave off pleasant aromas. Basil looked at the spread of food with delight.

"I've missed home-cooked meals. Life on the frontier is very different from New York City. Normally, if I can't beg a meal at the Lafontaine home, Joseph and I eat at a roadhouse. It can't begin to compare with the supper you've laid out, Mother."

"Don't they have chickens in the West?" Rosemary, one of the younger girls, asked.

"No, you silly girl," replied Valerian, the youngest boy. "They only eat buffalo and deer on the frontier."

Basil laughed and threw his hands up. "One at a time, please. We'll be here all night, and will answer every one of your questions. Yes, Rosemary, we do have chickens in the West, along with buffalo and venison. But nothing can compare with a meal that Mother is involved in." Basil smacked his lips in appreciation. "Now, who's next with a question? I think it would be Saffron."

The youngest Fitzpatrick child, Saffron was only seven, with a head full of yellow curls that matched her name. Her doll had a seat at the table with her. She smiled brightly at Basil.

"Are there any little girls in St. Louis I could play with?"

"I have a sister about your age, Saffron," Joseph replied. "Her name is Elise."

Saffron's blue eyes grew large as she surveyed the tall, dark man who was her brother's friend. "Really? Does she look like you?"

"A little bit. Her eyes are the same color as mine, but her hair is more the color of yours. And she has a doll, too."

"Could we have a tea party for our dolls together?" Saffron's expression was very serious.

Joseph held back his smile. "I am certain Elise and her doll would welcome your company. You are lucky to have so many sisters. Elise has only brothers."

Jasmine and Heather sighed in unison. These twins were due to be introduced into society next season. If his experience with them in the parlor was any indication, Joseph thought these two young ladies were much like two-year-old horses about to race for the first time. They were poised and ready, chomping at the bit to make their entrances. Joseph smiled inwardly as he thought of the havoc they would cause to next year's crop of unknowing suitors. Unlike Ginger, who despised every moment of her time in the spotlight.

"How many brothers do you have?" Jasmine, or Heather, asked.

They really are copies of each other, so my confusion in the library was not unwarranted, Joseph thought as he compared their skin tone, their brunette hair, and their brown eyes. Both sets of eyes were eagerly trained on him right now.

"I have three brothers, all younger than me."

"Oooh. What are their names and ages?" Heather or Jasmine cooed.

"There is Gaston, who is now twenty-three, Raoul is nineteen, and Etienne is the youngest brother at sixteen."

"Umm, Gaston...Raoul," they rolled the French names over their tongues. "Do they look like you?"

Joseph was glad Basil had enlisted his help only for Ginger.

"Gaston looks more like our father. He has hair the color of sand, sort of like Valerian's." Joseph nodded at Basil's youngest brother and smiled. "But Gaston's eyes are green."

"Raoul and I look most like each other, except he's not as tall as I am. He is living in Canada right now, with our grandfather."

"Raoul sounds perfect, if he looks like you, Joseph," Jasmine, or Heather, replied breathlessly.

"Jasmine, stop making a fool of yourself," Ginger said hotly. "I know it's hard for you to rein yourself in, but please try."

"Now, daughters, stop your squabbling. We have a guest this evening, so do try to be on your best behavior." Charlotte scolded her children. "Please go on, Joseph. Tell us about your youngest brother, Etienne."

"Etienne likes to think he's a man already. He's got my coloring and he will be tall when he completes his growth. But in many ways, he's still a child. He needs to spend a summer with our grandfather."

Joseph smiled to himself as he thought of how his brothers would react if the twins were within range. Gaston might be quietly interested in one or the other, but Raoul would bite their heads off and scorn their frivolous behavior. And, as for Etienne...he would be so flattered by all the attention, he would not know what to do with himself. *No, it would be best if my brothers and these troublesome young ladies never cross paths.*

Ginger tapped her finger against her lips thoughtfully. "Tell me why, Joseph, your name is not French like the other members of your family?"

Joseph looked up at her in mild surprise. He hadn't realized she'd been paying close attention to the conversation. "Actually, Joseph is a French name as well, if you place the accent on the second syllable. But I also was given this name because it was the name of my father's partner in the fur trade. He was Joseph Pearce, a British man who taught my father how to speak and read the English language. And, according to my father, Joseph Pearce was one of the most fierce and loyal men in the country."

Ginger's eyes glimmered with excitement. "He sounds like a most interesting gentleman. Does he live close to you in Missouri?"

"Sadly, Joseph Pearce died the year I was born. A bear

protecting her cub attacked him. According to my father's story, he, my mother, and I were with Joseph when the bear charged. Joseph wanted to protect me and my mother, so he gave his life to the bear in order for us to escape."

"He died doing the same thing as the mother bear. He was protecting his cub." Ginger put her hand over her heart, as tears glistened her eyes.

Joseph nodded in silent agreement as the table fell quiet, momentarily. Soon, though, the animated group began prying answers from Basil about his life on the frontier.

Although the Fitzpatricks all treated him amicably, Joseph felt a bit overwhelmed meeting the entire large family all at once. He'd already met Halwyn and Mr. and Mrs. Fitzpatrick the previous evening. However, the younger children hadn't been there. Halwyn, as the eldest son, shouldered the mantle of responsibility for the family business with great dignity, and a bit of stuffiness, Joseph thought. He could relate, being the eldest in a brood of four brothers and a young sister.

But Joseph liked to enjoy himself as well, with people such as Basil. From the looks of Halwyn, it had been some time since he'd had any fun. His manner was as formal as his evening attire. Halwyn spoke to the children with quiet dignity, not with the air of jocular familiarity Basil used. More than once during dinner, Halwyn lifted an eyebrow in the direction of an unruly child, who immediately corrected his behavior. Pepper, his twin sister, was the opposite of Halwyn, and not just in her coloring. She and her husband, Michael, sat close together, and their hands frequently drifting toward one another during the meal. Pepper's black hair blended with Michael's dark brown waves as their heads touched when they whispered to each other. Pepper was prettily pregnant with their first child. Joseph watched their interplay throughout the evening, with a feeling akin to envy.

"So, Joseph, tell me a bit about this family business of yours our bank has invested in," Halwyn turned toward him.

"We catch wild horses out on the plains west of St. Louis about twice a year, break them, and then sell them. It is a small operation started by my father, but it keeps all of us busy."

"To whom do you sell the horses?" Ginger asked.

"Right now, we are only selling to individuals who need new mounts. Mostly pioneers on the wagon trains heading further west, or men going to look for the gold fields. But soon, the city of St. Louis will have horse-drawn trolleys, and we will supply all the horses for the city to use."

Ginger's eyes gleamed as she digested this information. Halwyn noticed and grimaced.

"Now you've done it, Joseph. Ginger's trying to think of more ways you could wring a profit from your business. There will be no stopping her now."

Joseph caught Ginger's gratified look as Halwyn whispered "oof," and he assumed her foot had connected with poor Halwyn's shin. Their interaction reminded him of himself and his brothers, and it made him smile.

Ginger replied, "For your information, Halwyn, and unlike you, I do have other interests outside of the bank. I just met Elizabeth Blackwell the other day. She's the first female doctor in the United States, and she and her sister want to open a school here in the city for women to receive medical training. I've decided to take the introductory class she's offering this spring."

"Not if it cuts into your social obligations, young lady," Charlotte reprimanded. "You know what is really important this year."

It was Ginger's turn to grimace. "Yes, Mother. As if I could forget."

Joseph decided to take some of the pressure off by asking his own question.

"Mrs. Fitzpatrick, your children are all named for herbs and spices, I have noticed."

Charlotte took her husband's hand as she replied. "Yes, we did get carried away, it seems. We began with Halwyn, which is a family name on George's side. When we discovered it is also a name for salt, it seemed only fitting we name his twin Pepper, especially with her head of black hair, and Halwyn was so blond. We gave Basil his name just because we thought it was a nice name for a man. But then our next child appeared, with her mop of reddish-brown hair, and we had no choice but to name her Ginger."

Charlotte patted Ginger's finely coiffed hair, and then ran her hand down her daughter's arm. The small pause in her speech gave Joseph the chance to glance at Ginger. She wore a dinner dress with a wide skirt; its green velvet set off her emerald eyes and complemented her skin and hair. The sleeves were flounced in three sets of gathers, ending in wide cuffs of Maltese lace that fell from her elbows to just above her wrists. Her fine dress mattered little to Joseph—she could be dressed in a feed sack and still take his breath away. He reluctantly turned his attention back to Mrs. Fitzpatrick, who continued with her discussion of her children's names.

"Then came more twins, who were identical girls, so we gave them each the name of a scented herb—Jasmine and Heather." The girls giggled at their mother's words. "By then were locked into this pattern, and we finished off our children with Rosemary, Valerian, and Saffron."

The younger children preened as their names were announced. Rosemary was a quiet girl with lovely gray eyes, which perfectly matched her soft gray velvet dress, trimmed in a black braid that encircled her tiny waist and shoulders. Charlotte had insisted Rosemary put her book away before joining the dinner party. Otherwise, Joseph was convinced she would have read through the entire meal without lifting her lovely eyes to the family gathering once. A few times, she looked at Joseph covertly, but the minute his glance moved her way, she quickly ducked her head.

Valerian was the next in line, a raucous boy of thirteen. Even though this dinner was a family gathering, Joseph noticed Charlotte had sent Val back to the washroom to scrub his hands and face again before sitting down to the meal. His sandy brown hair and big brown eyes did remind him of his own brother, Gaston.

Charlotte asked her guest, "Do you miss your family, Joseph?"

He looked up at her, surprised she could read his thoughts. His years of living between two cultures had taught him to conceal his feelings, but Mrs. Fitzpatrick had cut through his mask.

"Yes, I do, for most of us still live and work together on the ranch. Raoul is the only one to have left home so far. We have many family dinners just like this in our household. But I have enjoyed this evening and getting to know your large and lively family."

He let his gaze fall on each person, and rewarded himself by letting his last look be of Ginger. Her eyes lifted as he looked at her and she ran her tongue nervously over her lips, like she had the previous evening. He mentally groaned as he watched her, and his body involuntarily clenched.

Chapter Eight

The next evening, the long table in the Fitzpatrick's formal dining room gleamed in readiness. The head housekeeper gave the place settings for twenty people a final adjustment. Charlotte positioned the centerpiece of flowers and stood back to make certain everything was in place. She clapped her hands together softly as she surveyed the room, looking for any dust motes at the corners or dried food on the silverware that may have escaped the housekeeper's attention. Everything was done, except to seat the guests to her liking.

Charlotte had been correct when she predicted this dinner would become the most talked-about event of the week. Not one person on the guest list had begged off. Now she just had to arrange the guests at the table, so as not to offend anyone.

She picked up the name placards and placed the ones she didn't need to think about first. George at the head of the table, herself at the foot. Annie Schemerhorn and her husband were on either side of George. Cornelius Vanderbilt, the railroad tycoon and his wife Sophia, were next. Her husband's best friend, Charles Gray, the wealthy industrialist who was also Quentin's father, and his wife, Eleanor, were seated on either side of Charlotte.

Then, she placed Basil, Joseph, Ginger, Halwyn, Pepper and Michael, Ginger's best friend Elizabeth Martin, and Elizabeth's parents. The three remaining spots at the table were assigned to Ginger's most ardent suitors—Quentin Gray; Richard Douglas, second son of an English duke who was visiting America; and William Davenport, an officer in the Army who had recently graduated from West Point.

Last night's meal was all about family. Following the meal, Ginger exposed the twins' bad behavior as she told Charlotte of their visits to see Joseph in the library. As the twins cried and howled at Ginger for tattling on them, Charlotte wrung her hands in dismay. She might have problems with Ginger this year, but she would *really* have her hands full next year, trying to keep her lively twin daughters in line for an entire social season, and keep the threat of scandal from their door.

Already, the danger of censure from society loomed close by, should Joseph's true identity be discovered. She hoped she, George, and Basil could put it to rest this evening with some fine acting.

Charlotte thought briefly of Ginger's behavior the previous evening. She had been excited for the entire day, waiting for the two men to arrive. She even helped plan the meal and arranged the centerpiece for Charlotte, which was totally out of character for her. But the minute Basil and Joseph set foot in the room, Ginger became subdued. Charlotte kept watching her daughter throughout the evening. She seemed to have a fever—bright eyes, flushed cheeks, a shortness of breath. Charlotte had even suggested she might want to retire early if she wasn't feeling well, but Ginger had elected to remain downstairs. Charlotte now realized Ginger had stayed in order to keep check on the twins until Basil and Joseph left to return to their rooms at the hotel on Broadway.

Well, tonight Ginger would be animated, if Charlotte had to prod her with a stick! This evening's dinner was meant to impress. Charlotte had arranged for the most handsome and available men of the season to be here and to have ample time with Ginger. She would not tolerate any of Ginger's antics this evening. Pleased with the way the room looked, she returned to her bedroom to finish dressing.

♦◊♦

Ginger looked at herself in the mirror as Colleen fussed with her hair. Her face flushed, just thinking about seeing Joseph again. He was, without a doubt, the most handsome, masculine, well-muscled man with whom she'd ever come into contact, and just looking at him made her lose her breath.

Even though Elizabeth had shared with her how madly in love she thought she was with the Englishman Cedric Smith, Ginger hadn't yet said anything to Elizabeth about how Joseph made her feel—or that they had met before the night of the Cotillion. She wanted to keep her emotions to herself for the time being, at least until she sensed some spark of interest on his part. She was glad she was sitting down last night, when he raked his eyes over her. Otherwise, she knew her knees would have buckled, making her look foolish in front of him. Her color rose as he gazed her way, and her mouth suddenly went dry as the desert.

She'd tried wetting her lips with her tongue, and then grabbed for her water glass instead, only to spill its contents on the tablecloth, causing a scene at the end of the evening. She had discovered over dinner he was French-Canadian. That explained his *"Enchanté, mademoiselle"* remark, which had caused her to swoon like a feckless female the night of the ball. If he was any indication of what French-Canadians looked like, she was going to have to rethink her idea of moving to St. Louis, and instead maybe travel to Montreal.

She examined her reflection in the mirror. Her dress was cut dangerously low in the front and off-the-shoulder. The swell of her breasts above the deep neckline was almost scandalous— she was amazed her mother had approved of the final version of the dress.

"You look wonderful this evening, my wee lass," Colleen answered Ginger's unspoken question. "I believe this is my favorite dress of the season so far. You'll surely be able to entice a man to become your husband in this one."

"Heather and Jasmine certainly agree with you. They both wanted to try it on before I donned it." Ginger giggled slightly. "Of course, I didn't let them. They can have their fun with it tomorrow—Lord knows, I won't be able to be seen in it again this season."

The copper-colored silk brocade caught the candlelight when she moved, and her layers of underskirts rustled as she stood and fiddled with last-minute adjustments to her attire. The fabric, draped in a crisscross pattern over her stomach, made her tiny waist look even smaller. Her earrings and necklace were a matched set of sparkling topaz stones, and her hair, piled on the top of her head, gleamed in the soft light. Surely, Joseph would notice her this evening, and give her some indication he was as interested in her as "the gnats" appeared to be.

"Thank you, Colleen. My hair looks quite lovely this evening, too."

"It's because we have been brushing it one hundred strokes each evening. That's what gives it that shine," Colleen announced proudly. "Well, that plus the fact that it's such a delightful color to begin with."

"The gnats"—Quentin Gray, Richard Douglas, and William Davenport—would all be in attendance this evening as well, she knew. Her mother couldn't resist providing them an opportunity to put themselves ahead of the pack in the quest for Ginger's affections. Although the rules of etiquette at any formal function dictated they not have more than two dances per evening with any one lady, those rules would be set aside for tonight's dinner. Which meant each would be given even more time to bore her senseless. She rolled her eyes and promised herself to get through the tedious evening on the horizon. Every time one of "the gnats" got on her nerves, she'd give herself the present of stealing a secret glance at Joseph.

She drew in a long breath as she gazed at her reflection one last time. She dabbed a bit of lilac water behind her ears.

"Okay, I guess I'm ready," she whispered to Colleen.

She ran a hand over her quivering stomach as she stood at the top of the stairs listening to voices coming from the salon, where the guests were gathering prior to dinner.

"You're more than ready, miss. Don't forget to have some fun this evening, too. Go on with you, then, down the stairs."

♦◊♦

"Basil, you look so handsome tonight," Ginger gushed as she entered the room and took hold of her brother's hands.

He leaned down and kissed his younger sister on the cheek. Then he whispered in her ear, "And you look like you forgot the top half of your dress. What are you thinking?"

She smiled up at him. "Don't be such an old fuddy-duddy, Basil. You know this doesn't begin to compare with the some of the shocking attire your actress friends wear. Besides, Mother approved of this dress."

"Well, then, I guess she does intend to marry you off this season. From the looks of the eager young men in attendance tonight, she'll have little to worry about."

"And where is your friend, Joseph?"

"I am here, Miss Fitzpatrick," Joseph said quietly from behind her.

Ginger turned around with a start, and looked up into his warm, brown eyes. His hand found hers. He wore a finely cut, short black wool coat layered over a silk brocade vest. The white ascot seemed to glow against his brown neck. Striped pants stretched over his muscular thighs and his boots were polished to a high gleam. His long black hair was sleeked back from his face and tied at the nape of his neck, bringing his exotic features into high relief. She caught her breath.

"Please, Joseph, call me Ginger. There's no need for such formality when we're in a private setting." He continued to hold her hand, and his eyes locked with her own. "You cut a dashing figure tonight."

Joseph's eyes left her face for the first time, and drifted slowly over her body. "As do you, Ginger."

The way he said her name made it sound almost like a caress. Ginger shivered slightly as his hand finally released hers. She closed her eyes briefly, to embed this moment forever onto her senses.

"There you are, Miss Fitzpatrick!"

The mood was broken abruptly as William Davenport muscled his way into the small group. Every society columnist in New York considered William to be the best catch of the season. The columnists even had ventured a guess he had already laid claim to young Miss Ginger Fitzpatrick. They did make a most handsome couple, with her unique hair coloring and small build and his blond hair topping his tall military-trained physique. He captured her hand, so recently warmed by Joseph, and kissed her wrist.

"Your dress is perfection, Miss Fitzpatrick. If I were proficient with verse, I'd write a sonnet about this gown." His eyes raked over her as he made his pronouncement. As he straightened he looked squarely at Joseph, whom he had met at the Cotillion a few nights back. "Oh, Lafontaine, you're here. Rumor has it you brought some horses to New York from the frontier. I'd like to see them."

Basil clamped Joseph on the shoulder as he answered William. "Yes, Joseph did indeed bring some horses with him. I'm not really a qualified judge of horseflesh, but these are fast, beautiful animals. Are you interested in buying a new one?"

William snorted at the suggestion. "My steed is the best money can buy. My father decided an Army horse wasn't good enough for me, and presented me with a thoroughbred Arabian horse when I graduated from West Point. Perhaps we could race my horse against one of old Joe's, here, and see who comes out ahead."

Basil rose to the bait. "I think a horserace would be a capital idea! Why don't we plan on it in July, when we all go to the country?" Basil continued.

"Why wait? We could meet tomorrow at Hangman's Tree and race through the park," said William.

Joseph objected. "The park is crowded during the day with buggies and people. It would be foolish to race there."

"Are you calling me a fool? I think you're afraid you might lose."

Basil replied anxiously, "Joseph makes a good point about the park. It is generally packed during the day. In fact, I know Ginger and Mother are planning to take the carriage out tomorrow. Perhaps, if you were exercising your mount in the morning, you could meet up with them? I'm certain Mother would be happy to give you some insight on the route they plan to take."

As they took their seats for dinner a few minutes later, Ginger's gaze flickered over William briefly, and then settled on Joseph. Her lips parted briefly, and her cheeks flushed. She moved her eyes away, and then back to him again.

William forced her attention away from Joseph as he began to speak to her. "Miss Fitzpatrick, it is settled, Joe here and I are going to race our horses. It should be the highlight of the Independence Day weekend at the Hamptons. Perhaps we could raise the stakes even further to include a private dinner with you for the winner?"

Ginger had read the society columns that claimed William had already selected her as his bride. And, considering his rivals, Quentin and Richard, he was probably correct in his thinking. After all, he had a solid career as an Army officer. His uniform accented his hardened physique, earned by years of discipline and exercise at West Point. But then Basil arrived with Joseph in time for the ball, and diverted her attention.

Now, William was forced to endure this dinner in Joseph's honor, and to watch as he was toasted and fawned over. Ginger almost felt sorry for him. Almost.

"I'll confer with Mother on the proper etiquette of a private dinner with a single man and let you know, Officer Davenport."

"Did you know the Opera House is putting on a performance this weekend?"

Ginger answered, "Yes, I am aware of it. The family plans to attend on Friday evening."

"Perhaps you'll have room in the family box for me? I have not been able to procure a ticket. It's sold out, I'm afraid."

"I—uh, I'm not sure. Mother?"

"Of course we have room in our box for a military man, Officer Davenport. We would welcome you, if you'd like to attend with us."

"Thank you, Mrs. Fitzpatrick, for your generosity. I'll plan on it."

William nodded slightly at Joseph. But Joseph merely raised an eyebrow. Ginger caught the exchange between the two men, and wondered what was going on. William had annoyed her long enough, though, so she gave herself the prize of looking at Joseph, just for a moment. When her gaze flicked back to William, he had a sour expression on his face. Uniform or no, there was no comparison between the two men.

She then turned her attention to Richard Douglas, the duke's son, who was regaling the guests on either side of him with a description of his father's land holdings in England. Ginger supposed he was pleasant enough to look at, with his light brown hair, blue eyes, and dashing clothing, but his body reflected his aristocratic upbringing—thin and pale. His melodious voice and accent, however, highlighted the culture and fine education he had been privileged to receive. *But it's not as soothing as Joseph's French-imbued speech.* She sighed softly and stole another glance at Joseph.

And then, there was Quentin. She let her eyes wander to him. She much preferred talking to his father, Charles Gray, who sat on her left. It was a shame Quentin had inherited none of his father's cleverness or personality. Or his backbone, for that matter.

She turned to the elder Mr. Gray. "Mr. Gray, how are your railroad investments holding up?"

"I took your advice, Ginger, when you first began pushing railroad stocks at me, and I'm proud to say the Pacific Railroad should have track laid between St. Louis and Jefferson City later this year. The big holdup was a massive bridge they had to build over the Gasconade River, which is now finished. The railroad is planning a huge celebratory train ride for all its investors later this year. Frankly, I'd like to see St. Louis, where Basil spends his time."

And Joseph as well, she thought. Again, she looked at him.

Joseph was paying attention to Elizabeth, of all people. Here she was, practically falling out of her dress in an attempt to capture his interest, and he was listening with rapt attention to her best friend who had declared to Ginger her undying devotion to Cedric just last night! Elizabeth was telling Joseph some inane tale about how she tripped over her dress and nearly fell into some bushes on her way here to dinner. Her dress may have a stupid train, causing her near-tumble, but the neckline was nowhere near as plunging as Ginger's own. So what did Joseph find so appealing? Suddenly, Ginger couldn't wait for this dinner to end.

The final toast of the evening soon followed. Joseph was welcomed to New York by everyone at the table, and Ginger was finally able to stand up. She waited until Joseph's gaze came her way, then she leaned over the table before rising from her seat, giving him an ample view of her assets. She watched with amusement as his eyes widened, and then narrowed, at her. *Take that, Joseph!* She stood and took William's proffered arm before heading back to the parlor.

Chapter Nine

Elegantly crafted carriages lined up for blocks in front of the newly rebuilt Opera House to discharge their passengers. Instead of Jenny Lind or Henrietta Sontag, tonight the patrons were excited to see the great French actress Rachel, who was gracing an American stage for the first time. Her performances had been sold out for weeks.

Ginger and Elizabeth sat in the front row of the box, along with Ginger's parents. The girls were admiring the gilt on the ceiling and the Venetian plaster reliefs adorning the crown of the room and the walls. A huge chandelier filled with hundreds of candles gleamed brightly overhead. In truth, they were using the gilt and chandelier as an excuse to throw their arms about and talk excitedly, hoping to attract some attention from the crowd below.

"Oh, look, Ginger. There's Richard Douglas. And his friend, Cedric Smith. My goodness, they're waving at us!" Elizabeth giggled. "Isn't Cedric handsome? I do love the way that one lock of hair falls over his forehead like it does. Don't you just want to brush it back for him?"

Ginger frowned at her friend. "Did you happen to notice it is the only lock of hair left on the top of his head? Goodness, the man is nearly bald! Please don't do anything to encourage him."

"Don't be so stuffy, Ginger. You're beginning to sound like my mother." Elizabeth looked again at the two English gentlemen and waved back enthusiastically, nearly falling from her chair. "I do hope they come up here at intermission, so I can hear his lovely accent once again!"

Ginger laughed before she replied, "I love your enthusiasm, but should you not be a little more reserved? After all, you don't want to make Cedric think he has a chance with you. Your father has already said he'll not welcome a penniless Brit into the family."

"Hang my father. I find the thought of adding a titled young British fellow to the family exciting, especially if the young man is Cedric Smith!"

♦◇♦

Basil and Joseph walked through the gilded hallway of the Opera House on their way to the family's box. Basil said to his friend, "You'll have to keep an eye on Ginger tonight, Joseph. I'll be distracted watching my latest conquest up on the stage."

"You only met Mademoiselle Rachel last night, Basil. I would hardly consider an evening's amusement a conquest."

Basil gave Joseph a wink and a sly grin. "Ah, but you don't know what we did during last evening's amusement. I'm surprised the woman has the stamina to perform tonight. She was a French delight. I'm so glad you broke the ice by speaking her language to her. But, it was obvious from the start I was the one she was interested in. Sorry you missed out. *Ooh la la.*"

"You are welcome to your actress. I have no interest in her. And, as for your sister, I have no doubt she can handle herself just fine without either of us rushing in to save her."

"Maybe so, but the men who are making plays for Ginger seem to be a bit unruly, especially that young Cavalry officer William Davenport, so it's best we keep watch."

"Yes. Let us discuss Cavalry officer William Davenport. Why did you encourage him when he brought up the idea of the horserace?"

"I apologize for putting you in a tough spot. Had I known how quickly he would react, I would not have agreed. Can you imagine, he actually wanted to race through the park? It was all I could do to get him to agree to hold off until we go to the country."

"And now I am forced to push my horse to his limits to

satisfy this senseless challenge. It is all so unnecessary. After all, we are not chasing buffalo." Joseph shook his head.

"No, and again, I'm sorry. With any luck, William will be otherwise occupied this evening, so we won't have to put up with him."

"I do not think our luck will hold. He does not seem to be the type of man who lets an opportunity slip through his fingers. He went out of his way to invite himself here tonight, so I doubt we will be lucky enough to avoid seeing him this evening."

Basil and Joseph entered the box quietly, and watched the two young ladies run their hands over their dresses and fuss with their jewelry, much to the delight of the young men who were watching from adjacent boxes and from the floor below.

Ginger turned in her seat and glimpsed the two men standing at the back of the box. Smiling, she rose gracefully and made her way to them. Her green dress complemented her eyes. Her hair was caught up in curls, in a show of fine craftsmanship by her talented maid. Each curl was held in place by small emeralds. Matching stones dangled from her ears. The dress fell off her shoulders, revealing her swell of bosom, which was accentuated even further by an emerald necklace.

"Basil! Joseph! How nice to see you again." She kissed her brother lightly on the cheek and took Joseph's hand, feeling the sparks race up her arm as her fingers touched his dark skin. "Come, sit with us." She tugged on Joseph's hand, pulling him forward. "Elizabeth and I were just talking about the upcoming horserace at Roslyn. We're so excited at the prospect. How do you feel about it, Joseph?"

"I feel it is foolish and childish, much like the young man who suggested it."

Perplexed, Elizabeth said to Joseph, "But Officer Davenport is so dashing. I mean, with his uniform, and all. Do you feel your horse is at a disadvantage, then?"

Ginger sputtered, "Of course he doesn't. Joseph's horse is

going to win!" She looked at Joseph. "Won't he?"

Joseph glanced at the two young beauties before he replied. "I came here to sell my horses and have accomplished my mission already, except for two of them. One I plan to take back to St. Louis with me. So I am left with only one to sell. I do not need a race to draw attention to my horses, or to myself, unlike Officer Davenport. Any man who knows horseflesh can tell mine are superior."

"See, Elizabeth, I told you his horse will win!" Ginger said. "Elizabeth is picking Officer Davenport's horse to win, but I am backing yours."

Joseph nodded briefly at the compliment before Ginger continued, "But why are you taking one back to St. Louis instead of selling them all here?"

"Because I plan to ride back home on horseback. I do not like these railroads."

"Frankly, I can't wait to ride the train to St. Louis. It's going to be my reward for behaving myself through the season." She smiled at Joseph and Basil.

Before Basil could reply, a voice broke through the din. They glanced around to see William Davenport entering the box, in full military dress. They stood as William greeted Mr. and Mrs. Fitzpatrick, Ginger, Elizabeth, and the two men. As the theater began to darken, they all took their seats. William snuck into the seat next to Ginger where she'd hoped Joseph would sit. Joseph said nothing, and took a seat in the row behind them, where he could watch every move William made.

♦◊♦

At intermission, Joseph stood silently at the back of the box. Basil had stepped out for some stronger refreshments than the lemonade provided in the box. He also wanted to greet other friends whom he had spotted and had not yet talked to since his return from St. Louis. And Joseph knew he was hoping to get backstage during intermission and steal a kiss from the lovely

Rachel. The box was crowded as people milled around, saying hello to George and Charlotte, or, if they were younger, stopping by to see Ginger and Elizabeth.

The ladies were among the most popular of this season's debutantes, and the parade of young gentlemen had not ceased all during the break. Joseph kept watch, as Basil had requested, thinking he much preferred the mating rituals of his mother's people. A young Indian man, before taking a woman as a wife, first had to prove he could take care of her, which meant demonstrating his strength mentally and physically. He must take part in a buffalo hunt and go through the manhood challenges, including a vision quest. After those rites of passage, a young Indian male needed to assemble gifts to take to his chosen one's father. The more comely the maiden, the more gifts he needed. A man could take months assembling a cache of presents to exchange for his wife, consisting of bison meat, deerskins, horses, and furs.

Joseph looked around at the pasty faces and soft bodies of the men in the box, and thought none of them would have been able to survive the most basic of Indian rituals. He grabbed a glass of lemonade as the waiter made his way through the box.

He waited. And watched.

William took Ginger by the hand and led her to a corner. She seemed to go willingly enough to begin with, until she realized she was about to be trapped. She turned, only to discover he was mere inches away from her, with an arm on either side of the wall at her back, corralling her into the corner. Joseph quietly glided over near them.

"Officer Davenport, what are you doing?" Ginger's eyes widened as she realized her dilemma. She grabbed his forearms and tried to push him away.

"I'm only trying to capture your heart, my sweet. It's too difficult to express my feelings for you if you never allow us time to be alone together." He attempted to lean in and steal a kiss from her, but Ginger dodged his lips and he kissed the air next to her ear.

Surprised by her adroitness, William growled, "So, you like to play hard to get, do you? Well, I like things a little rough myself at times."

He narrowed his arm span on either side of her, and boldly moved his mouth toward her plunging neckline. Ginger stomped on one of his feet in protest. He let out a yelp and backed away a few paces. Ginger quickly skittered around him, freeing herself from the corner, just as Joseph appeared at her side with a glass of lemonade.

"Here is the lemonade you requested, Miss Ginger."

He handed her the glass and gazed into Ginger's eyes. He then looked at William, who glared at him. Joseph calmly returned the glare of the young man before turning his attention back to Ginger.

She laid her hand on his arm. "Thank you, Joseph, for the refreshment. Perfect timing, for I'm absolutely parched. The second act is about to begin—we should take our seats."

Joseph maintained his stance until William turned to follow Ginger back to their seats. Joseph took his seat immediately behind them once again, being certain to bump William's chair slightly during the remainder of the performance, reinforcing the fact that he was being watched.

Chapter Ten

May, 1855

The two Englishmen, Richard Douglas and Cedric Smith, huddled over the roughly hewn table at a small tavern off Broadway. As Cedric raised a foamy mug of ale to his mouth, Richard's hand came down on the table.

"Damn it, Cedric. We are running out of time. It's already been two months' worth of dances, that boring opera, and calling on young ladies in their parlors at tea time—and we have gotten nowhere."

"I know," Cedric said as he rubbed his stomach. "It seems there's not a good scone to be had in the Colonies."

"I'm not talking about food, you oaf. If we don't make some progress toward finding a wealthy young American woman who wants to be affiliated with English royalty, we are doomed! Our fathers will yank us home in another month or so, and we will have to live in poverty."

"What do you suggest? Surely, we're doing all we can."

"Well, since our natural English charm seems to be falling on deaf ears, we need a strategy. Our two best bets are Ginger Fitzpatrick and her sidekick, Elizabeth Martin."

"Yes, I agree. I rather fancy that Elizabeth Martin," Cedric replied.

"And both of their fathers have loads of money, so we can continue to live the lives to which we are accustomed, should we marry one of them."

"But they are the most sought-after women this season. We have never even been alone with them."

Richard's eyes took on a gleam of excitement. "Unless I miss my guess, both of these young women seem to be adventurous. Suppose we issue them an invitation to join us for an evening's entertainment at Niblo's Theater. Then, we can entice them into the Pleasure Garden for some night air."

"And what good would come from having them join us for some air, pray tell?"

"For God's sake, Cedric, do I have to spell it out for you? All we have to do is be discovered by someone while we have these ladies in a compromising position, and they'll have to marry us in order to preserve their reputations!"

Cedric scratched his head, running his hand through his thinning blond hair. "So, how do we get them into these 'compromising' positions? The ladies seem to be joined at the hip."

"We separate them from each other. When we get them into the Garden, you'll stroll one way with Elizabeth and I'll go the other direction with Ginger."

Cedric thought for a moment. "Although the idea of getting Elizabeth alone in a dark garden is making me hard as a rock, I still don't see how it will advance my cause of getting her to marry me."

Richard sighed. Sometimes Cedric could be so thick. "I will arrange for our good friend and patron, Mr. Harris, to find us once we have sufficiently undressed the ladies. He knows our purpose for being here this season, and he knows we are running out of time. He'll be more than happy to be able to report back to our fathers of our success in finding heiresses to marry."

"All right, then, if you think this is our only option. I do rather fancy Miss Elizabeth, and I'm happy for the opportunity to see more of her." He winked at his friend. "If you know what I mean."

Richard groaned. "Okay, then, let's put together an invitation."

♦◊♦

Between dinners, the opera, and the other events comprising the high social season, Basil and Joseph had been kept busy. Everyone who hosted an event needed available single men to balance out the young ladies who attended. The Pleasure Garden at the corner of Broadway and Prince was their chance to mingle with all types of people, not just the elite. It was a place where people could have some fun without worrying about always being proper.

Etiquette took a back seat to fun when one was in the Pleasure Garden, an outdoor entertainment complex with wandering gravel paths leading past candlelit sculptures. Songbirds in gilded cages filled the air with sweet melodies, in counterpoint to the string quartets placed in gazebos around the park. Basil had an assignation later in the evening with his French actress, Rachel, but for now, they were just two men on the prowl, as was often the case during their many evenings together in St. Louis.

The strapping men soon attracted the attention of a lady of the evening. "Hello, handsome," she said saucily to the men. In unison, they examined the voluptuous strumpet before them. She was scantily clad in an off-the-shoulders blouse with a band of ribbon around the top, holding it up over her bosom. A long, slim skirt hugged her hips. The skirt was slit up to her thigh. Basil gave her an easy grin, and replied, "To which of us are you referring?"

"Either one. It makes no difference. You're both quite handsome, Lordy, and a sight for these sore eyes."

Basil replied, "Well, then, you'll need to pay attention to my friend, here, as I have a prior engagement."

Basil took his leave, and Joseph was left alone with the comely woman.

"Come with me, handsome. Let's go some place where the light is not so bright." She took Joseph's hand in hers and led him into a darkened corner of the garden, surrounded by tall hedges that afforded them some privacy. They sat on a bench that had been conveniently placed in the corner for just such encounters.

Joseph thought these New Yorkers had strange habits when it came to wooing and bedding a woman, and tonight's events proved no different. The Pleasure Garden's sole purpose was to give people a place where they could engage in disreputable behavior, made all the more exciting because they might be caught at any time by others in the garden. He had never seen anything like it. His Indian ancestors, whom these people referred to as savages, did not behave so flagrantly.

"For two bits, I'll let you suckle my breasts," the woman whispered.

Joseph jumped up from the bench, as if he had been burned. "I will give you some money if you want. You are a most lovely woman, but I am not interested in getting to know you better."

"It matters not to me, so long as I get my money." She sighed as he dropped the coins into her hand. She got to her feet and laid a hand on Joseph's broad chest. "Although you are a most attractive man." She sashayed away, in search of another conquest.

Joseph sat back down on the bench as he watched the harlot walk away.

"Isn't this delightful?"

A voice—an achingly familiar one—pierced the fog surrounding his mind. He shook himself to clear his head. Ginger's voice had been in his head for days now, but this voice was coming from the garden, not from within his mind. What in the world was Ginger doing in this den of iniquity? His mind and body went on high alert.

"Oh, look, Mr. Douglas. There are some songbirds!" Again, the voice wafted through the air.

"I am hoping you'll see something else tonight you will like equally well." The cultured British accent floated over the hedges.

Joseph listened closely, straining to hear what Richard Douglas and Ginger were doing on the other side of the bushes. Why was Ginger in the unruly Pleasure Garden, alone with Richard and seemingly without a chaperone? Joseph was steeling himself to pounce from behind his cover of hedges when he heard Ginger's voice raised in anger.

"Mr. Douglas, what are you doing? Let me go!"

Joseph sprang to his feet.

"I am attempting to seduce you, darling. You can't tell me you're unaware of the steps one takes in seduction. You have an audience of men dancing around you at all times. It's extremely difficult to get you alone and to let you know the true depth of my feelings, so I am not about to lose this opportunity."

"Where did Elizabeth and Mr. Smith get to?"

"She has been taken down another path by my friend, who offered to help separate the two of you, to give me some time to be alone with you."

Joseph strode quietly from around the hedge. Richard had pushed Ginger down on the seat of the bench and was attempting to climb on top of her, while busily trying to free her breasts from the bodice of her dress. Ginger beat him with her hands, and was agile enough to slip away from Richard. She stood facing him angrily just as Mr. Harris came around the hedges on the opposite side of the clearing.

As Ginger opened her mouth to speak, Joseph took her arm and pulled her gently to his side.

"Why are you here, and alone?"

Ginger's eyes sparkled with anger as she looked at Richard. "I am not alone. Elizabeth and I came here together for an evening's amusement in the theater, at the invitation of Mr. Douglas and his friend, Mr. Smith.

"They brought us out into the garden for some air, and we, after all, were curious to see the Pleasure Gardens that we've heard so much about. Elizabeth and Mr. Smith got separated from us, on purpose as it turns out, so Mr. Douglas could try to have his way with me. But he didn't get far!"

"All I needed to do was to put you in a compromising position, my dear, and be discovered. It would have worked, too, if this giant French slug hadn't come along." Richard spat the words at her, and then glared at Joseph.

"Ginger bested you," Joseph said. "I think you should leave right now."

"So you can be alone with her? How do I know you won't try to do the same thing?" Richard growled. "After all, you could be after her for her father's money, too."

"She is the sister of my best friend. We must go rescue Elizabeth now from your cohort in crime before he does to her what you tried to do to Ginger."

Joseph put his hand on Ginger's waist and attempted to guide her away from the Englishman. But Richard grabbed his arm to prevent his departure.

"Not so fast, Frenchie. It took a lot of planning and work to make tonight happen. I might have failed in my attempt, but Cedric still has a chance."

Joseph shrugged off the aggressor with a slight shift of his shoulder. Richard lost his footing and fell to the ground.

"Bless my bloomers," Ginger gasped as Richard slumped to the soft earth. "Have you hurt him, Joseph? Not that he wasn't asking for it."

"No, he has merely lost his advantage. Let us leave him and go find your friend."

"You're right. Let's hurry and find her. After all, it's because of me she got waylaid. My goodness, I hope we're not too late. Hurry, Joseph."

Chapter Eleven

As Joseph and Ginger walked quickly through the park, they came upon several couples in various stages of undress, so wrapped up in each other they had no qualms about being discovered. The Pleasure Garden was living up to its name this evening, it seemed. Joseph had the keen eyes of a hunter and managed to see most of these couples first and to steer Ginger from the most flagrant acts being committed. However, she was able to view a few indiscretions, and her eyes widened as she took in sights she hadn't seen before. She uttered not a sound, but huddled closer to Joseph as they hurried along.

From behind a hedge came the sound of a woman's full-throated moan of delight. Joseph put his hand on Ginger's arm as they stood motionless, and waited.

"Yes, yes. Oh, Cedric, I've never felt like this before." The woman moaned again, and Ginger caught the sound of fabric being ripped. She tugged on Joseph's arm.

"Cedric Smith is the man who was with Richard Douglas," she whispered. "Most likely, we've found Elizabeth."

As one, they moved around the hedge. Elizabeth lay sprawled on a bench with her breasts exposed. Cedric knelt by her side, one hand creeping up her leg while he suckled her breast. Elizabeth's eyes were closed in rapture, but popped open as suddenly Cedric wrenched his mouth away. Her moan of dismay became one of despair as she spied Joseph and Ginger.

Joseph took hold of the man's jacket and pulled him off, shoving him to the ground. He removed his coat and placed it over Elizabeth's exposed bosom.

"Get up and cover yourself please, Miss Martin. It is past time for you and Ginger to be home. Both of you have caused me nothing but trouble this evening."

Joseph's gruff voice made Elizabeth blush in embarrassment. Cedric still lay on the ground, but had propped himself up on his elbows.

Grasping Joseph's coat to her chest, Elizabeth rushed to his side. "Are you all right, Cedric?" She turned back to Joseph. "I had no wish to be saved by you, Mr. Lafontaine, so if my being here has caused you trouble, it's of your own making. I am quite happy to be with Cedric."

Ginger went to her friend's side and pulled her up off the ground. "Get a hold of yourself, Elizabeth. This man has manipulated you into a most compromising position. Richard Douglas told me of their plan to destroy our reputations this evening, just so they could get their hands on our fathers' money. It's fortunate only Joseph and I found you. Otherwise, you'd have to marry this lout."

Elizabeth gazed at Cedric, with a look of adoration on her face. "He is no lout, Ginger. I would happily marry him, should he ask for my hand. I've never felt this way toward any man." She ran her hands through Cedric's tousled wispy blond hair as she helped him to his feet. She then put her arms around him and raised her mouth to his.

"What would your mother say, Elizabeth?" Ginger wailed.

Elizabeth took a deep breath and unwrapped herself from Cedric's body. "You are right, Ginger. Mother would not approve of my behavior. But then, she never met a man like Cedric, either."

Cedric took one look at Joseph's stormy face and apparently decided not to take a stand.

"I'll call on you tomorrow, Elizabeth, at your home." He kissed her hand before he disappeared into the night.

Elizabeth sighed deeply as she turned her back to Joseph and

Ginger and slid her arms into Joseph's jacket.

Ginger could contain herself no longer. "Cedric? Really?"

Elizabeth looked at her best friend and shrugged. "What can I say? He's not like any other man I've known, Ginger. I can't expect you to understand—you don't like men."

She turned away and missed the look of desire on Ginger's face as she stole a glance at Joseph. Together they left the Pleasure Garden, and walked to the Fitzpatrick household.

♦◇♦

When Ginger and Elizabeth received the invitation from the English gentlemen to attend Niblo's Theater, attached to the Pleasure Garden, they hid it from their mothers. They hoped they could take a quick stroll through the infamous garden, but if their mothers found out where they were headed, they'd be forbidden to leave the house. Even if their mothers did agree to the outing, the young ladies would have been chaperoned, and would never have been able to set foot in the Pleasure Garden.

Elizabeth and Ginger concocted a plan: Each would tell her mother she was being accompanied to the theater by the other girl's mother, and they would spend the remainder of the night together at Ginger's home. Their plan had worked until things got out of hand in the garden.

They quietly made their way to Ginger's bedroom and changed into their nightgowns. As they crawled into bed, Elizabeth chatted away about her newest conquest, and how wonderful Cedric was.

Ginger reiterated, "I repeat what I said at the Garden— Cedric? Really? Isn't he a bit, well, old? And balding?"

"Being older just means he's had time to experience women. A lot of women. And I found out tonight his years of experience have resulted in his ability to do wonderful things with my body." Elizabeth sighed dramatically. "I tell you, Ginger, if you ever were to find a man like Cedric, whose fingers can do the most magical things, whose mouth is so hot when it touches my skin, you'd understand what I'm talking about. I can imagine myself in his bed, with him doing wicked things to my body, for the rest of my life. I don't care if he is balding. It just means I'll have more of his delectable skin to cover with my kisses."

"Elizabeth Martin, you are shameless!" Ginger threw a pillow at her, and then wrapped her arms around her best friend. "That's what I love about you. We did have some fun tonight, didn't we?"

"We always have a good time together. Even the dramatic rescue by Joseph to save my reputation was rather, well, divine," Elizabeth said as she drifted off to sleep.

Restless, but not wanting to disturb Elizabeth, Ginger got out of bed and strode quietly to the window. Elizabeth had carelessly tossed Joseph's jacket on a chair nearby as she undressed for the night. Ginger carefully picked it up and draped it over her body. She inhaled Joseph's scent and her mind went back to the scene of Elizabeth and Cedric in the garden. She wondered if she would feel the same about Joseph if he touched her intimately the way Cedric had Elizabeth. Would she be here waxing poetic about him?

She longed to tell her best friend about her feelings for Joseph, but he had shown no indication he harbored similar intentions toward her. He had only been cordial and friendly, what she would expect from her brother's best friend. Until she knew that he shared her feelings, she would keep her desire to herself.

Ginger wrapped herself tighter into the jacket, inhaling the sweet scent of hay mixed with musk and another, uniquely Joseph smell. She fell into a troubled sleep, dreaming of Joseph touching her as Cedric had touched Elizabeth, kissing her deeply and possessively, and stealing her breath away.

Chapter Twelve

The Intersection of Broadway and Bond Streets, June 1855

Broadway was the showiest, most crowded street in New York City. Not only was it the main artery, it also was where trade and fashion intersected. Storefronts and businesses butted up against private homes; churches nestled next to theaters and barrooms. The sidewalks teemed with men, women, and children from all walks of life. Streets were packed with carriages, horses, and mule teams. Maneuvering from one side of the street to the other required finesse, quickness, and sure-footedness. Many a person had slipped and fallen while trying to dodge the droppings left by the horses or attempting to avoid running headlong into people, animals, or buggies.

It was the perfect place for Ginger to take to a soapbox in her bloomers. She knew if her mother or father ever discovered she had become such an outspoken advocate of women's rights, she would surely have every one of her few remaining privileges stripped away. But she was not content with the pace of Amelia Bloomer's movement toward equality of the sexes, and wanted to do her part to speed up the cause.

She had carefully orchestrated her outing. She feigned an upset stomach at Elizabeth's home, in front of Mrs. Martin. Then, instead of directly walking the few doors down the street to her own home, she took advantage of the extra stolen hours of freedom. She ran to Broadway, along the way stopping in an alley to divest herself of her crinolines and skirt and pick up the box she had placed there earlier.

She staked out a position on a busy corner and set the box

down. No one paid any attention to her at first. She stood on top of the soapbox and began to speak loudly over the cacophony, cupping her hands around her mouth to make her voice carry. A few nearby shoppers uneasily looked her way. Satisfied she was making at least some small impact, she grew emboldened. Her cries became more insistent, as she rattled off the reasons why women should be treated as equals to men.

She had worked herself up into a full head of righteous steam and a small crowd gathered at her feet. She knew a few of the men were there just to leer at her in her bloomers, but she hoped at least some of her message was getting through their thick heads. She stood a better chance of making an impact with the women in the audience, whom she hoped would heed her advice not to bend to the wishes of their husbands and to develop their own voices.

From behind her, someone yelled, "Runaway buggy!"

Ginger turned in time to see the out-of-control horse and buggy, along with its frightened passengers, hurtling down the street. From her position on the box she saw Joseph approaching her, directly in the line of the buggy, and her heart clenched. She yelled out to him as she jumped from the box and into his hard body. The collision of their two bodies knocked them out of the path of immediate danger.

She opened her eyes just as the horse and buggy smashed into the box on which she had been standing. Wrapped in a solid pair of arms, they rolled out of harm's way as the runaway buggy hurled past, mere inches away. She looked up into Joseph's dark brown eyes, and fainted.

♦◊♦

The sweet scent of hay wafted into her nostrils as she struggled to regain consciousness.

"There, there, little one, *ma petite*. Crazy *zhaagnash*. You are all right."

The soothing sounds were murmured like a chant. A cool damp cloth was laid across her forehead.

She opened her eyes and looked at Joseph. For a long minute, they merely stared at each other. Ginger's heartbeat escalated with every second their eyes were locked. Neither spoke or broke their gaze. When she knew she would explode if she didn't move, she finally lowered her eyes and struggled to pull herself up.

"Where am I?"

Joseph helped her to a sitting position, and then leaned her back against the stall.

"You are in the livery, with my horses. What were you doing standing on top of a box in your underclothes in broad daylight?"

She squirmed as his bold gaze took in her scantily clad body. His touch as he helped her to sit up had heated her body, but his eyes raking over her barely clothed form scorched every inch of it. She struggled to breathe. How was it that she could consider herself adequately dressed in her bloomers as she stood on a soapbox in the middle of a busy street, but here, alone with Joseph, she felt like a wanton strumpet? She turned away from his gaze.

"I—uh, I was trying to advance the cause of women's rights. And, if I hadn't been on the soapbox, we would right now be picking up your body parts from under the wheels of that buggy. So, you're welcome."

Joseph swore softly under his breath, in a language unfamiliar to her.

"What language is it you are speaking? I know a thing or two about the French language, and it doesn't sound like any French I've ever been taught. What is *zhaag*...whatever you said?"

Joseph's eyes narrowed as he sidestepped her question. "Do your parents know where you are?"

"Of course not. What kind of fool do you take me for? And what is *zhaag*…whatever that word was?"

"It is a phrase we use in St. Louis." Again, he tried to circumvent her questions. "Where did you leave your skirt and petticoats? I will go retrieve them so you can properly clothe yourself and return to your home."

"In the alley, near where I was standing. Of course, someone could have already taken them."

"Stay here and I will go fetch them."

Ginger struggled to get to her feet, but was still unsteady. Joseph knelt by her side, his arms holding her in position.

"Stay seated and do not move until I get back. Do you understand?"

She looked up at the chiseled face, so near to hers that she could reach out and touch it. Her fingers tingled at the possibility and she gulped in an unsteady breath.

"You won't tell my mother, will you? Or Basil? If they knew what I was doing, I'd be in serious trouble."

"No, I will not tell them you were here," Joseph's voice changed to a gentle tone. "And it is quite possible that if you had not thrown yourself on me, I could have suffered serious injuries, so I am grateful you were."

Ginger laid her head back against the stall boards and took a deep breath. "Thank you for your silence. I owe you."

Joseph groaned. "Now you sound like Basil. You owe me nothing but to behave yourself and stop parading around in public in your bloomers."

Joseph's hair was caught up loosely at the nape of his neck and tied with a thin strip of leather. Several strands had worked their way loose from the tie and were brushing his cheek. Ginger reached out a tentative hand to him, and ran her fingers down his long black hair. At her touch, Joseph flinched and grabbed her hand.

"What do you think you are doing?"

Ginger's stomach was doing cartwheels as her hand was caught in his. "I've wanted to touch your hair since our first dance together. It is unlike any hair I've ever seen. So black it's almost blue, and very straight and thick."

Joseph's eyes blazed. "And I have wanted to do this since our first dance together."

He seized her chin in an iron grip as he captured her lips with his. Ginger's stomach stuttered in response to his rough, possessive kiss. Before she had time to process what was happening, he backed away, and hurried from the livery as if the very devil himself were at his heels.

♦◊♦

Joseph stopped outside of the livery, leaned against the wall, and closed his eyes, willing his stomach to calm down. It had been in an upheaval since Ginger had pushed him out of the way of the buggy in just the nick of time. His heart raced as he thought of what almost happened to him. It was not like him to be oblivious to his surroundings, but his mind had been full of Ginger at the time.

Still, it was no excuse for losing control of himself with her like he had. What evil force had taken possession of him? He never should have touched her. She was forever forbidden to him, he knew. He should have left town, as he wanted to, after the Cotillion and his first dance with Ginger. For too many weeks now, she had tormented him every time they were together. The swell of her breasts in her low-cut gown at the dinner party made him feel like a dog with his tongue hanging out. He had to force himself to look away, and then keep away, from her all evening.

And then there was the night of the opera. William Davenport had backed down without too much of an argument when Joseph made his presence known, yet he had remained by her side all evening. A hot flash of jealousy had stabbed

Joseph's chest then as he wished he could change places with William.

What was it about this one woman that made all others dull by comparison? Indian, French, white, Canadian, American. What did it matter? She was the embodiment of everything he had ever wanted or hoped for. Spirited, lively, lovely to look at. She would lead a man on a merry chase for the rest of his life, and any man would welcome the challenge. But it could not be him. It could never be him. He took several deep breaths and pushed himself away from the wall.

A few minutes later, he found Ginger's skirt and her petticoats in the alley, where she had stashed them earlier. He tossed the garments over one broad shoulder and returned to the livery. But she wasn't in the empty stall where he had left her. He walked to the stall that contained his most spirited stallion—and found her there. She stood beside the big, powerful animal, caressing his neck, absolutely ignorant of the potential damage a horse of this magnitude could do to her. Joseph's heart began to stutter again as he considered the danger in which she had placed herself. Quietly, he approached her and put his hand on her shoulder.

She jumped, startled, and turned to him. He got a whiff of lilac, combined with the straw mingled in her hair before he backed away from her.

"What are you doing in this stall with my black? Did I not tell you to stay put? This is a most forceful animal."

She smiled fetchingly up at him. "I wanted to see him again. Everyone is talking about the horse you'll be racing. It's all I hear at every blasted party I've been to this last week." She turned back to the horse and brushed her hand over his mane. "But now I see all the talk is not misplaced. He is truly a magnificent specimen. Does he have a name yet?"

When Joseph shook his head, she ran her hand once more down the stallion's black neck.

"Then I shall call him Midnight." She turned to Joseph again, with a smile on her face. She reached up and wove her fingers into his hair. "His hair is as dark as yours. But it is more than just your hair that sets you apart. What is it about you, Joseph? You are not like any of the New York men I've met."

She lost herself in his dark brown eyes, which had grown stormy.

"If you know what is good for you, you will get dressed at once and leave here, never to return," he growled at her.

Her fingers tightened their hold on his hair and she brought his head closer to her. She whispered in his ear, "Or else what?"

"Or else, I will strip those bloomers off your beautiful body and put an end to your teasing." He tossed her skirt and crinolines at her. "It would be best if you clean the straw from your hair before you return home. Otherwise, your mother will think I have done just that."

He then turned on his heel, leaving the livery once again.

Ginger's knees felt weak and her body warmed as little shivers of excitement worked their way to the very core of her being. He had threatened to ravage her! The thought left her breathless with excitement. She backed away from the magnificent steed and returned to the empty stall where she lowered her quaking body to the floor.

Well, bless my bloomers.

Ginger made her way back to her home, even though her legs were a bit shaky. She had almost lost her life today, as the runaway buggy nearly mowed Joseph and her down. But that wasn't what was making her knees weak. Joseph had finally shown that he was as infatuated with her as she was with him. That show of emotion from him, that crack in his stern control, was all she needed. He cared for her!

She put a hand on her heart as she walked rapidly down the

street to her home, skirting past Elizabeth's house, because she had told Elizabeth's mother hours ago that she felt unwell and was going straight home. She let herself in the back door quietly and made her way upstairs to her room, where Colleen was starching and pressing her petticoats. The maid looked up when Ginger came in.

"Hello, my wee lass. Did you have a good time at Elizabeth's this afternoon?"

Ginger searched for a sign that the maid was on to her, but could find nothing of significance. "Could you please arrange for a bath for me, Colleen? I'm very tired."

"Most certainly, miss. Right away."

The water was quickly heated, and the tub filled. Ginger removed her clothing and sunk into the hot water with a sigh of true pleasure. Colleen took the pins from Ginger's hair as she relaxed in the water, and began to brush her waist-length hair.

"What's this, miss? How ever did you get hay in your hair?"

Ginger blushed from her toes to her hairline, grateful that the hot water had already reddened her skin a bit. She scrambled for an answer.

"Uh…I guess I must have picked it up in the livery. We went there to see the horse that Joseph is going to race in a few weeks."

"Ah, I see," Colleen replied, as she continued to brush Ginger's hair.

"You see what?" Ginger prodded, wanting to make certain her story was sound.

"Well, Mr. Lafontaine is devilishly handsome, if I do say so myself."

Ginger sat up in the tub and turned on Colleen. "That's not why I went to the livery. I truly did want to see the horse."

"Whatever you say, miss."

Ginger sank back into the tub, covering her face with her hands. Her cheeks were inflamed. Colleen had seen through her feeble story too easily. Well, she would just deny it, should Colleen ever feel the need to tell Mother or the house staff of her suspicions.

But she was right. Mr. Lafontaine *was* a devilishly handsome man.

Chapter Thirteen

The Hamptons, July 2, 1855

Roslyn Harbor, eighteen miles east of New York City proper and on the north shore of Long Island Sound, was quickly becoming the summer playground of New York's finest families. With its scenic beauty and harbor views of the Atlantic Ocean, Roslyn Harbor was the place to be seen from June through August. The newly wealthy Americans sought out land to convert into grand estates to show their peers a tangible expression of their affluence and status. They hoped their displays of wealth would reinforce or establish their place in society, and each new estate became more opulent than its neighbor.

One of these newer estate homes belonged to Mr. and Mrs. Nathaniel Curran, who, along with their daughter Georgiana, opened their home to their friends for the Independence Day weekend events. The estate was in the middle of a 250-acre tract of rolling farmland and woods—the perfect setting for the big horserace between Joseph Lafontaine and William Davenport, the Cavalry officer.

New Yorkers had been buzzing about the impending race for weeks, and an invitation from the Currans was one of the most sought after for the Fourth of July weekend. People not fortunate enough to receive a formal invitation planned to line the race route, as word of the big contest spread to everyone who had seen or heard about the two horses.

The rudimentary road between New York and Long Island quickly became overcrowded with carriages, as people interested in getting away for the holiday began the long trek to the harbor from the city. Joseph and Basil were on horseback, so they were able to wind their way between the many carriages, exchanging pleasantries with those less fortunate people who were stuck in the traffic.

Along the way, many men stopped the pair to study Joseph's mount up close and to decide which horse to bet on. Women also called out to the two men, flirting outrageously with Basil and Joseph. Spirits were high as the festive weekend commenced.

Joseph had studiously avoided any contact with Ginger since his encounter with her in the livery several weeks before. It was not like him to lose control of his emotions as he had done that day. Her ability to make him throw caution to the wind surprised and tormented him. Kissing her was the worst possible thing he could have done. Not only did he break his best friend's trust, but instead of diminishing his desire for the beautiful woman as he had hoped, it only made him long for her more. When he finally gave in and kissed her lips, he was like a drowning man who had been given a lifeline, and only Ginger could pull him to safety.

This little slip of a woman managed to infuse him with desire every time she was near. He was no stranger to the pleasures of women, although his experiences had mostly been with other Indians or saloon girls in St. Louis. But none had ever tugged at his heart this way. He had always been able to dismiss women from his mind as soon as he left their beds. He knew to his core the nearness of Ginger would probably destroy the fragile hold he still had on his control, so he made one excuse after another to avoid attending the opera, ballet, and musicals—so much a part of the Fitzpatrick family's entertainment in the past month. If it were not for this blasted race Basil had roped him into, Joseph would have taken his leave of New York weeks ago.

Now he could avoid her no longer. The time had come to face her. He and Basil had just ridden abreast of the Fitzpatrick carriage, and Basil reined in his horse to keep pace with the buggy. Joseph had no choice except to fall in with him, or risk being seen as ungracious. Despite himself, he eagerly looked toward the carriage and spotted the reddish-brown locks of the woman who invaded his dreams every night.

♦◊♦

Ginger's eyes rested on Joseph's familiar face as he sat astride the large stallion—the same horse she had been standing beside when he revealed his desire to strip off her bloomers and ravage her. The horse she had named Midnight. That day had been the most momentous, fateful day of her life. The past three weeks had been excited torment for her, as each event approached where Joseph might be seen in her presence without raising any eyebrows. But her excitement was repeatedly dashed as he declined one invitation after another.

Her stomach flipped over as she looked at those chocolate eyes. They were smoldering, and she knew he could probably see the desire in her eyes too, before she lowered her gaze. She felt strangely short of breath, and was warm and damp in places she barely knew she had. She wove her fingers into the fabric of her skirt, remembering how she had threaded them into his hair in the livery. That day would forever play in her mind as the one when she lost her heart, and she knew her life would never be the same again.

Basil and Joseph rode alongside the carriage for ten or fifteen minutes, making idle conversation with her parents until they tired of the slow pace.

"We're going on ahead, Mother. Joseph is anxious to get to the Currans' and let his horse rest before the big race. We'll see you when you arrive." As they rode off, Ginger melted back into the seat.

"Are you all right, my dear?" Charlotte noticed her daughter's flushed cheeks and labored breathing. She took one of Ginger's hands and held it between her own. "Did you bind yourself into your corset too tightly?"

"No, Mother, I'm fine. I'm just restless and eager for the weekend's festivities, I guess. I wish I could have ridden out here like Basil and Joseph are doing. At least I would have been able to get some exercise."

"You'll have plenty of time for exercise." Charlotte smiled at Ginger. "Between a dip in the ocean, croquet on the lawn, and the hide-and-seek games, you'll be able to stretch your legs to your heart's content once we arrive at the estate. Your father and I will be looking at some properties while we're here, too, and you're welcome to come along with us, if you'd like."

"Thank you, Mother, but no. For a change, I don't want to think about investments of any kind. The horserace will be the highlight of the season, and I want to ride out for a front-row seat. I am beside myself with excitement. I just want this blasted road to end so I can get there and enjoy the weekend."

"Well, it's nice to see you're excited about something. You've been so moody these last few weeks I was beginning to wonder whether the long season was taking too much out of you. It's nice to see my Ginger has her snap back." Charlotte brushed a hand over Ginger's hair and kissed her on the forehead. "We'll get there soon enough. Put your head back and try to nap for the rest of the trip."

Ginger melted back into the seat and closed her eyes. A vision of Joseph on his mighty steed immediately popped into her head, and she sighed. She was too wound up to fall asleep, but replaying visions of Joseph would be just the thing to make the time pass faster.

Chapter Fourteen

To give both horse and rider enough time to recover from the journey from Manhattan to Roslyn Harbor, it had been decided the race would take place on the Fourth of July, with fireworks following in the evening. So the day after the long trek to the country, the guests indulged themselves in a most luxurious and decadent manner. Most of them were not expected to rise until late in the morning. A breakfast buffet was set up in the long dining hall, where guests could avail themselves of all manner of muffins, eggs, bacon, and toast whenever they did manage to stumble out of bed. They could spend the day at the beach or at lawn bowling and croquet. In the evening, there would be a formal dinner and dancing.

Joseph did not plan to attend any of these events. He wanted to be near his horse at all times. He did not trust William Davenport. He had seen the gleam in the man's eyes when Joseph reluctantly agreed to this race, and knew William would not be above putting Joseph's steed in danger in order to win. Until the race, Joseph would stay in the stables to ensure the stallion was fed the proper food, and nothing untoward took place. On the racecourse, he would let his common sense and his years of riding experience take over as he bested his competition.

He quietly entered the house early to help himself to the spread of food in the dining hall. As he predicted, he did not encounter any of the other guests. It was too early for these pampered New Yorkers to be up and about. He filled a napkin with food and took the improvised sack back to the stables and to his horse.

Immediately upon entering the building, he sensed there was someone else in the barn, someone other than the stable boys and grooms. Someone the horses didn't know, for they were on edge. Joseph's ears quickly registered the pawing of the horses as they nervously clawed their hooves at the straw in the stalls. Joseph went on high alert, set the bag of food on a bale of hay, and crept silently toward Midnight's stall.

He peered over the railings and caught sight of a boy in the stall, standing next to his horse, causing the horse to nicker and bray. He dragged the intruder out from the stall, balling his hand into a fist as he prepared to deliver a crushing blow.

But suddenly his senses told him he had hold of a woman's arm, not a man's. And he knew who the woman was. He pulled her to the center aisle of the stables and dropped his hand as if she were a hot coal.

Ginger looked up at Joseph, questioning. He finally blinked and exhaled a long breath as he unclenched his fist. He shook his head to clear his thoughts.

"Do you realize how close I came to knocking you senseless? What are you doing here? And why are you dressed as a boy?" His voice was gruff and clipped, but his eyes blazed.

"I wanted to see you, and your horse, before the race. I figured dressing as a stable boy would be the best way to get out here unnoticed. Besides, it's early, and I knew no one will be stirring for hours."

"And what could be so urgent that you would risk the possibility of me hitting you?"

Ginger blushed at his harsh words. "You're obviously in a foul mood, so I'll just go back to the house." She straightened her spine and began to stalk away, then turned back. "No! It took a lot of planning and effort for me to borrow these clothes and to get out of the house undetected, so, I *will* ask you the questions I came here to ask. What I want to know is why, Joseph? Why have you avoided me since the day in the livery?

Was the experience of kissing me so dreadful for you?" She broke off as her eyes filled with tears and her voice choked.

Joseph sighed softly as he noticed how the boy's outfit did nothing to hide her lovely curves. His heart pounded as he said the words he knew would cut her to the quick. "It is for the best you think nothing more of the day in the livery. I regret it happened. That is all you need to know."

"But, Joseph, I know you felt as I did when we kissed. After all, you threatened to ravage me!"

Although she had whispered these words to him, Joseph still glanced around the stables to make certain no one was listening. He turned back to her and spoke softly. "As I said, I regret it happened. It would be for the best if you would forget about it, and forget about me. I beg you to select one of the many young men who are better suited to you and accept his advances. Now, leave me and Midnight and get back into the house before you are discovered."

Ginger's breath caught in her throat, and she placed her hand over her heart. "Oh, are you calling him Midnight? That means you do care for me, in spite of what you say, if you let me name your precious horse." She wiped her tears away. "Well, bless my bloomers!"

Her laughter filled the air as she skipped out of the stables.

Joseph went to his horse and put his head on the steed's neck, stifling his groan. It was true he regretted the day in the livery. He knew Basil's anger would be uncontrolled if he discovered Joseph had kissed Ginger. If Joseph had lost all of his control and taken her, as he wanted to do, Basil would surely cut him out of his life in St. Louis, and would cease doing business with Joseph and his father. For the sake of the family business, and so as not to lose Basil's friendship, he must never touch her again. He had been trying to tamp down his feelings for her since the day he had lost his senses and kissed her in the livery, and thought he had regained his control.

But seeing her today, in the clothes of a stable boy—so

typical of her lively spirit and her sense of adventure—brought his desire to the surface once again. Not to mention her beautiful face and curvaceous body, which a boy's attire only accentuated. He thought he had been successful over the past few weeks, forcing her from his mind and keeping his distance from her physically, even though she played a starring role in his nightly troubled dreams.

He replayed the scene in Niblo's Garden when Richard tried to seduce Ginger. He had managed to undo her bodice before Ginger fought him off and Joseph had caught a momentary glimpse of her exposed bosom. The vision of her creamy swell of breast and that luscious pink nipple played in his head nightly as sleep overtook him. On the evenings when he could sleep. He spent many a restless night in the livery, bestowing extra attention on his horses as he relived the afternoon when she rescued him from the runaway buggy. Their close encounter had caused him to take advantage and kiss her. If not for his rigid self-control, he would have given in to his need to plunder her there and then.

His manhood had sprung to attention today the very second he grabbed her arm and pulled her out of Midnight's stall. He did not need to look at her or to see her telltale reddish locks to know it was Ginger in the clothing of a young boy. His body knew the minute he put his hand on her.

With his head swimming, he pondered what to do next, and decided. He would leave New York immediately after the race, and head back to St. Louis. Once he got out of this privileged and cultured environment of New York City, which was totally foreign to him, and fell back into his hard routine of finding and breaking horses, sheer exhaustion would put Ginger forever out of his mind. At least, that was what he had told himself every day since their kiss in the livery.

He grabbed a brush and began to groom Midnight to a sleek, coal-black sheen worthy of his name.

Chapter Fifteen

Later in the day, Ginger and Elizabeth, along with the Englishmen Cedric and Richard and the other guests, took their places on the wide expanse of carefully manicured lawn in front of the large estate house, in preparation for a game of hide-and-seek. In actuality, the game was an excuse for couples to steal away from the crowd for a few moments of pleasure out of the view of the mothers and other chaperones who were constantly in attendance.

Ginger knew she could not count on Elizabeth to run interference between her and Richard. Elizabeth and Cedric were among those couples who wanted to find a hidden spot where they could kiss. And she knew Joseph would not leave Midnight alone in the stables until after the race. Even if he were free, she could not imagine him playing such a foolish game. So, it was up to her to defend herself against Richard's unwanted advances. Fortunately, it was an overcast day, so she thought it wasn't too unseemly of her to carry her parasol with her as she ran lightly over the grass with the others in search of a place to hide.

She ducked behind one of the large, squat boxwoods running along the side of a stone wall. Their pungent smell filled the air, reminding her of cat urine. Perhaps their odor would keep other people away. After all, it wasn't nearly so romantic to crouch behind stinky boxwoods as it was to lie in a field of sweet-scented lavender.

She sat quite still and enjoyed hearing the whoops of laughter as one person after another was found, or tagged home. She had no desire to leave her spot and rejoin the game.

Doing so would just mean she'd have to be the one to find the others, and she had no wish to intrude on intimate scenes like the one she knew Elizabeth and Cedric were having, maybe even at this very minute. She had to admit she was a bit jealous of Elizabeth. Cedric may not be the man she would have picked for her friend, but at least he hadn't sent her away from him and told her to forget his existence! No, Cedric was more than willing to kiss and fondle Elizabeth. Ginger propped her head on the stone wall and closed her eyes, imagining being kissed and fondled by Joseph. Her lips parted as she thought of his mouth touching hers again.

"Aha, there you are, my little minx."

Her eyes popped open as she recognized the cultured British accent. She had only a second to brace herself before Richard fell on top of her, pinning her to the ground.

"Get off of me, you big oaf," she said as she pushed against him.

"Not this time, my love. I made sure the Frenchie is nowhere near us before I came to you. This time, you will be mine." His hands moved over her breasts as she continued to struggle. "I must admit, even though your money is what I need, your body is what I lust after. It will be no hardship to be married to such a comely lass as yourself."

He captured her mouth with his as one hand began to creep down her body.

Ginger wrapped her hand around her parasol and pushed its pointed tip into his ribs with all the force she could muster. At the same time, she bit into his lower lip.

Simultaneously, his mouth and his ribs exploded in pain as he doubled over, trying to catch his breath. Blood spurted over his fine white linen shirt.

"What have you done? I was just trying to have some fun."

Ginger scrambled to her feet. "Yes, I know the kind of *fun* you have in mind, Mr. Douglas. Your form of seduction comes very close to rape. How do you think my father would react if I tell him what you're trying to do? Do you think he'd open his arms, and his bank, to you and welcome you into the family? I'm sorry for your plight, but I won't be your way out of your financial problems. Nor will my father, I'm sure. He did not have money handed to him, which is what you're anticipating."

Ginger's eyes glimmered in anger as she continued. "Papa worked hard to get where he is today, and he expects each member of our family to work hard as well. So, you see, Mr. Douglas, you'd never fit into the Fitzpatrick household. You don't know what an honest day's labor is."

A picture of Joseph and his family, working on their ranch, training and breaking horses, flashed through her mind. *Joseph knows what an honest day's labor is, though,* she thought.

Richard tried once again to grab her in a last futile effort to overwhelm her. But, she had grown up with brothers and knew the best place to aim to do the most harm. She raised her knee and hit him squarely in his crotch. Richard crumpled to the ground, grabbing his inflamed testicles and moaning in agony.

Ginger chuckled. "Men. You're all crybabies."

She helped him get to his feet. She felt only a tiny bit sorry for inflicting such pain on him.

"If you can ever find a woman who considers herself lucky just to have you, and she can afford you, you can continue on with your dissolute lifestyle. But this is America, not England. People don't mind working and getting their hands dirty, if that's what's needed to get ahead. That attitude enabled us Americans to beat the pants off you British during the Revolutionary War, and it's why we're here this weekend, celebrating our independence from louts such as yourself!

"Come on," she said. "I'll help you back to the house where you can take care of your nasty cut lip. And maybe get an ice pack to soothe the...ahem...other parts of your body that are hurting. And, if I were you, I'd come up with a really good story about how it happened. You don't want everyone to know it was the result of a failed attempt at lovemaking."

Richard leaned on her and Ginger laughed as they walked toward the house. On the way back, Ginger noticed he had pieces of boxwood hanging from the back of his suit. She playfully poked him with her parasol, in an attempt to free the clippings from the cloth. When the parasol failed to dislodge them, she brushed his back to clear all signs of debris. Soon they were laughing together, as Richard returned the favor and picked some boxwood clippings from her hair. Ginger was almost sorry for Richard and his attempts to land an heiress. It must be a horrible position to be in, to either marry for money or be forever dependent on the benevolence of an older brother.

♦◊♦

William Davenport had been attempting to feed Joseph's horse moldy hay, in the hopes of making the horse sick, when Joseph crept up behind him. William swore the man appeared from nowhere—he hadn't noticed his moccasined entrance. Joseph said nothing, he simply emptied the crib of the bad hay and glared at William.

Foiled in his attempt to put Midnight off his game tomorrow, William backed away from Joseph, and then barreled out of the stable. He ran straight into Ginger and Richard, nearly knocking Ginger off her feet. His stormy eyes took in the scene, and already angry, he turned a malicious gaze toward Richard.

"So, have you finally succeeded in compromising Miss Fitzpatrick, eh, Douglas? When you first boasted several weeks ago that you would be the one to take her, I thought she'd see through you. Yet, here you are, still in my way. And from the looks of it, you two have been rolling around in the grass."

"Officer Davenport, please! Mr. Douglas has not compromised me. How dare you even think such a thing?"

"Unlike you, William, I don't need to compromise Miss Fitzpatrick in order to win her hand. I don't see a whole lot of competition here," Richard taunted.

William bristled. "That's it, man. I've taken one too many of your fancy English slurs. Put up your hands and let's fight like men."

The two men circled each other, fists raised. They bobbed and weaved, each gauging the other, yet neither took a punch. Ginger thought it was more posturing than anything. And, if they were trying to impress her, they needn't bother. Shaking her head in exasperation, she stepped between them and raised her own hands, just as William let go an upper right, aimed at Richard's jaw. Richard ducked out of the way, and the blow landed on Ginger's shoulder, knocking her off her feet. Richard gasped as Ginger fell to the ground, absorbing the blow meant for him.

When William struck Ginger and she fell, Joseph rushed at them, fists clenched. He was at her side in a heartbeat, and helped her to her feet.

"Are you hurt? Is your shoulder all right?" Joseph asked.

"I'm so sorry," Richard said.

"It wasn't your fault, Richard," Ginger replied. "I'm fine. It was not much of a punch."

Richard and Joseph both turned on William.

"Such gentlemanly behavior, Officer Davenport. I'm sure Miss Fitzpatrick will be enamored with you now, if she wasn't before," Richard said, his voice dripping with sarcasm.

"Miss Fitzpatrick, I do apologize. It was never my intent to hit you, only the cowardly Richard Douglas, who was hiding behind your skirts. However can I make amends?"

Ginger dusted herself off and rolled her shoulder to assess the damage. Satisfied it had been just a glancing blow, she replied, "You can make amends by ceasing this childish behavior. I am more than capable of watching out for my own virtue. I don't need either of you to do it for me. Please stop this foolishness."

"We are not just fighting to protect your virtue, Miss Fitzpatrick," William replied. "We are in a battle for your hand."

"Well, then, by all means, stop. My hand is not yours for the taking. I do not have romantic feelings for either one of you." She stole a quick glance at Joseph.

The duelists stopped in their tracks and looked at her in disbelief.

William coughed out a laugh. "You're full of fine talk now, but after I win the horserace in the morning, and have women swarming all over me, you'll change your mind. You will want me then. And despite your words today, I will still welcome your attention tomorrow."

Ginger looked at the West Point officer and raised an eyebrow. "I hardly think it will sway my opinion. I couldn't care less who wins a stupid and ill-advised horserace. But if you want to believe the outcome of the race will change my stance, go ahead."

She turned to Joseph. "I'm unhurt, so please return to Midnight's side. I know you're concerned about his safety. Thank you for your efforts. Mr. Douglas will accompany me to the house."

Joseph silently walked back to the stables as William glared after him. Then, William puffed himself up, and followed Richard and Ginger to the house.

In a voice filled with indignation, he spoke to their backs, "All right, Miss Fitzpatrick. I can wait until tomorrow to claim you as my prize."

Chapter Sixteen

Ginger took her seat at dinner, silently stomping her foot underneath the expensive mahogany table. She'd hoped to be seated near Joseph, but he was not at the table. She and her maid, Colleen, had taken extra care with her grooming this evening. Her new dress, with its full skirt of patterned blue organdy, complemented her hair beautifully. The sleeves fell just below her elbows and were finished off with a wide band of creamy Maltese lace. The bodice was cut in a low V, with another band of lace inset at the middle. The tight bodice made her waist look even smaller, and her hair had been brushed until it gleamed. Ginger knew she looked her best, but it seemed her dress and her grooming were all for naught, for there was no one at dinner she wanted to impress.

She was seated between Basil and Mrs. Curran, their hostess, and across the table from William, who would be racing the next day.

"Basil, where is Joseph this evening?" Ginger asked.

"He's eating with the stable hands tonight."

"But why would he eat in the stable, instead of feasting on this wonderful meal Mrs. Curran has provided for us?" Ginger smiled at Mrs. Curran, who accepted the compliment with a nod of her head.

"Maybe he doesn't want to show his face, knowing how soundly I'm going to beat him tomorrow," William sneered.

Ginger flicked an angry glance across the table at William, then turned back to Basil. "Well?"

"He's worried about his horse, and doesn't want anything more to happen to him."

Ginger caught her breath. "Anything more? Has something happened to Midnight?"

"No, but only because Joseph is never far from him. Someone tried to slip moldy hay into the horse's feeding trough this afternoon."

She glared at William, who would not meet her gaze. "Why, moldy hay would make the horse sick for at least a day! Who would do such a thing, knowing that the big race is tomorrow?"

William straightened in his seat, pulling his body into military erectness. "Are you accusing me of foul play? I have not been anywhere near the stables since this morning. And I don't need to resort to trickery to win the race."

"But you nearly ran into me this afternoon as you were hurrying away from the stables! Surely you remember? It was right before you punched me."

Basil turned to his sister. "William punched you? What are you talking about?" He rose from his seat and reached across the table, grabbing William's arm. "You hit my sister? I'll beat you to a bloody pulp!"

Ginger pulled on her brother's arm and hissed. "Sit down. There's no need to cause a scene. I'd be happy to show you the bruise, Basil, if you'd like. It's of no consequence, really—he certainly didn't have much power behind his punch. I've received harder blows from you and Halwyn when we were just playing. But Mr. Douglas and I did see Officer Davenport leaving the stables this afternoon, so his claim he hasn't been there since morning is indeed false." Basil took his seat once more, but he continued to glare across the table.

William glared back. "So now you're accusing me of lying as well as insinuating I'm trying to harm a horse?"

Basil covered his sister's hand with his own. "Despite the fact that you hit my sister, I'm certain Ginger did not mean to cast aspersions on your character. She knows you are a horse lover, as is Joseph. But in addition to the moldy hay, one of the workers tried to take Midnight out for a run this evening. When Joseph caught him leading the horse out of the stall, the stable boy said he'd made a mistake and had the wrong horse. So, Joseph thought it for the best he take off his fancy dinner suit and stay in the barn for the night, in order to avoid any more mix-ups."

William's hand flexed into a fist on top of the table. His eyes flashed as he stared at Basil. "It seems to me Joseph is finding one excuse after another for why his horse will lose tomorrow. Why doesn't he just accept the fact his is the lesser horse and he is the inferior rider instead of trying to pin blame on someone other than himself and his steed?"

"Believe me, William, Joseph is not trying to point fingers. He would never have said anything about it, but I felt an explanation for his absence from the table this evening was owed to our hostess."

Mrs. Curran nodded her head as she accepted the explanation.

William would not back down. "Well, tomorrow will tell the tale, won't it? When we were out today, both of us going over the course, he merely walked his horse through the race, and let him sniff around, rather than keep the horse on task and get to the finish line. I don't think much of the mount myself, and can't understand why he's gained so much attention from everyone. You'd think all of New York had never seen a horse before, until Joseph came to town with his steeds."

"But Midnight is the most handsome horse I've ever seen." Ginger's voice was almost a whisper. *And the rider the most handsome man I've ever seen.*

"Handsomeness has nothing to do with performance. We'll see what tomorrow brings." William gulped a long swallow from his wineglass.

"Indeed, we will," she replied. "I can't wait."

Chapter Seventeen

The Fourth of July dawned cloudy. A hard, steady rain had fallen during the night, making the ground spongy and soft. Guests on horseback, as well as the two racers, assembled in the front yard, gouging holes in the finely manicured lawn, so recently the scene of spirited croquet and bowling matches.

As the horses milled about, Nathaniel Curran explained to the excited crowd what was about to happen. Standing on the front steps of his home, he cleared his throat dramatically before he began speaking.

"Essentially, there are no rules for this race, other than the starting and ending points. It can be run in any order and on any route the riders choose so long as they cross the four major obstacles—the great stone wall, the ravine, the creek, and the wooden fence. We will begin here at the door to the estate, and end at the steeple of St. George's Episcopal Church in Hempstead. The course is approximately four-and-a-half miles long and consists of a flat but rough terrain portion, a heavily wooded area, several small fences, and a creek. Officials are already positioned at each of the four chosen obstacles to make certain they are crossed by both riders."

Mr. Curran looked out over the crowd. "We will give the spectators ten minutes to get into position before we send the racers off. This will be a difficult and dangerous course, which adds to the excitement. Good luck to both of our riders, and have a safe and clean race."

The crowd dispersed with a cheer, riding off to vie for the best positions along the route of the race. Ginger and Elizabeth rode together, along with Cedric, who had not been far from

Elizabeth's side in the weeks since their passionate encounter in Niblo's Garden.

It's so like Elizabeth to jump into romance with both feet, as she's done with every other experience since we were just young girls, thought Ginger. If it had not been for Elizabeth's influence, Ginger would have missed out on some of her most treasured escapades. Like the night in Niblo's Garden, when Joseph saved Elizabeth from certain ruin. That night, anyway.

She sighed briefly reliving in her mind every detail of that evening. She'd caught his quick glance at her exposed bosom before she could realign her bodice, and, despite the circumstances, had hoped that furtive glance would be enough to enflame Joseph's lust. But, alas, he had remained aloof. At least until the moment she snatched him from certain death when she threw herself at him, knocking him out of the way of a speeding buggy. And then he forever changed her life by branding her with his kiss.

Elizabeth and Cedric paused their horses and exchanged a kiss, leaning precariously over their mounts to do so. Ginger caught her lower lip in her teeth as tears came to her eyes. She knew, deep in her heart, Joseph's feelings for her were as strong as hers were for him, but he kept mounting a resistance. The other day in the stables, he nearly tore her heart out when he told her not to think of him anymore and to select one of her many suitors. Then he referred to his horse as Midnight, the name she had bestowed upon him.

Why had Joseph not taken her into his arms and kissed her again, like Cedric was doing with Elizabeth right now? She truly didn't understand his reluctance. Or his strong will. She had tried coquetry, brazenness, helplessness, and every other feminine wile she could think of to break down his resistance, all to no avail.

Cedric and Elizabeth were whispering to each other as their horses stood side by side. Elizabeth looked like she was ready to leap from her sidesaddle and into Cedric's arms.

"You two are moving much too slowly for my tastes," Ginger said. "I want to be at the finish line to see Joseph take it all. I'm going on ahead, if you don't mind."

Elizabeth didn't turn her eyes away from Cedric, as their horses continued to bump up against each other. "We don't mind at all, do we, my love?"

Ginger needed no further encouragement. She tugged on her top hat to position it squarely in place. She nudged her horse into a trot, then a canter as she sped away from the two lovers. She pondered whether to stay on the path and follow the crowd to Roslyn Harbor, or to take the shorter route through the woods. Because she wanted to be the first to make it to the steps of St. George's, she dug her heels into her horse's sides and turned him toward the woods.

Chapter Eighteen

Joseph and William glared at each other, their horses pawing the ground in readiness.

"I have looked forward to this day for weeks, Joseph Lafontaine. Today I am going to show everyone what you're made of."

Joseph glanced over at his rival. He put his hand on Midnight's withers. The horse's body was shivering in excitement; Joseph knew he was eager to race, and race hard.

"We both have fine steeds. This will be a good race."

William tightened his grip on his horse's reins as he swirled in a circle. "And after you lose to me, Miss Ginger Fitzpatrick will be lost to you as well. She will realize her loyalty is misplaced and I am the better man to claim her hand."

"I thought the race was to prove which was the better horse, not which of us is the better man."

William's lip curled in disdain. "I grow weary of you, pretending not to realize what's going on here. I will win this race, and I will win Ginger's hand and heart as well, before this season comes to an end."

Joseph extended a hand to the man, as Nathaniel Curran mounted the steps of the estate house to signal the start of the race. "Best of luck to you then, on all counts."

William ignored the hand stretched out to him. "I will not soil my hand by touching yours, you filthy Frenchie. I cannot wait until I have bested you and can celebrate with a bottle of the finest cold champagne and Ginger's warm body."

Joseph pulled his hand back and straightened in the saddle. "So be it."

Mr. Curran fired a gun into the air, and both horses took off at a gallop.

The first obstacle on the long course was the barrier separating the Curran estate from the neighboring property. It was constructed of stone and about four feet high—a good test of both horse and rider. William and Joseph pounded toward it side by side. As the stone barrier approached, William cut in front of Joseph and sailed over it with a victorious yell, his fist raised to the sky.

Joseph had to pull his horse sharply to the right in order to avoid a collision with William, yet Midnight cleared the barrier with room to spare. Joseph shook his head at the impetuous young man whose actions placed both horses in jeopardy. Joseph raced along in the other's wake, content for the time being to avoid further peril to his horse by letting William take the lead.

The horses' hooves pounded over the soft ground of the neighboring estate. As the rolling hills gave way to the woods, both riders had to slow their mounts. Footing became more treacherous, and low-lying branches threatened to unseat the two riders. The rain, which had held off all morning, began again. The horses easily leaped over a downed tree and continued their pace along a narrow path through the woods. William's horse momentarily lost his footing on some wet leaves, allowing Joseph to slip into the lead. He marked the way for William as he sped through the last of the wooded area.

As Joseph cleared the forest, he kicked Midnight into a gallop. He had only a few minutes before he came to the next obstacle—the creek, which by now was swollen with last night's downpour. Yesterday, during their inspection of the course, it had been an easy matter to run the horses through the creek, which had been no higher than the horses' fetlocks, but today it was a swirling torrent of brown water. Joseph spied the best opening at the bank for him to cross, and looked over his shoulder. No sign of William yet, but he should be clearing the woods at any second.

Joseph rode downstream to the slight opening on the bank and quickly plunged Midnight into the rapidly running current. As he cleared the water on the other side, he caught a glimpse of William attempting to take his horse into the creek at the same point he had yesterday. The horse whinnied and backed away from the crushing water. Joseph did not wait to see the outcome of this standoff between horse and rider, but instead urged his horse toward the next hurdle in his quest to be first to the steeple.

Midnight's muscles bunched as he jumped the waterlogged ravine, gaining a foothold on the other side in a long easy stride. The cries of the crowd gathered at this obstacle, yelling out encouragement from both sides of the ravine, reached Joseph's ears in a blur of noise as he sailed past. He looked back to see if he could spy William and caught sight of him coming up quickly behind him. He spurred Midnight on to the last obstacle. A wooden fence was the only obstacle left before the horses would race across open fields to the steeple in Roslyn Harbor.

Midnight cleared the fence as Joseph sensed the pounding hooves of William's horse behind him. He glanced over his shoulder and saw William's horse clear the fence with no problem. The ride across the field was on.

Joseph steered Midnight away from the most direct path, losing some ground to William as he did so.

William narrowed his eyes against the rain and yelled to Joseph, "Hey, French slug. The finish is this way." He pointed across the field.

However, Joseph had taken his time yesterday at this point of the course, and let Midnight choose the best route through the field, which was riddled with woodchuck holes. He knew his horse could make up any lost ground with a burst of speed at the end. As Joseph and Midnight galloped along their chosen route, Joseph watched William and his horse go down. He sped on and, within a few minutes, reached the finish line and acknowledged the roar of the crowd as he crossed the line alone. He turned in his saddle, but William was nowhere in sight.

Joseph accepted the congratulations of the well-wishers, many of whom had put money on the outcome of the race. He scanned the crowd, looking for Ginger, but she was not in the group, which troubled him. He knew she would be here to support him unless something happened to prevent her from doing so. He turned his attention back to the crowd hovering around him and Midnight, yelling questions to him and making offers to buy the horse.

A shot rang out from the vicinity of the field where Joseph had last seen William. The crowd fell silent, and Joseph spurred Midnight back the way they had just come. Several men from the crowd jumped on their horses and galloped in the same direction, eager to see what had caused the shot.

Joseph carefully picked his way back over the muddy field. He came upon William, standing beside his horse. William turned to him, revealing his barely controlled anger.

"This is all your fault! I had to shoot the best horse I've ever had, and it's all because of you!" His eyes blazed as he stared at his foe, the smoking gun still in his hand.

"If you had taken your time to examine the course yesterday, you would have noticed all these woodchuck holes and steered your mount clear of them," Joseph replied. "I consider this unfortunate waste of a good horse *your* fault, not mine."

"We will see if the race officials agree when I tell them that while I was at dinner last night, you were out here digging holes to endanger my horse. You will be disqualified."

"Any fool can see this is the work of a woodchuck, not of man."

"Are you back to calling me a fool? We will see about that. I'm going to lodge a complaint against you."

"May I offer you a ride back to the estate, then?" Joseph stared down at the other man, who was soaked to the skin. William looked bedraggled in his now sodden military uniform.

"I will find my own way. I do not want to hazard a ride back with you. Lord knows what cutthroat idea you have up your sleeve to prevent me from seeing justice done."

"As you wish, then." Joseph saluted the officer and turned Midnight in the direction of the warm stables.

Chapter Nineteen

The rain, which had started off gently, had become a classic summer deluge before the racers were halfway through the course. By the time Joseph got back to the Curran property, hard, driving torrents slammed to the ground, obliterating the tracks of the many horses and creating fields of mud where only the morning before lovely grasses had glistened in cultivated splendor.

Although during the walk back to the stables Midnight had sufficiently cooled off from his grueling race, Joseph took his time wiping down the horse completely and checking him over for any signs of cuts or bruises from the rigorous steeplechase. Other than blowing hard, the horse appeared to be in good shape, and ready to take on another challenger.

Joseph took a peppermint candy from his pocket and fed it to the horse before he filled the trough with fresh hay and a cup full of oats. He patted Midnight's neck and spoke softly to him in a mixture of French, Ojibwa, and English.

"*Migwetch, merci*, thank you, my gallant one. You have proven to everyone here that your heart, your *odayin*, is as big as the rest of you. My only regret is that the horse of a foolish man had to be put down." He rested his face against the black's neck, inhaling the familiar odor of horse sweat and hay. He sighed. "Now, we are free to leave New York and return home."

His heart lurched at the thought of never seeing Ginger again after tonight. Even though he knew it was for the best if he left and allowed her to marry one of her own kind, he also knew he would never find another woman like her, even if he searched for the remainder of his life.

He remembered she had not been at the finish line, nor had he seen her on the ride back from the harbor. She had not been among the flurry of riders that befell the stables as people returned their soggy mounts to the stable boys and made their way into the estate house to dry themselves and to get a hot cup of tea or buttered rum. Feeling a sudden sense of urgency, he left the stables and started across the lawn to the Currans' house in hopes of finding Basil.

He spied a stable boy in the yard gathering up the reins of a riderless horse. Ginger's horse!

He grabbed the boy's arm. "Where did this horse come from?"

"I don't know, sir. I found him out here just now, with no rider."

Joseph dropped the boy's arm and hurried to the house with a feeling of foreboding. He followed the sound of male voices into the library. Basil was there with several of the other men. They had changed into dry, casual clothing, and were smoking fat cigars, drinking brandy, and reliving the race from their various perspectives. Joseph's muddy boots left wet stains on the floorboards, but he didn't notice, as his troubled mind accelerated from worried to frantic. He waved off the shouts of congratulations from the men and rushed to Basil's side.

He spoke quietly, for only Basil to hear. "Do you know where Ginger is? No one has seen her, and her horse just came back to the stables without her."

"Excuse us, gentlemen," said Basil, and he and Joseph left the library.

They dashed to the parlor where the ladies had gathered after changing their clothing and drying their hair. Basil's eyes scanned the room, until he located his sister's best friend.

"Elizabeth, you were with Ginger when the race began. Do you have any idea where she is now?"

Elizabeth blushed, then said, "She parted from Cedric and me a few minutes after we left the yard. She said she wanted to get to the finish line before Joseph did, not after, and we were moving much too slowly for her. I haven't seen her since we got back. She hasn't been in the room, either, to change clothes."

Basil then explained to Mrs. Curran that his sister hadn't returned from the race and asked her to organize a detailed search of the house. Staff and guests searched every room and outbuilding for Ginger. But their search came up empty.

"We'll have to search the race route, then," Basil insisted. "There are twelve of us men, so let's split up and each take a part of the course to look for her. Joseph, you're the most accomplished tracker among us, why don't you try to follow her trail?"

William snorted at this suggestion. "There is no trail, Basil. In case you haven't noticed, it's been raining since the middle of the race, and all signs of a trail have been washed away. Not that anyone could distinguish one set of hoof prints from another, anyway."

"I can," Joseph replied, as he hurried from the room and ran to saddle Midnight for yet another ride.

Chapter Twenty

Joseph slowly picked his way through the forest, following Ginger's tracks, which were rapidly fading under the relentless rain. Her horse's hoof prints led into the woods, and he was certain he would find her there. But what had happened? She was a superb rider, and quite comfortable with horses. His sense of dread heightened with each passing minute, but he still moved slowly, all of his senses on high alert.

He plucked a small piece of cloth from a branch near the path and knew instantly it was from her riding outfit. The scent of lilacs still clung to the scrap of fabric. He inhaled the smell as he closed his eyes, relying on his senses, feeling her close to him. He tucked the scrap of cloth into his shirt, and bent over his horse to follow the trail. A few minutes later, he found what he was looking for. A bit of white against the dark needles of the forest floor.

Joseph rapidly dismounted. Ginger was trapped underneath a large branch, which must have fallen suddenly as she rode under it. Her white blouse was like a beacon, allowing him to see her body in the forest's gloomy shadows. Joseph's years of tracking game in the woods to provide food for his family worked to his advantage now. A person less skilled in reading the forest would have ridden right past her, unaware there was anyone trapped underneath the huge pine.

"Ginger," he yelled at the top of his lungs, as the rain continued to pound the earth. "Ginger, are you hurt?"

No sound came from the crumpled form under the branch. She was either unconscious—or dead.

Joseph assessed the situation and plotted the best course of action to remove the branch, which must have weighed hundreds of pounds. Fortunately, the bulk of it had missed Ginger, but it was too heavy for him to pluck off her. With the rain still pounding relentlessly, he unfurled his rope from the saddle. He quickly tied one end around the branch and the other end around the saddle horn. Speaking quietly to Midnight, he slowly began backing up the horse, until the branch was pulled out of the way. Joseph let the line go slack as he dismounted and rushed toward Ginger again, using all his strength to tear the remaining branches away.

His hands slid over her body, checking for broken bones. He took a deep breath when he could find no outward signs of injury, although she was burning up with fever. His heartbeat slowly returned to normal. She was unconscious, but he could detect no skeletal damage. He untied his rope, and then carefully picked Ginger up off the soggy ground. He cradled her in one arm as he swung himself back into his saddle and rewound the rope.

While riding over the course route yesterday, he had spied a small hunter's cabin not far from their location. It would not be much, but it could provide shelter until the rain stopped, so he headed Midnight in the direction of the cabin. He knew Ginger should be tended to by a doctor, but he worried more about the amount of time she'd already been exposed to the elements. It seemed imperative to get her to immediate shelter.

Several minutes later, he kicked open the door of the tiny cabin and laid Ginger on a bunk in the small, dusty room. There was a stash of dry wood in the cabin, so he started a fire to remove the chill from the room. He found several blankets and wrapped a couple of them tightly around Ginger, while he rubbed her arms and legs to promote blood circulation. He brushed her hair away from her face with gentle movements and dried it with another blanket. He ran the cloth over her face, drying it, too.

As his large hands moved over her, he sighed. She was safe now. He could breathe again. He cupped her face in one hand, leaned down, and allowed himself the small luxury of kissing the lips that had haunted him for weeks. Chastising himself for his weakness, he straightened back up again. There was much to do. She was still in danger from exposure to the elements. He must get her warmed up.

He added more wood to the fire. He had to take care of his horse, too, which he'd left standing in the rain. He picked up another blanket and went outside again. He led Midnight onto the small covered porch where the horse could at least get some shelter from the storm, and tied him there. He removed the saddle and rubbed Midnight down with the blanket.

"Good job, Midnight. We found her. *Migwetch*, my friend." He pulled an apple from his saddlebag and fed it to the horse.

When he went back into the cabin, Ginger was still unconscious. She was shivering violently, and he knew he had to get her out of her wet clothing if she was to get warm. He tugged on her muddy riding boots and pulled them and her stockings off, then dried her feet. In an attempt to protect her modesty, he undressed her while she lay under the blankets. Her tailored, close-fitting jacket was the first to go. He held her in a sitting position while he worked her arms out of one tight sleeve, then the other.

Throwing the sodden jacket to the floor, he pulled her white blouse out of her riding skirt. As he unbuttoned the blouse, his hand moved over the swell of her breasts, and he groaned as he steeled his mind to accomplish his task. Her damp blouse finally was unbuttoned, and he again pulled one arm at a time out of the garment before he dropped it to the floor.

His hand returned to her waist as he unhooked the skirt. His callused hands caressed the smooth curve of her hips as he pulled the full skirt down and off her legs. He lingered over his task for a moment longer than he needed to, enjoying the feel of her body in his hands. Like a man coming out of a dream, he shook himself from his trance and divested her of the remainder of her outer clothing with relative ease.

It was the undergarments that caused a problem. He was not accustomed to the fancy under things these Easterners wore, and he had no idea how to unclasp them, especially without looking at them. Taking a deep breath, he removed the covers from Ginger—and what he observed made his mouth water.

She was quite simply magnificent. Creamy skin with a sprinkling of tiny freckles dotted the landscape of her upper body. The corset she was wearing pushed her bosom up, enhancing her cleavage. His eyes raked over her curves for a moment, and the image was burned into his mind forever. He turned her over gently and undid the binding, releasing the wet undergarment. As her breasts tumbled free of their constraints, Joseph's heart leaped. He yearned to cup one in his hand, but knew any dalliance was dangerous in more ways than one. He still needed to strip off her bloomers, and whatever else was on her bottom half of her body and warm her, or she might catch a dreadful cold—or worse. With a blanket he dried the top half of her body.

He finally finished removing all her garments and wrapped her naked form back into the blankets. He laid each article of her clothing near the fire, which was now roaring. The small room was beginning to heat up—as were Joseph's thoughts. He ran his hand lightly over Ginger's beautiful hair just as she shivered again, and moaned softly. Cursing himself as some kind of fool, he removed his wet deerskin shirt and leggings, draped them over the hearth, and lay down beside her. As he took her into his arms in an attempt to warm her more quickly with his body heat, he whispered words of endearment into her hair, praying to his mother's gods as well as to his father's God she would wake up soon.

The feel of her skin against his was almost his undoing.

Accustomed to always keeping his emotions hidden, he now let them surface as he held his beloved for the first time. As his senses reveled in delight, he was surprised to realize, although she was much smaller than him, they fit together beautifully. He drew her head under his chin as he pulled her closer and wrapped his arms around hers and threw one leg over her hips. He ran his rough hands up and down her arms, hoping to get her blood flowing to her extremities faster. While he was relishing the sensation of lying next to the one woman he loved more than life itself, he knew if he did not get out from under the covers soon, he would never be able to.

Chapter Twenty-One

Joseph had managed, with his body heat, to get Ginger to stop shaking during the night. But being so close to her, feeling her soft breasts against his naked chest, and luxuriating in the rise and fall of her body as she took each breath was torment for him. For his own safety, as soon as he got her warmed, he left the bed and dressed, but stayed by her side, indulging himself by watching every flicker of her eyelids and listening to every small sigh from her lovely mouth. A mouth he wanted to possess again and again.

Since the day they first met, he felt he could only sneak quick glances at her. Basil had warned him not to touch her, and he was trying with all his might not to betray his best friend. But now, after a long night of watching her and worrying about her, he realized this small woman had wound herself around his heart.

Slowly, Ginger awoke. Joseph watched her eyes moving under her lids as she struggled to wake up. Breathing a sigh of relief, he gazed at her as she blinked and looked around the strange room, lit only by the glow of a small fire. She attempted to sit upright, but fell back again. She grabbed her head, as if to slow its spinning.

Joseph sat beside her. "It is all right, little one. You are safe now."

"Where am I? What happened?" Ginger tried to focus on Joseph's dark eyes as the dizziness passed.

"I found you in the woods, where a tree branch had fallen on you. Your horse came back to the stables by himself, so we sent out parties of men looking for you. I found you and brought you here to get out of the rain. We are in a hunter's cabin in the middle of the forest."

Ginger jumped as Joseph laid his large hand on her forehead. "Your fever has gone down. This is a good sign. How does the rest of your body feel? I checked for broken bones and could not find any."

Ginger slid her hands under the covers and ran them up and down her body, realizing for the first time she was naked. Her eyes widened, and she gasped.

"Did you remove my clothes?"

"Yes," he admitted. "They were soaking wet, and I had to get you warmed up."

Ginger's blush rose from her toes to her cheeks, which became inflamed with color. She stared up at him again and gasped. "You threatened me on our fateful day in the livery, saying you would like to strip me of my bloomers and have your way with me. Did you ravage me?" She squeaked out the question.

"You were unconscious, and ill. I would not take advantage of you under such circumstances."

"Damn," she whispered. She pummeled her hands on the covers. Then she smiled up at him.

"But I'm awake and well now." She let the covers slip from her shoulders as she tried once again to sit up.

He pulled the covers up over her. "Awake, but still ill. We will head back to the house at first light."

"Good. I'm still so tired." She lowered herself back to the bunk.

"You must not sleep again. You were knocked out, and now you must stay awake for a few hours, until we can return to the house."

Ginger gave Joseph what she hoped was a coquettish smile. "Then it will be up to you to keep me awake somehow. And if you refuse to seduce me, and destroy my reputation so I'll be forced to marry you, I guess we'll be reduced to having conversation. Tell me about the race. Did Midnight win? I'm so disappointed I missed it."

"Yes, Midnight came in first. William's horse stepped into a woodchuck hole during the last section of the course, and broke his leg. William had to put him down."

Ginger gasped. "Oh, the poor horse. William must be so upset."

"You might say so. He is lodging a protest with the authorities about the outcome."

"Why? Isn't it enough his horse had to be put down? What a waste of good horseflesh."

"He is accusing me of digging the holes."

Ginger snorted. "What a ridiculous notion. And what a ridiculous man. Well, I'm glad you won fair and square, and anything William says or does will only show what a sore loser he is." She sat up straighter in the bed and pulled the blankets to her shoulders.

"I don't want to talk about William, though. I want to talk about you. Tell me about your life in St. Louis. All I know about you is that you and your family raise horses. Where do you find them? Do you race those you don't sell, or breed a line of champions? I know so little of your life there."

He shrugged. "It is not such an exciting life. There are no formal balls or affairs, like here. Most of the work we do is hard and dirty. We chase wild horses, mostly, catch and break them, and then sell them to the settlers who are traveling west."

Ginger drew her knees up under her chin and wrapped her arms around them. "It sounds exciting to me! What kind of profit margin do you have on each horse you sell?"

As he stared at her, she shrugged her shoulders and continued, "I am good with numbers. And I'm curious about your business, and would like to explore ways to make it more profitable. It's what I do. Didn't Basil tell you I've been working with Father and Halwyn at the bank for some time now?"

"He did tell me. And my reply was to say women belonged in the home, not in a bank."

Ginger pounded her hands on the bed, and her green eyes sparkled. "This is exactly the kind of backward thinking Amelia Bloomer and I are trying to change. Would you rather I was home, barefoot and pregnant?"

Her eyes blazed at him. His eyes blazed back, not in anger, but in lust.

His quiet reply spoke volumes between them. "I would let you wear moccasins."

Chapter Twenty-Two

Without speaking, she opened the covers and stretched out her arms to him. He groaned as he drank in the sight of her, like a man dying of thirst. He closed the gap between them and lost himself in her warm embrace. His hands slid over her breasts as he finally took one of them in his hand and lowered his mouth to kiss its tip.

Joseph was drowning in a sea of delicious torment. He wanted to touch every part of her body as fast as he could, yet he wanted to take his time with her and explore every inch of her luscious body. He had an urgent need to press his finger in the dimples he had spotted on her derriere when he took off her bloomers. He wanted to run his thumb along her instep and the back of her knee, just to see her response to her touch. He cupped her upturned face in the palm of his hand and blew a light breath up her nostrils, much like he did with his horses to gain their trust. He captured her mouth in a long kiss, his tongue flicking against her lips until she opened her mouth to him. His tongue greedily entered, and then withdrew, only to enter again, setting up a ritualistic rhythm. He smiled in satisfaction as she gave a small moan of delight.

He wanted to do the same with the rest of her body, and touch her in a way no man had done. To be the one to bring her to her first orgasm and to watch her eyes fog over in ecstasy. He wanted to be the first, and the only man to teach her the ways of sexual fulfillment. But for now, he slowed the pace of his heart, and his thoughts, and enjoyed the leisurely exploration of the woman who had so long been denied to him.

His hands recaptured her breasts as his mouth continued to

ply hers. He ran his thumbs over her nipples, causing her to catch her breath. She innocently arched her body up to him, granting him even greater access. She pulled him nearer and returned his kisses. Her moans of delight became louder as he once again moved his mouth to a nipple and resumed the same sensual rhythm he had been using on her mouth. As her passion rapidly mounted, he backed off from his exploration of her breast.

Her moan of dismay made him smile.

"Be patient, *ma petite.*"

He ran his hands up her body to her face and kissed her again. His gentle kisses continued, first very slow and light as a feather, then intensifying in force and duration, until he sensed her heat rising once more. He backed off again, teasing and tormenting her, as well as himself. He wanted them both to remember this night forever.

He positioned his leg between her thighs, and began to lightly pulse his thigh against her sweet spot. The deerskin of his leggings added an extra tactile sensation, and she began to react to the motion Joseph was setting for her. She wrapped her thighs around his leg and rose up to meet him each time he pressed against her. Her moans became louder and more insistent. Feeling her body tightening, he glanced at her face. Her eyes were tightly closed, and she was running her tongue over her lips.

"Open your eyes, *ma petite.* I want to watch you."

Her green eyes locked with his brown ones and he watched them go wide with pleasure and then cloud over. She moaned one final time, and her body shuddered. She released the blanket from her fists as her body relaxed into a puddle of satiation.

As her breathing returned to normal, she pulled Joseph close again. "Is it always like this? This lovemaking?"

He smiled. "Most of the time I would have my clothes off as

well, which would make it much better."

"Oh, having you naked too *would* make it better. Shall we try again?" She began to tug on his shirt. He laughed, and kissed her again. "I think you need a few minutes." His kisses were gentle, but he never stopped touching her.

She gazed lovingly up at him. "Tell me, Joseph, what does the word 'Giz-ah-gin' mean? I know some of the French language, but I have never heard of it."

"How do you know that word?"

"You whispered it to me during the night, sometime. I woke up a little and felt you next to me, whispering softly, the word 'gizahgin' over and over. Is it Canadian, or something?"

His lips curved up slightly. "Or something. It, ah ... it means 'I love you.'"

Ginger's breath caught in her throat. "Do you mean it, or were you just saying it to get me to wake up?"

He brushed a strand of hair from her face and captured her lips in a long, passionate kiss. "*Gizahgin,*" he murmured, taking her in his arms again.

She ran her fingers through his hair and pulled him close to her.

Just then, the door crashed against the wall, and Basil stormed into the room.

As Ginger screamed, Joseph rolled out of the bed and landed on his feet, like a cat. He stood protectively over Ginger, who had drawn the covers up to her neck. Basil surveyed the room with Ginger's clothing laid out near the fire. He ran his hand through his hair and then locked his angry stare on Joseph.

"What have you done to my sister?"

"Saved her from dying in the forest. A tree branch fell on her, knocking her off her horse and pinning her to the ground. Even if she had not been unconscious, she would never have been able to get out from under the branch without my help. You are most welcome."

"And then you brought her here and took advantage of her?"

Ginger rose from the bed, wrapping the blanket around her. "He did no such thing, much to my regret, Basil. While I was unconscious, he stripped off my wet clothes and got me warmed up. Joseph has been a perfect gentleman." She strode to Joseph's side.

"It doesn't look like it from my vantage point. Were you going to bring her back, once you were finished with her?"

"We were about to return to the house, now that it is first light."

"We've all been out looking for you all night. The ladies even joined us in the search once dawn broke. It's fortunate I'm the one who walked in here, or your reputation would be in tatters, Ginger. We'll leave you to get dressed. Joseph, you will come with me outside."

Ginger cried out in frustration. "No, I will not get dressed! Joseph and I aren't finished here. I don't need to listen to you. We want you to leave and pretend you've not seen us. Right, Joseph?" She turned to him with a look of confusion on her face.

Joseph quietly replied, "Do as your brother asks, Ginger."

Basil turned on his heel, and left the room. Joseph let his gaze flicker over Ginger's face briefly, one last time. He reached out to run his fingers through her hair, but stopped in mid-air and dropped his hand. He sighed and walked from the room without saying a word.

Chapter Twenty-Three

Joseph walked outside to find Basil pacing in the small clearing, pounding one fist into the palm of his other hand. Basil's enraged glare moved up from the forest floor to meet Joseph's face.

Joseph nodded at Basil's curled fist as the two of them circled one another. "Would you like to take a swing at me?"

"More than anything, but I won't, because you'd probably knock me senseless and take advantage of the situation to go back inside and continue to seduce Ginger."

"I will offer no resistance to you. Go ahead and hit me if it will make you feel better."

"No, I'd feel worse if you let me take a cheap shot. Neither outcome is a prospect I find enticing." He dropped his gaze to the ground and then looked back at Joseph. "How could you?"

"I have done nothing to harm your sister's reputation, Basil. She is still pure."

Basil ran his hand through his hair again. "You were in bed with her while she was naked, for God's sake! How is that 'still pure'? If anyone other than me had found you, her reputation would be destroyed, and she would be forced to marry you."

"We would not need to be *forced*. It would be my honor to marry her, Basil."

Basil's expression changed from anger to incredulity as he glared at the man he had called his best friend. "It's one thing to be my friend, but quite another to toy with the affections of my sister. She will marry someone worthy of her. I allowed you to come with me to New York and welcomed you into my family. This is my fault. I never dreamed you would force yourself on one of my sisters."

Joseph's defenses rose. Basil's reaction to the scene in the cabin, to be told Joseph was not worthy, was an insult he had been dealing with his entire life. Somehow, his Indian blood overruled the French blood when it came to finding his place in society. He had entered into his friendship with Basil tentatively, knowing Basil had a naïve approach to life on the border and that his friendship with an Indian could change at any time. It seemed the moment was at hand.

"So you are showing your true colors after all, Basil. You had a great deal of fun with the 'Indian' though, did you not? Amusing yourself with the people you know here in New York and wondering what their reactions might be if they only knew my true bloodline. You and your family have regaled each other with the joke you were playing on your friends. You all have had a great deal of fun this summer, at my expense. I thought all along it was a bad idea, did I not?"

Basil shrugged his shoulders uncomfortably. "I'll admit, I believed it was a great joke to have you here. I thought most of New York's high society was a bunch of old fuddy-duddies and I did want some fun at their expense. Little did I realize the joke would be played on my family. Well, it can't be helped now. As much as I regret my foolish choices, at the end of the day, you are an Indian, my sister is a blueblood, and the two of you will never unite. I'm sorry I brought you here at all. I regret I got you involved in this wretched horserace. I've been going out of my mind all night, worrying about Ginger and fearing my foolishness at accepting William's taunt might result in my sister's death." He looked up at Joseph. "But it seems my senselessness has done far greater damage than I ever thought."

"Are you saying that Ginger and me being together would be worse than her death?"

"If she was to run off with you, neither of you would be welcome in the family, which is the same thing as her being gone from this Earth. And I have no doubt, from what I saw in the cabin, the two of you would have been on the road to St. Louis this morning, if I had arrived an hour later."

Joseph sighed, knowing Basil was correct in his assessment. The thought had certainly crossed his mind during the night to just pick her up, set her on Midnight with him, and ride off toward the West. And he knew it was what Ginger would want—at least until she knew his true heritage.

Ginger, still wrapped in a blanket, yanked open the door to the cabin and joined the men in the clearing. Rushing to Joseph's side, she turned to face her brother.

"Basil, please leave us alone."

"Not until you hear the truth. Joseph has to know his place."

"What do you mean, *his place*? His place is here, with me! You're the one who should leave, not Joseph."

"No, his place is not with you, sweetie. It never has been. It never could be. Tell her, Joseph."

"Tell me, Joseph."

"I am only half French-Canadian. The other half is Ojibwa Indian. And I am equally proud of both halves."

"So? What does it matter what your heritage is? The only thing that really matters is the nature of the man you are."

Basil sighed. "It is the way of the West. He will forever be treated as an Indian, despite being half French-Canadian. He will never fit into society, especially the portion of society you belong to. You must forget about him, and pick a husband who is worthy of your station. It's fortunate I was the one who discovered you, so we can salvage your reputation and one of your more patient suitors can still lay claim to you."

"I will not pick another for my husband. Joseph has my heart, and has had it since the first night you brought him into our midst. I knew the moment he led me to the dance floor at the Cotillion that we were destined to be together for all time."

Joseph's smoldering gaze lit on Ginger. "You can come with

me right now. I will take you home with me to St. Louis."

"Ginger, please, think carefully about this." Basil's glance bounced from his friend to his sister. "If you go with Joseph, and marry him, our family's reputation will be destroyed. Father's customers at the bank will leave and the family will be destitute. You know how fickle the wealthy are. One hint of scandal and they'll go running, so as not to be tarnished themselves."

Ginger's eyes filled with tears as she listened to her brother's logical remarks.

Basil continued. "Please, listen to me. I thought it would be fun to have Joseph accepted into our society as my friend, all the while knowing he was an Indian. I wanted to show everyone how hypocritical New York high society was and to have a good laugh."

"But instead, you've only shown *yourself* to be the hypocrite. I thought he was your friend. Why would you want to make a joke of him? What was the story you told about him saving your hide when you first arrived in St. Louis? Was that a big joke, too?"

She began to cry in earnest as Basil watched her put a hand on Joseph's arm. Both men remained silent, waiting for her choice.

Her eyes raked over Basil. "Joseph and I share a very deep bond, much like you and he do. We saved each other's lives a few weeks ago. We were in the path of a runaway buggy on Broadway. I saw it coming and jumped into Joseph's arms, knocking him out of the way. Then he rolled us to safety at the last second. I knew he would never brag to you about how he saved both my blasted reputation and me, but I will. I literally threw myself at him time and again, and he would not be moved, until this morning. Even then, he made certain he did not violate me and I remain a virgin, capable of marrying another." She spat out the words to her brother, her green eyes blazing.

"Mother and I had 'the talk' before the season began, Basil, so I know what I'm speaking about. I gladly would have given myself to Joseph in a heartbeat. I still want to."

"But think about Father. And your sisters. What will their chances be for a successful marriage if you follow your heart instead of your head? Please, I'm appealing to your logical nature. Don't compound my mistake by making one of your own."

Ginger drew in a deep breath as she pondered her situation. "Basil is right, Joseph. If I went with you—and you know I want to beyond reason—I would be placing my family's reputation and future livelihood in jeopardy. I'm sorry."

She raised tear-filled eyes to him, and inched up on her toes to kiss him softly.

"We are not yet done, *ma petite*." Joseph ran his hand down her cheek, wiping her tears away. "I will see you again."

Without another word, she walked inside the cabin.

Basil turned to Joseph. "I want you to leave here, right this minute, and not return. When I get back to St. Louis, I am going to close your father's account. The bank will cease doing business with Tall Feather Enterprises. And as for you, I never want to see you again. Do you understand?"

Joseph looked at his former friend, sadly. Basil was just a white man like any other. Already, he missed their friendship. He sighed.

"I understand. You are like all the rest. Forgive me for thinking you were someone special. I ride out now knowing it is not yet time for Ginger and me to be together."

He saddled Midnight, untied the reins, and jumped on his back. He nudged the horse into a trot.

"It will never be time!" Basil yelled after him.

♦◊♦

After a few minutes of pacing in the clearing, Basil returned to the cabin where Ginger was dressing. She glared at him as he entered the room.

"Well, he's gone now, thank God, and you can forget about him."

Ginger ran to her brother and began to pummel him with her fists as her tears of anger became sobs of remorse. Basil said nothing more and let her cry herself out.

Finally, she turned her back to him. "I need some help getting laced back into my corset. If you would, please, Basil."

She allowed Basil to tighten the laces. Her sobs had diminished and now sounded like a kitten mewing.

Basil laid his hand on her shoulder. "Gin—"

She cut him off and shrugged out of his grasp. "I have nothing to say to you, Basil."

"All right then, have it your way. If you are sufficiently put back together, I'll take you to the estate, and we can call off the search. Everyone will be so relieved."

"Yes, I expect they will. I'm nearly ready. I want to say this while we're alone, though. If you want to blame someone for destroying my hopes at making a proper marriage, blame yourself, Basil, not Joseph. He is the only man I want, and if I can't have him, I'll have no one."

"Please don't say that, Ginger. It would break my heart if you martyr yourself because of my stupidity."

Ginger took one last look at the room where Joseph had touched her with his scorching hand and branded himself on her heart. Where he finally declared his love for her. Tears slid down her face as she realized she had not had time to return the declaration to him. With a final sob, she turned her back on the cabin and on the life that might have been hers.

Chapter Twenty-Four

As they rode back to the Curran estate, Basil began to think of an explanation he could offer for how he managed to find Ginger—and what had become of Joseph. He needed something plausible to quell the spate of questions sure to come their way as soon as they arrived. A plan formed in his mind and, as they neared the large house, he spoke quietly.

"I know you don't have anything to say to me, but we need to get our stories straight. I'm thinking we should tell everyone Joseph found you, got you to the cabin, and told you to stay there until daylight. He knew that staying with you would cast you in a bad light, so he went back to St. Louis, having finished the race and his work here in New York. I came upon you walking through the woods this morning, trying to find your way back to the house. Will you agree to align your story with mine?"

She thought for a moment, nodded in agreement, and then added, "So long as you say or do nothing to disparage Joseph, I will agree. But, if anyone thinks he left because of the outcome of the race, or because William was going to file a protest, or if anyone tries to otherwise blacken his name, I will tell everything as it truly has happened, family reputation notwithstanding. Unless you come to his defense."

"Hopefully, the race is old news by now. Your disappearance and now subsequent return will surely put it out of everyone's mind. You have had all of us quite frightened out of our wits, me especially."

"As Joseph said, the race was a foolish and childish thing to do, an idea put forth by two foolish and childish men—you and William. It resulted in one good horse being put down, and me nearly perishing out in the forest. So once again, Joseph has proven to be the better and smarter man, even though his skin is brown. Is that what you're saying?"

Basil groaned. "Not exactly in those terms. I can tell I'm going to have a hard time getting back into your good graces. I remember how long it took you to forgive me the last time I truly upset you."

"What you have done in this instance does not begin to compare with the time you put all my hair ribbons in the ink well. You have broken my heart, and ripped my one true love from my arms. My life will never be the same, and I may never forgive you."

"Then you would break my heart, Ginger."

"I wish I could say I am sorry, but I'm not." She slid off the horse as it came to a stop and walked into the house without waiting for him.

Her mother, father, and Elizabeth all hurried to the door when they heard Basil's horse approach the house. Tearfully, they wrapped her in a group embrace.

"We were so frightened for you. Since Elizabeth's last glimpse of you was as you headed into the forest, we had horrible visions of you, alone in the dark woods all night, cold and frightened. Why, anything could have happened to you! Come into the parlor and tell us what went wrong."

Ginger smiled weakly at them. "Could I first have a bath and change clothing? And, I am a bit weary from my ordeal. I wish for a nap. I'm no worse for wear, just tired."

Charlotte bustled around her. "Most certainly, dear. You do look pale. I'll order a bath be drawn for you. Come with me, I'll comb out your hair while we wait for hot bath water."

Charlotte took Ginger's hand and they climbed the stairs, leaving the relieved group to bombard Basil with questions. Basil followed George and Elizabeth into the parlor and helped himself to some hot tea while the other guests gathered to hear the details.

"I don't know how the accident happened," he began, "but, as Ginger was riding through the forest, a branch snapped off a tree and hit her. She was knocked from her horse and pinned underneath the huge fallen branch. Joseph was able to track her trail through the woods and found her, still trapped and unconscious. He freed her and took her to a small hunter's cabin in the woods nearby and built a fire there to warm her. When she woke up, he urged her to stay in the cabin, out of the rain, until morning, and gave her directions back to the estate. I found her walking in the woods this morning."

"How fortunate we are to have a knowledgeable tracker in our midst," said Mrs. Curran. "I shudder to think what would have happened to poor Ginger if Joseph hadn't found her. Where is our hero?"

"He didn't want the acclaim he knew would come his way, so he took off sometime during the night and began the long ride back to St. Louis."

William's lip curled at the mention of his foe. "He left because he was going to be disqualified from the race, not because he was a hero. Who would believe such nonsense?"

"Joseph saved Ginger from a certain death in the woods last night," Basil said angrily. "She would never have survived being out in the rain. Even if she had made it through the night, who among us would have been able to find her before she perished from cold, or from an animal attack? So, he is due the moniker of 'hero' although he would never admit to it."

♦◊♦

Charlotte brushed Ginger's long locks. Ginger closed her eyes, enjoying the pampering her mother was bestowing on her. How long had it been since her mother brushed her hair? Tears dampened her eyes as she looked at her mother's reflection in the mirror.

"Darling, it's all right now," Charlotte cooed softly to her daughter. "You're home, you're safe, and you can put this harrowing experience behind you."

"That's just it, Mother. I can't. I'll never be able to." Ginger began to cry in earnest.

Charlotte put down the brush and took her daughter into her arms. "Did Joseph behave inappropriately or take advantage of you in the woods? Is this why you're so upset? You can tell me anything, you know."

Ginger patted her mother's arm, and sighed in defeat. "Don't worry, Mother. I'm still as pure as the driven snow, unfortunately. The story Basil is telling the guests is quite different from what actually happened, and I have agreed to go along with it to save our family's reputation. But the truth is, he sent Joseph away. I love Joseph with all my heart and he loves me, and Basil can't stand the idea I would fall in love with his best friend—his *Indian* friend!"

Charlotte raised her hand to her forehead. "Oh, no! I was afraid from the day we started this deception something like this would happen. But, I was hoping we could get through the season playing out the ruse Basil forced us to perpetuate on our friends."

Ginger stared at her mother in amazement. "You mean, you knew about Joseph's heritage, too? How could you go along with this? And how could I be the only one who was unaware?"

"I not only knew about it, I'm the one who unfortunately put us in this spot, by first suggesting you dance with Joseph. And, I'm the one who came up with the plan we've been playing out all season. When Basil brought Joseph to the Cotillion and all of society danced with him, we had to think of something to protect our reputations and those of the young ladies who danced with him after you did. So, we chose to ignore his Indian heritage and passed him off as a French-Canadian. You weren't the only one who was in the dark about his true origin. How could Joseph have so abused our family's trust by forcing his affections on you?" She cupped her daughter's face in her hands.

Ginger pulled away angrily and stood up. "He did not take advantage of me, Mother, although I would have welcomed his advances. Did you not hear me say unfortunately I'm still as pure as the driven snow? Instead of seducing me when he had every opportunity, he saved me from a certain death! William and Richard—the two 'suitable' men, in your view—are the ones who have been attempting to compromise me!"

Charlotte gasped at Ginger's claim about two of the finest men of the season. But Ginger barely slowed in her tirade.

"I literally threw myself at Joseph time and again, but he has a will of iron and would not taint my blessed reputation. Unfortunately, the same cannot be said of William and Richard. I have been fighting off their advances all season. I will not listen to any criticism from you, or anyone else, when it comes to Joseph!"

She turned on her heel and stomped away to the waiting bath. Ginger divested herself of her dirty garments with the help of her maid. The she sank into the bathwater up to her chin.

"Will there be anything else, Miss Ginger?"

"No, Colleen. I'd just like to soak the coldness out of my bones. You may leave me."

"Would you like me to heat some more water for you, to warm up the bath in a few minutes?"

Ginger smiled. "You know me well by now, don't you? Yes, I'd like a long soak today."

As Colleen left to tell the kitchen staff she needed even more hot water, Ginger relaxed against the high back of the slipper tub. The warm water was finally leaching the chill from her body. She sighed deeply, as her tears dropped into the warm water.

How could Basil have done such a thing to the family? Maybe his year in the West made him forget the strict conventions of society everyone in New York held. Perhaps he just needed to grow up a bit more. Whatever the reason for his idiocy, he had done one thing for which she would be forever grateful. He had introduced her to the only man she would ever love. She could be thankful for their one night together. She knew she would remember every moment of it for the rest of her life. She closed her eyes and relived the evening, from the moment she had awakened to find herself alone with Joseph in the cozy little cabin in the woods.

She had sensed his presence before she had opened her eyes, as he knelt by the bed. The love and the protection radiating from him, as he watched over her and warmed her, gave her such a strong sense of safety. When she realized she was naked, and he had gazed upon her nude body without her knowledge, powerful and previously unknown feelings washed over her. She knew she would die happy if she could just see and touch his naked body, too.

But those thoughts came before Joseph finally gave in to his feelings and climbed into bed with her. His caress had aroused flames of torment within her that she had not realized her body was capable of. She closed her eyes and remembered.

Ginger inhaled sharply as she recalled the feel of his mouth on her breast and how his touch seared her heart. She knew at that fateful moment only Joseph would ever be able to claim it. Her fingers had roamed over his clothed body greedily. She wanted him to be as naked as she was so she could caress his tawny skin. Her nightly dreams of being close to him were finally coming true. She sensed his hardness pressing up against the core of her being and was pleased she had such a profound effect on him.

She changed her mind about dying happily if she could just touch his naked body. As his hands roamed over her, she realized there was much more to lovemaking and she wanted to experience it all. When he put his leg between her thighs and began to press against her, it took her breath away. The explosion within her was more potent than any emotion she had ever had. All thoughts left her except the realization that she was more alive than she had ever been, and she wanted to live forever if she could have Joseph by her side. Her tears began afresh as she remembered how the heat had risen within her at his touch. To never have those feelings again was too heartbreaking to contemplate.

Colleen knocked on the door, and then entered before Ginger could splash water on her face. The maid rushed to Ginger's side when she spied the tears streaming down her face.

"Why, you're crying as if the world has just come to an end, miss."

"For me, it has."

"Nonsense, missy. You've just had a scare, 'tis all. It must have been so frightening to be alone in the woods, and unable to free yourself from those branches. I hate the forest."

Ginger lay back in the tub while Colleen poured in the hot water. When the water was toasty again, she became drowsy. As Colleen washed her hair, Ginger asked, "I can't believe I don't know this about you, but have you ever been in love?"

Colleen smiled. "Yes, miss. I was married for a while, to a wonderful man."

"What happened?"

"He was a woodsman. He and a crew of men were working in the woods one fine day when one of the trees they cut didn't fall properly. My husband was crushed to death."

Ginger gasped. "Oh, I'm so sorry."

"Ah, but that wasn't the worst of it, miss, on what was the blackest day of my life. When the men came out of the woods with his body, I went into shock at seeing my man dead. I was pregnant with our first child, and I lost the baby. So, in one day, I went from being a wife and soon-to-be mother to being alone in this world and having to fend for myself."

Ginger took hold of Colleen's coarse hand, and looked up at her. "Oh, how heart-breaking. I never knew. You must be so sad."

"Well, I figured life out after losing my man. You, and only you, are responsible for your own happiness, and no one else can tell you what's right, or how you should be feeling. I came to work for your family soon after my tragedy, and I've been quite happy. I have a sense of belonging with both your family and with the other servants in the household. And, I even have taken a shine to a new man—the iceman who comes around several times a week to the house in the city. He's quite a handsome lad, and so strong and muscled. Who would have thought a man who makes his living delivering blocks of ice would turn my head?"

"You give good advice about making your own happiness. I need to heed it."

Ginger sunk into the water completely, rinsing the soap from her hair one final time. Colleen stood with a towel at the ready for her.

"What would you do if the iceman whom you fancy told you he fancies you back, and then is forced to leave the area? Would you follow him?"

"Lordy, my wee lass. What a question! Would I leave my good job and blindly follow after a man without him asking me to come? No, I think not."

"But what if you truly loved him with all your heart?"

Colleen smiled. "So, it's true love then, is it, miss? With the Frenchman?"

Ginger nodded slowly.

"Well, Miss Ginger. I am a firm believer in true love finding a way. Be patient."

"Thank you, Colleen. You've made the most sense of anyone I've talked to since I came out of the woods. After you comb out my hair, I think I'll try to sleep for a while."

"All right, miss, as you wish."

Chapter Twenty-Five

Ginger changed into an afternoon dress of purple taffeta, with ribbon woven into the fabric to form a plaid design. The bell skirt and wide pagoda sleeves set off her figure, as did the waist-cinching corselet, but she only sighed deeply at her image. There was no one downstairs whom she hoped to impress. She tugged on boudoir slippers made from purple velvet, and tears clogged her eyes again. She leaned toward the mirror and spoke softly to her reflection.

"You have to stop this. Many women never find their one true love, and you have been fortunate enough to do so. The fact you can't have him is beside the point. You have known what it feels like to be cherished and protected. For the sake of the family's reputation, and to save Papa's business, your one night will have to suffice for the remainder of your life."

She straightened up as she heard a quiet knock on the door. She called out, "Enter," and Elizabeth bounded into the room. She grabbed Ginger in a huge hug before she threw herself into a chair and burst into tears.

"I am so sorry Cedric and I let you go ahead on your own. I was frantic last night, with worry. I was sick, thinking that my selfishness at wanting to be alone with him caused this!" Elizabeth placed a hand over her heart, for effect. "Tell me everything!"

"There's truly not much to tell. I got knocked off my horse and trapped under a tree branch. Joseph dug me out from under it, found a cabin in the middle of the woods where I could recover overnight, and took off for St. Louis. This morning, when I woke up, my clothes were relatively dry, so I put them on and was walking home when Basil found me."

"So you and Joseph weren't alone in the cabin all night? What a pity. It could have been your golden opportunity. I had so hoped he would be the one to find you and the two of you would be forced to spend the night together. Who knows what might have happened? I think he's so handsome. And quiet. And big. And mysterious." She smiled at Ginger. "Of course, he can't compare to my Cedric, but you must admit, he is still very good-looking."

Ginger smiled back. "So, he's 'my Cedric,' now, is he?" She pried a bit, hoping she could steer the conversation away from herself and Joseph.

Elizabeth sighed dramatically and smiled wickedly. "Oh, Ginger. He's just the most magnificent man. When you left us, we went into the woods by ourselves and he introduced me to all the pleasures of a man and a woman!"

"*All* the pleasures?"

"I'm quite certain we covered every single one of them. My clever Cedric had packed a blanket and some food into his saddlebag. We found a lovely little gazebo in a clearing in the woods and he laid the blanket out. Then, he reached up and took me from my mount. His hands slid down my body as he put me on the ground, and I simply melted in a pool of desire!"

"So all he did was run his hands down your body?" Ginger mentally compared it to what she and Joseph had been doing.

"Oh, no, he didn't stop there. But his mere touch was all it took for me to become a raving, moaning woman who wanted to have him touch me all over!"

"And he did?" Ginger's voice dropped to a whisper.

"Ever since the night at Niblo's, when Joseph pulled him off me—much to my dismay—I've longed for Cedric to touch me again. But we were never able to be alone very much. So, when he touched my breasts again yesterday, I was ready for more. I wanted to know what lovemaking was all about."

"So you and he – ?"

"Yes, yes, yes. That's what I've been dying to tell you. I was so excited at just the thought of being alone with him, without my mother prying us apart. I forgot all about the food he had brought, until much, much later. Oh, Ginger, it was just the most wonderful way to be introduced to lovemaking." Elizabeth sighed at the memory.

"And now we must get married because I've so willingly let him have his way with me. We are going to elope to Illinois tomorrow, after we return to New York. We'll take the train and head for Galena and the DeSoto House."

Ginger stared at Elizabeth in amazement. "Elope? Whatever are you talking about?"

"Well, Father has already told me he would never approve of Cedric, as he has no money of his own. But, I truly do love him, Ginger! What else can we do except elope, now that he's claimed my virginity?"

"But I'm sure if you explained the situation to your father, he would recant in his disapproval. And why Galena? Isn't that where Agnes St. John went when she decided to marry her poet? Will you be creating a new scandal then?"

"It's the very same hotel. Agnes, bless her heart, was my inspiration. The DeSoto House is supposed to be gorgeous, and it's brand new. And, they specialize in helping eloping couples. Oh, Lord, yes, I long to be shocking, don't you?"

If you only knew how very close I've come. Ginger bit her lip, trying to hold back her tears.

"But, I've always wanted to be in your wedding, Elizabeth, and for you to be in mine. You remember, we planned our special days way back when we were children. You were going to marry Basil so we could truly be sisters, and I was going to be your maid of honor. Whatever happened to those plans? What of Basil? I don't want you to elope!"

Ginger could hold back her tears no longer as she grasped

their childhood plans were being dashed. She ran to her friend's side and clasped her hands.

"But think how delicious it would be though, to steal away in the dead of night and board a train to a new, unknown place. Not to mention, romantic. Maybe we can get a sleeper car on the train and have our honeymoon happen before the wedding. Mmm." Elizabeth closed her eyes.

"But why not Basil? What happened to your undying devotion to him?"

Ginger knew she should be deliriously happy for her friend, but tears streamed down her face as she realized their relationship would never be the same after tomorrow. She tried to reason with Elizabeth.

"You told me, just last year when he left for St. Louis, you would love no other. Of all people, Basil would understand if you came to him after being with Cedric. Lord knows he's dallied all summer with his French actress."

Elizabeth merely rolled her eyes at the suggestion.

Ginger pummeled the pillows on her bed. "But if you and Cedric marry, I'll never be able to see you. You'll move to England, and we will no longer be neighbors," she wailed as she gathered Elizabeth into her arms again. "Oh, I hate the Cotillion and all it stands for! I can't wait for this dreadful season to come to a close."

"There, there, Ginger. We can still be friends. We'll always be friends. But I can't marry Basil. He has shown not one speck of interest in me since his return. I spent most of my time talking to Joseph when the two of them were near me."

Elizabeth patted her friend's hand before she continued, speculatively. "Basil seemed off in his own little world this summer, trailing after his flamboyant French actress with his tongue hanging out. Who, if we can believe anything we hear about her, has many men other than Basil at her beck and call. It's a wonder the woman has any time to perform. On the stage,

I mean." Elizabeth giggled. "So, it is Cedric, not Basil, to whom I have given my heart, and we will elope to Illinois and spare Father from going back on his word. And, if my actions create a scandal, so be it. Are you not tempted to do something outrageous and delicious, too, before the season ends?"

"No, I think I'll leave any devilment up to you, my friend. I'm going to content myself with working with Papa and Halwyn for the rest of my days."

Elizabeth looked at Ginger with speculation. "I've never known you to be a bore. If you had been, I would not have been a friend to you since forever. But the life you've just described for yourself is tedious beyond reason. Surely there's another option for you. Are you certain you can't tolerate one of your suitors? What about Richard Douglas? He seemed so attentive early on. And it would be such fun if the two of us married the two Brits. We could tour England together!"

Elizabeth flopped on the bed beside Ginger and rolled onto her stomach. She crossed her ankles as she raised them off the bed.

"Richard is only interested in Papa's money, not in me. In fact, he told me this weekend even though Papa's money is what he needed, he did lust after my body, and so it would be no hardship to be married to me! What kind of backward compliment was he giving me? Does he think a woman longs to hear such idiotic remarks?"

The two girls giggled at Richard's awkward behavior.

"Okay, then, what about William? True, he lost the horserace in a most dramatic fashion, but nonetheless, he is a cavalry officer in the Army, and a really good catch."

"William is a senseless fool. Because of his need to be the best, he placed his horse in peril. The outcome of the race and the fact he wants to protest the result only prove what an immature man he is. I could never tolerate being married to someone like him."

"So you will finish the season with no husband? What a pity. Will you try again next year?"

"No, next year, it's Jasmine and Heather's turn. I have no wish to go through this agony again. I'll just pray I get through the remainder of July and August without too many social obligations. Then, I'll rejoin Papa at the bank, and be content."

"Oh, Ginger. If you only knew what I now know about men, you'd think differently. Nothing can compare to making love to the man of your dreams. To feel him deep inside of you, and pounding his body up against yours." She sighed dramatically once again. "I get damp just thinking about Cedric!" Elizabeth giggled softly and gave Ginger another wicked look.

"I'm happy for you, Elizabeth, truly I am. But it's not meant to be the life for me. My work at the bank, and with Amelia Bloomer, will suffice. Will you need my help in managing your getaway with Cedric tomorrow?"

"As a matter of fact, I will. It's why I came up here."

Laughing delightedly, as they had done since they were children, they began to plan Elizabeth's escape into marriage and scandal. Ginger put her thoughts about Joseph away for the time being, and launched wholeheartedly into creating a magical memory for her friend.

Chapter Twenty-Six

Following a light supper in her room, Ginger helped Elizabeth plan the details of the elopement. Then, before retiring for the night, she decided to find her father. As she expected, he was in the yard, walking on the once finely manicured lawn, which was now in serious need of repair after all the horses' hooves had chewed the ground. She joined him and locked her arm in his.

"I do miss having a yard to tend," he said, with a trace of longing in his voice.

"Well, this one looks like it could use your touch," Ginger said, ruefully. "I do so enjoy spending time at Grandmother's home in the country, where you grew up. She has the most beautiful rose gardens. But I also love being in New York City, with its hustle and bustle. Did you and Mother get to look at houses this weekend? Perhaps if you find a home here in the Hamptons, you can have your own gardens to tend."

"We saw a few the day after we got here, but nothing we liked. We'll come out again for a weekend before summer ends." He patted his daughter's hand. "But tell me how you are feeling. You look a lot better than when you first came in with Basil. Are you recovered?"

As she gazed at her father, tears filled her eyes again. He moved his arm to her shoulder, and embraced her.

"I know it was a frightful experience for you, and I was worried sick—as were we all—praying nothing was seriously wrong. Do you wish to talk about your experience? I've found talking about things often helps."

"Oh, Papa," she choked out. "Although I feel badly for all of you who worried about me, it was the most wonderful experience of my life. Right up until Basil ruined everything."

"What are you talking about? Basil didn't ruin everything. He found you."

"No, he didn't. Joseph found me. He took me to a small hunter's cabin in the woods, stripped off my wet clothing, and built a fire to warm me. I was unconscious, so I had no idea what was going on."

"Did Joseph compromise you?"

Ginger shook her head, as her tears fell. "I only wish it were so, but no, Papa, he was a gentleman. What more would you expect? He's the most wonderful man I've ever encountered."

"Spending time alone with Joseph while you were unconscious is the most wonderful experience of your lifetime? Forgive me, dear. I know you've led a fairly sheltered life, but I'm not following."

She laughed, a little. "Well, I did wake up eventually. Just before Basil kicked in the door, Joseph told me he loved me."

"And then, what happened?"

Ginger sighed heavily, and brushed the tears from her face. "And then Basil appeared, accused Joseph of taking advantage of me—which, to my disappointment, he did not—and told me of Joseph's Indian blood."

"Did Basil then send Joseph away?"

"Yes, and I concurred, since I never want to do anything to compromise your position at the bank. I can't believe everyone in the family but me knew Joseph is part Indian." She stomped her foot in her frustration. "It doesn't change my feelings for him, though."

"What exactly are you saying?"

"I'm saying the only reason I did not tell Joseph I loved him as well was because we were interrupted during what should have been the most cherished moment of my life. But I *do* love him, Papa, and if you will let me, I want to go to St. Louis right away and find him."

It was George's turn to sigh heavily. He took his willful

daughter's hand. "You know I love you, and, as your mother says, I have been most indulgent with you, allowing you to work with me at the bank. But this is one time when my word must be upheld. You cannot have Joseph. He was never meant to come here. You were never meant to meet him. Basil did a very immature and selfish thing by bringing him into our midst, and forcing us all season to perpetuate a lie about his heritage. But the lie stops now, as does any involvement with Joseph and his family."

Ginger's tears started anew at her father's pronouncement. "So what am I to do with my life, if I can't be with Joseph?"

"You are to find a nice young man here in New York and settle down with him, into a life of privilege, not one of hardship. I don't think you realize how difficult life with Joseph would be. He lives on a ranch at the edge of the frontier. He catches and breaks horses for his living, dodging the Osage Indians who are after his scalp, because he is aiding the settlers who are invading the Indian lands. His mother probably delivered her babies without the assistance of a doctor, or even another woman in attendance. Her life is one of hardship, dressing and salting meat for winter, constantly worrying if there will be enough food stored away to get through a harsh Missouri winter. There are no butcher shops near their ranch— they themselves must trap and slaughter animals for food. And that's just the practical side of things. You would face constant criticism and would be ostracized by a large portion of society for marrying an Indian. Have you considered any of this?"

He studied his daughter to see if his words were making an impression. All he noticed was the same look of determination she got on her face when she spoke of women's rights or her desire to join him and Halwyn at the Stock Exchange. In frustration, he finished his argument.

"I know Joseph is a strong, capable man, and you think he could shield you from any harm. Surely, he wouldn't let you starve. I can read your mind, Ginger, and I know, right now, you're plotting ways to join him. But, I'm telling you, the Fitzpatricks will not tolerate an Indian in the family. It was bad enough we allowed Basil to bring Joseph into our midst for as long as he did, but we were more or less forced into creating the charade after the Cotillion. Please, don't make things worse by thinking he's the only man for you. You will break your mother's heart, as well as mine."

"But he is, Papa. If I can't have Joseph, I'll have no one."

"I don't wish a solitary life on you, Ginger. But on this point, I remain firm. He will never be welcome in our home again. And, if you should do something as foolish as run to his side, you will no longer be welcome in our home, either. Can't you see how this would hurt our bank's reputation, if it were to become common knowledge we are doing business with the Indians? Not to mention our standing in the community, if word ever got out we entertained one and passed him off as a Frenchman, only to make fools of New York's best families? No, it's best to leave Joseph to his own kind, and you to yours."

George gazed at his precious daughter. "I'll tell you what I will do for you. If you stay in New York City and forget your foolish notions of running off to be with Joseph, I'll make you an officer in the bank. You so admire Elizabeth Blackwell, whom you met last spring, because she's the first female doctor in the United States. You will be able to advance women's rights in your own way by becoming the first female bank officer in the country. How would you like that?"

Ginger sighed. "Three months ago, if you had made me that offer, I would have jumped up and down in joy, Papa. Now, I don't know. I need to think about it."

"That's all I ask, Ginger. I only want your happiness, you have to know that."

George took his daughter's arm again, and they completed their stroll around the grounds in silence, wrapped up in their own thoughts.

Chapter Twenty-Seven

A few days later, all talk of Ginger's miraculous return to their midst and Joseph's sudden departure disappeared amidst the talk of Elizabeth and Cedric's elopement. Charlotte consoled Elizabeth's mother as best she could, while breathing a sigh of relief that her own subterfuge this season was now taking a back seat to Elizabeth's scandalous behavior. Ginger had been extremely quiet upon their return from the country, but Charlotte thought they could claim her attitude was a result of her brush with death, and of the loss of her best friend to a shocking marriage, should anyone ask.

Charlotte was worried about Ginger, though. She had thought her spirited daughter would change her life-long rebellious behavior when she finally entered society and settled into adult life, with a husband and children. But Ginger now had no interest in entertaining suitors, and she was going to let this season slip away before she could find a suitable mate. Ginger's eyes had lost their luster, and she was merely going through the motions of daily life. She stayed in her room and read books. More than once, Charlotte had entered her daughter's room to find her in tears. Charlotte's heart ached for her child, and she tried to find a way to give Ginger back her love for life.

"Why don't you and Basil go for a ride in the park? The exercise will be good for you, and we just got your new riding outfit from the dressmaker."

"I have no wish to spend time with Basil, Mother."

"But he's leaving soon to go back to St. Louis, and I will not abide the two of you still quarreling with each other when it comes time for him to leave. You need to make amends."

Ginger glanced at her mother briefly, then dropped her eyes. "We are not quarreling, Mother. It's not quite so simple. Because of him, I have had my heart broken. How can I forgive something so momentous?"

"You know your brother feels terrible for what he's done."

"But it doesn't change anything, does it? He put Papa's bank in a perilous position, and he played all of society for a fool. And you and Papa went along with it! Because of him, my life has been destroyed, and all he can do is laugh at how he got away with it. Basil has a lot of growing up to do, and until he does, I have nothing to say to him."

Charlotte sighed. "I know you and your brother will eventually reconcile. Maybe it is still too early. But I think a ride in the park will do you both good. You need to get out of this house and get some color back into your cheeks. And you do need to be seen in public again. Would you consent to a ride if I agree you don't have to talk to him?"

Ginger heaved a heavy sigh. "I know you won't give me any peace until I do, so all right, Mother. I'll change into my riding habit."

♦◊♦

Ginger rode a bit behind Basil on the gravel-covered walkway through the park, in order to avoid conversation. Basil seemed to accept her reticence, and rolled his shoulders as his horse trotted sprightly down the long path. Only a few other riders were out on this muggy afternoon. Most of society was cloistered in drawing rooms and parlors at this hour, huddling over their teacups as they discussed the latest tidbits of news and gossip.

A lone horse and rider approached from the opposite direction, and hailed the pair as he came close to them. Quentin Gray doffed his hat after pulling his horse to a stop.

"Miss Fitzpatrick, Basil. It's so good to see you out and about again. I thought I was the only one riding today. The park looks deserted."

"Well, it has been awfully hot, even by July's standards," Basil replied.

"Will you be heading back to the frontier soon?"

"Yes, in a week or so, I'll board the train and go back. I know I left the bank in good hands when I came here, but I do need to return to the business world. I have a few more things to take care of here, though."

"Such as the memorial service?"

Basil frowned at Quentin. "What memorial service? For whom?"

Quentin's Adam's apple bobbed before he continued. "Why Mademoiselle Rachel, of course. You haven't heard?"

"No, man, I have not." Basil appeared as if he were about to throttle Quentin. "Tell me what has happened."

"Evidently, she caught pneumonia a week or so ago, and perished shortly after our return from the Hamptons. I thought you knew, because you and she were frequently in each other's company."

"I haven't been able to see her since I got back to town. I called on her once, and was turned away. Her maid told me she was too sick to see anyone. Oh God, poor Rachel."

"They are taking her body back to France for the burial, but the Opera House will hold a memorial service for her tomorrow evening. I'm certain all her suitors will be in attendance." Quentin had a smirk on his face as he glanced slyly at Basil.

"I'll not have you speak ill of her, Quentin."

"I'm sorry, Basil, but I'm merely stating a truth all of New York knows. You were not her only suitor, despite what you've been led to believe. She was entertaining three or four men at the same time, and each thought he was her one true love, according to what I hear." Quentin sighed. "She must have been some woman, to garner all that attention."

Basil's voice was gravelly. "She was definitely one of a kind."

The three of them rode in silence for a few minutes. When Basil said no more, and Ginger remained quiet as well, Quentin cleared his throat.

"I…uh…just remembered, I've been invited to tea at Jane Livingstone's, so I'll be off." He tipped his hat to Ginger, and sped away, relieved to put the awkward situation behind him.

Ginger watched Basil as he rode ahead of her. His body was bowed, like an old man's, and he stared at the ground instead of the beautiful scenery. She ached for her brother, even though she was still angry with him.

She decided to call a truce. "Basil?"

Basil turned in his saddle, and glanced at her, sadly. "I truly did love her, you know. I don't even care if she had other men. I have never met anyone quite like her before, nor will I ever again." His eyes gleamed with unspent tears as his anguish took hold.

"But surely you knew your relationship with her was fleeting? She would have gone on to the next town soon, or back to France to perform, and left you behind. Even if she hadn't, is it not true she would never fit into society, especially the portion of society you belong to, just as Joseph would never fit?"

"You're throwing my own words back in my face? Can't you see I'm in pain?"

"Your pain is no greater than the pain I've been in these past weeks, not having *my* love by *my* side. Now you know how I feel. You see why I have had such a difficult time forgiving you."

Basil nodded. "Yes, now I understand. I have been a self-centered ass most of the summer. Will you come with me to the memorial tomorrow evening?"

Ginger smiled gently at him, and held out her gloved hand. "I'd be honored."

Chapter Twenty-Eight

New York, August 1855

Ginger sighed when she turned the page in her calendar over from July to August, and observed the notation she had made there months before. In the August 31st square, she had written, "Leave for St. Louis!!!" Although she and Basil had reached a tentative truce before he returned to the frontier, she had no desire to see either him or St. Louis now. Her lonely life stretched out before her like railroad tracks. Blinking rapidly to quell the tears that suddenly sprang into her eyes, she put the calendar aside.

At least, the season was whimpering to a close. It seemed, after people returned from the holidays in the Hamptons, they were reluctant to continue the revelry for yet another month. The climate played a large part in their hesitation, as New Yorkers suffered through an unbearable August heat wave. Folks were not so eager to layer on undergarments and heavy clothing to stroll in the park. They usually ended their exercise with sweat pouring down their faces and rushed home to get away from the relentless sun. There were only a few musicals to attend, and several theater performances in the evenings, after the day had cooled off somewhat.

Ginger agreed to accompany Quentin to Buckley's Opera House to see a burlesque of Don Juan. Burlesque had been introduced to New Yorkers the previous year by the Buckley troupe, but because it bordered on the outrageous Ginger had yet to see it. Her spirits lifted at the thought of doing something different. Charlotte and George were to accompany the young couple, as would Quentin's parents.

"I'm glad to see some color in your cheeks again." Charlotte patted Ginger's face and looked her over to make certain all parts of her elaborate dress were secure.

The dress was a pale cream crepe, the exact color of Ginger's skin. Around the off-the-shoulder neckline a band of black lace dripped over her arms. Three wider flounces of similar black lace graced the skirt. Five layers of petticoats, each a bit shorter than the other, finished off the bottom. Each petticoat was edged in a violet band of velvet, and a wide band of violet velvet was cinched around her small waist.

"You are lovely, my dear. Quentin is a most lucky man."

"Quentin is a buffoon, Mother. You know as well as I do he is totally lacking in poise and refinement. But his father is a wonderful man, and I agreed to this evening so he and I can talk about the railroads."

Charlotte pursed her lips. She had hoped Ginger would forget all about Joseph Lafontaine and find a suitable husband before the season ended. She knew Ginger would never allow William near her again, and Richard, charming as he was, was penniless. Quentin was Charlotte's last hope.

"Please be certain to show some attention to Quentin, too."

Ginger smoothed the band of velvet around her waist. "Do not worry, Mother. You have taught me well. I'll not say or do anything tonight to cause harm to the family's reputation, or to cause you embarrassment. I'm not like Basil. I just don't want you to get your hopes up about Quentin and me ever being more than friends. I have decided to continue my work with Papa at the bank after this abysmal season creaks to an end."

Her mother's eyes filled with tears at the thought of her daughter never getting married. "Oh, Ginger, I do want the best for you, you know I do. And, even though a woman's role is changing slowly, it's still best if you marry and have children. Only then will you be truly fulfilled."

"But I only want to marry if I truly love the man, and I certainly would never be happy with a man like Quentin. And there is none other in sight. Besides, I can't very well give my heart to another when I've already given it to Joseph."

Charlotte used a fine lace handkerchief to pat her cheeks and dry her tears. "Why can't you just accept it was a mistake for Basil to bring the Indian into our midst in the first place, and your paths should never have crossed?"

"Because he did, and we did. I don't care if he's an Indian, a Frenchman, or a rancher, for that matter. He has taken my heart with him back to St. Louis, and I'll not pretend to fall in love with another, just to satisfy society's interpretation of what a woman should be in the nineteenth century! I'll work with Papa at the bank, and make lots of money for our customers. It will suffice."

Ginger wrapped her arms around her mother and said, "I know this is not what you planned for me, but it's the best I can do. I don't like to see you in tears, so let's leave well enough alone, can we?"

Her mother straightened and fussed in front of the mirror to repair the damage her tears had caused to her makeup. "I still say buffoon or no, Quentin would be better than a miserable spinster existence. Will you at least try to look at him with a new set of eyes this evening?"

"All right, Mother. If Quentin can manage to get through the evening without doing anything ridiculous, I'll reconsider, just to please you."

The carriage carrying the Grays was late pulling up to the Fitzpatrick house. Charles Gray came to the door to announce their arrival. "Sorry about the lateness. I hope we'll still be in time to make the opening of the show."

As he hurriedly led the trio out to the carriage, he confided, "Quentin split his pants in two as he was getting into the carriage this evening and had to rush back inside and change.

Then, of course, changing the pants meant he needed a different jacket, too, and the hat and the shoes. You know how it is."

Ginger glanced at her mother, and raised an eyebrow. Charlotte pretended not to see the look, and fussed with her fan.

The carriage had two bench seats facing each other. Quentin, Ginger, and Charlotte sat on one bench. Mr. and Mrs. Gray and George were on the opposite side. Charles Gray and George eagerly began to talk business, and Ginger leaned forward to hear what they were discussing. Charlotte tapped her on the knee with her fan. With a small sigh of defeat, Ginger sat back on the bench, struggling to think of something to say to Quentin.

"Are you as glad as I am that this season is almost over, Mr. Gray?"

He tried to turn in his seat to face her, but they were packed together so tightly she could still only see his profile. She caught his startled look, however, at being addressed.

"Have you not enjoyed the season then, Miss Fitzpatrick?"

"I've had enough of this charade. Please, Quentin, call me Ginger. We've been friends for years, but suddenly and sadly, this year, because of our introduction into society, we are no longer able be on a first name basis. I find it totally ridiculous, as I have found everything else about the season. Although I have enjoyed portions of the past few months, I grow weary of it now, and just want to be done with it."

Quentin smiled a little before he replied, "I, too, am a bit tired of it, but I do plan to attend again next year, in hopes of finding an appropriate wife, if what's left of this season doesn't net me one."

He again tried to turn to look at her squarely, and almost succeeded this time. His eyes raked over her fine dress, and she burned with embarrassment.

"Jasmine and Heather are so excited about coming out next

year. I'm certain they'll both beat me to the altar."

"You will not be returning, then?"

"Gracious, no. One season was brutal enough for me. I plan to make a career for myself at the bank, alongside Halwyn and Papa."

Quentin took one of her hands in his. "A finely bred woman such as yourself should not have to work for a living. You need a husband to take care of you." His pale blue eyes gazed into hers adoringly.

Ginger removed her hand from his sweaty palm and surreptitiously wiped it dry on her velvet waistband. "I have no plans to get married, Quentin. You'd be wise to look elsewhere."

Charlotte rapped her fan on Ginger's knee again.

Ginger smiled up at Quentin and finished her statement. "Although I am looking forward to this evening. I have never seen burlesque, have you?"

She and Quentin continued to make halted conversation until the carriage pulled up at the door to the Opera House on Broadway. The two sets of parents exited first. As Quentin was stepping from the carriage, one foot got caught in a rung of the steps, and he crashed to the ground. Ginger was crouched at the door of the carriage, waiting for Quentin to exit and turn to help her. As Quentin scrambled to his feet, her gaze caught her mother's. Charlotte shrugged her shoulders, and Ginger grinned.

Chapter Twenty-Nine

New York City, October, 1855

When Elizabeth returned from Illinois shortly after the big elopement, she and Ginger fell back into their same familiar routine of late afternoon visits. The scandal Elizabeth had caused entertained society for only a few weeks before it died down. But now that Elizabeth was a married woman, Ginger found their talks had shifted from girlish fun and games to include more adult topics. Hurriedly, the two women made their way to Ginger's bedroom and closed the door.

"Oh, thank you. I'm starving!" Elizabeth exclaimed as Colleen wheeled in the teacart. Ginger poured the tea and handed Elizabeth a gooseberry tart, which she knew was her friend's favorite.

"Okay, what secret are you dying to reveal?"

Elizabeth's smile could have lit up the room. "You're so clever. I never have been able to keep a secret from you for long. I am with child!"

Ginger grasped her friend's hands and they jumped up and down in a circle, squealing with glee, like they'd done since childhood.

"Well, it didn't take you very long."

Elizabeth grinned. "It's because Cedric is insatiable. We make love whenever we can, sometimes several times a day. My trip to Galena was one long sensual ride." Elizabeth threw herself onto the bed, where she rolled languidly from side to side. "I do believe I got pregnant on the train."

Ginger experienced a flash of jealousy at Elizabeth's

announcement. She knew she would never again feel a man's embrace, much less have children of her own.

Elizabeth caught her look of yearning, and reached for Ginger's hand. "You know I want the same for you. I remember how, when we played with our dolls, you were always so patient, long after I'd lost interest. You'd be a great mother. Have you truly found no one who interests you?"

Ginger shrugged and gently removed her hand. "No, no one. What were my choices? Richard Douglas, Quentin Gray, or William Davenport? Not a really outstanding field from which to draw. I guess it's not meant to be my lot in life." She looked sternly at her dearest friend. "Well, Elizabeth, since your elopement took away my opportunity to be in your wedding, may I at least be your child's godmother?" Ginger asked with a touch of wistfulness in her voice.

"Of course, silly. But you may have to travel to England for the christening ceremony."

"What? Are you moving?"

"Cedric and I have discussed it, and yes, at the very least we'll go for a visit before I'm too much further along, so I can meet his parents. And we may stay there, for the quality of life provided by the English society would be so beneficial to our children."

"You're not wanting to move just to get away from your parents, are you? They have forgiven you for running off with Cedric, haven't they?"

Elizabeth smiled. "As soon as they found out about the baby, all hard feelings were tossed aside. We're on very good terms now. If we decide that England is where we want to raise our family, Mother and Father have said they'll make the trip at least once a year, after I have the baby. Will you help me pack for the trip to England?"

"Of course I will. But are you feeling well enough to travel, with the pregnancy and all?"

"I must admit, I do get a bit queasy in the mornings, but one has to expect a bit of morning sickness."

Ginger and Elizabeth spent the rest of the afternoon talking about what garments she should pack. They chose some books on the United Kingdom to read up on the area where Cedric's family lived.

"After all, the last thing I want is to have his parents think I'm an uneducated girl from the Colonies!" Elizabeth declared.

The two young ladies giggled in unison, as they'd done for years. Ginger tucked the memory away, knowing it might be one of the last times she and Elizabeth would share tea and conversation like this.

♦◊♦

The following morning, Ginger sat behind her desk and surveyed her little office at the bank with pleasure. She had fallen back into a familiar pattern when she returned to her work two months ago. Her mother encouraged her not to return to the bank, but rather to continue her social schedule of attending the opera and accepting invitations to formal teas. Charlotte still held out the hope Ginger would attract the attention of some of the young men who remained unattached after the season. Ginger emphatically declined, reminding her mother she had fulfilled the request of last February, and she had no intention of shirking her duties at the bank for another minute.

Looking around her office, Ginger sighed softly. Losing Elizabeth to England was the final blow in this long Cotillion season. She longed to rewind the clock back to last February, and knew she would do everything differently. Beginning with putting her foot down when the suggestion first arose about her participation. Considering how close her parents had come to losing their reputations among their peers, would it really have been so bad if she declined the invitation to be part of the

Cotillion ball? She thought not. If her family had waited one more year and begun the Fitzpatrick Cotillion tradition with Heather and Jasmine, who were certain to be quite successful in their quests to find husbands, what difference would it have made? Yes, Ginger thought, her younger sisters would shine throughout every moment of their time in the spotlight, and would thoroughly enjoy their season.

She sighed as she turned back to her work. She picked up a report from the Pacific Railroad, detailing the steady progress they had been making laying track west of St. Louis. Within a month, rail service would extend all the way to the state capital of Jefferson City. She would need to add the Pacific Railroad to her list of recommended buys for the bank's clients, rather than keeping it an exclusive for Charles Gray's portfolio.

She glanced up from the report when she sensed someone at her doorway. "Why, Mr. Gray, how nice of you to stop by. I was just thinking about you. Please, have a seat."

"I have to admit, Ginger, it's good to see you back at the bank. I've missed having your keen insight when selecting companies to add to my portfolio."

"It does feel good to be working again."

"So, you're glad the season is finished?"

She smiled. "I could actually feel my mind melting during the flurry of drivel I had to endure. I think both Quentin and I breathed a huge sigh of relief when August came to a close. How is he?"

"Doing well, and surprise of surprises. He's now seriously courting someone."

Surprised, Ginger inquired, "Who might that be?"

"Jane Livingstone seems to have taken a liking to my boy. They've been stepping out together for the past month now, and she's not tired of him yet."

"Jane Livingstone, eh? Well, bless my bloomers!" Ginger grinned at the thought of the overpowering Jane taking Quentin to task. "Maybe she'll be the one for your son."

She sighed softly. It seemed she was losing yet another friend to the marriage game. Another twinge of jealousy rippled through her body. Not because she had set her cap for Quentin herself, but because another of her friends would be able to experience married life, and she never would. A marriage to someone other than Joseph would leave her with an empty heart and an empty marriage.

Mr. Gray nodded. "What are your plans now?"

"To stay here at the bank, and make money for all of us. Papa has offered to make me an officer of the bank, and I'm considering it. If I accept, though, it would mean longer and more consistent hours, with no days off for shopping with Mother and Pepper. Or time for anything else. So, I don't know. It's kind of exciting though, don't you think? To be a trailblazer in the world of finance?" She looked at Mr. Gray for the approval she needed.

"Well, I think it sounds downright boring, especially for a spirited young woman such as yourself. You need to expand your horizons a bit more. Which is why I'm here today."

"Whatever do you mean?"

"If you've read the full report from the Pacific Railroad, you know they are hosting an inaugural train ride from St. Louis to Jefferson City next month."

"I did see the notation, yes."

"And, since, at your advice, I've invested a lot of capital with them, I'm among the invitees—as are your father and Basil. We'd like you to join us for the grand affair."

"Papa is going to St. Louis? This is the first I've heard of it."

"He just made the decision. I talked to him about it before stopping in here to speak to you."

Ginger turned her head toward the wall, hoping Mr. Gray would miss the sudden tears sparkling in her eyes. "I have no wish to go to St. Louis," she replied in a monotone.

Charles Gray shifted in his seat, in obvious discomfort. "My dear Ginger, I know something took place between you and your brother while he was here this summer, and you're not on the best of terms right now. But, this is the biggest event in the railroad's history. All manner of dignitaries and investors will be in attendance. There will be music, drink, and laughter. Partially because you've been such a strong advocate of the railroads, this bank—and I—have invested heavily in the company, and helped get it to this milestone, which is cause for celebration. Why not set your rift with your brother aside for now and enjoy some of what your faith in the railroads has helped bring about? Reap the fruits of your labor, as it were."

Ginger fiddled with her fountain pen, pensively. At the start of the season, she had longed to see St. Louis, but Basil ruined those plans for her. She had done her best to mend their relationship before he headed back, but it was still a raw, open wound. She sometimes thought they'd never get their strong bond back—a rock-solid relationship that had been there since her birth for both of them to rely on.

And then there was Joseph. Her heart ached anew as she thought of him, knowing she could never see him again. She knew in a town as large as St. Louis, her chances of running into him were slim, especially if they were on the celebratory train most of the time. She might be able to sneak into and out of town without his knowledge. A trip to St. Louis might be exactly what she needed to help get her and Basil's relationship back on an even keel. And, Mr. Gray was one of the bank's most loyal clients. She certainly did not want to do anything to jeopardize *that* relationship. She glanced up at him, and smiled.

"Since you put it in such a way, I'd love to accompany you and Papa on the trip. It might be fun, after all. Thank you for extending the invitation."

"Good! Then it's settled. We'll leave in a few weeks. And who knows, you just might find you like to travel and will want to venture even farther west. I hear San Francisco is quite charming."

"It does sound exciting. But, I think I'll take it one trip at a time. St. Louis first, then maybe England, to see Elizabeth."

♦◊♦

Charles Gray stood, doffed his hat to Ginger, and exited her office. He stopped back at George Fitzpatrick's office before he left the building.

"You owe me, George," Charles said quietly.

"You got her to consent to the trip, then?"

"Yes, but it took some work."

George's eyes twinkled. "I knew Ginger would never agree to the trip if the suggestion came from me, but coming from one of the bank's most prestigious clients is a different matter. And you are one of her favorite people."

"Well, it's done. And I even think she's looking forward to the adventure. Before I left her office, I noticed a bit of a sparkle in her eyes."

George got up from his desk and clamped Charles on the shoulder. "You're a good friend, Charles. Thank you. Maybe Ginger can find a way to be happy yet."

Chapter Thirty

St. Louis, November 1855

St. Louis surprised Ginger, with its tall buildings and busy streets. The town had witnessed a rapid expansion during the first half of the 1800s, and was no longer considered just a frontier town, but rather a bustling scene of commerce. She enjoyed the bumpy ride of the omnibus streetcar over the cobblestone road that stretched from the National Hotel to the bustling waterfront, where steamboats were lined up and waiting for patrons, or to be loaded with goods.

Basil told her the town was going to add rails on the city streets for horse-drawn carts to replace the omnibuses, which would result in a smoother ride; he was considering investing some of the bank's money into the venture. If horse-drawn carts on tracks were to be the future, she was glad she was able to take at least one ride on the omnibus before it faded into history.

Immediately after agreeing to the trip, she had begun a countdown of the days, then the hours and minutes before their departure from New York. When she was alone in her room at home, she fantasized about running into Joseph and falling into his welcoming embrace. She again shed some tears as she acknowledged the life she would never have. She would never be as happy as Elizabeth, and now Quentin, and the dream of having children of her own faded the moment Joseph had fled New York.

She longed to walk on the sidewalks of St. Louis, knowing Joseph had trod on those same boards many times. Even with her trepidations of ever being able to set things to right with Basil, she couldn't quell her mounting excitement as their departure date neared.

Charles Gray was right. She was far too spirited to sit in her lonely office at the bank, watching life pass by her window, feeling sorry for herself and refusing to partake in any new experiences. Traveling would be an excellent way to fill the voids in her life. She'd roam this vast country and then the world, speaking to women in every station of life about women's rights, expanding hers and Amelia Bloomer's cause. It might be a male-dominated world at present, but that would not always be the case, she was certain. Maybe she'd go to England next, and see Elizabeth after she had her baby. Ginger could not wait to see what experiences life would throw at her next. She had been walking in a fog since Joseph galloped out of her life in July. But she now had a renewed outlook and was once again ready to grab life by the horns.

Standing on the platform—even sandwiched between her father and Basil, with Charles Gray in front of them—Ginger was still jostled as hundreds of patrons jockeyed for positions on the train cars, trying to get out of the persistent rain. This was the first time the train would go the entire distance from St. Louis to Jefferson City, and Ginger found herself caught up in the gaiety and frivolity of the crowd. She had been giddy with anticipation about this trip since talking to Mr. Gray, and it was at last here.

Ginger turned her focus back to the festivities taking place on the railroad platform.

"Well, it may have taken four-and-a-half years to lay this 125 miles of track from St. Louis to Jefferson City, but at last, we can celebrate!" St. Louis's mayor, Washington King, announced to the milling crowd.

Six hundred invited guests jostled for space on the platform and hundreds of other spectators spilled onto the street below.

As the heavy downpour continued, the guests began to board the train and slowly filled the fourteen railcars. Even the rain could not dampen their spirits, as everyone caught the festive nature of this milestone event.

Ginger finally boarded and took a seat on the train, grateful to be out of the rain at last. She deposited her parasol under the seat and smoothed the green-and-brown-striped silk of her skirt. Her many layers of starched petticoats held the wet fabric away from her body. She shook her shawl, removing most of the moisture, and then wrapped the heavy green velvet more closely around her shoulders. Even though it was wet, it provided her some much-needed warmth.

"At least it's raining, not snowing," Basil joked as he settled in next to Ginger. "This time of year in St. Louis, it could easily be the heavy white stuff, and at the rate it's falling, it would amount to a couple of feet. Then none of us would be going anywhere."

"True enough, Basil," his father replied. "The cowcatcher on the front of the engine can clear the track somewhat, but it would be no match for two or three feet of snow. We'll count among our blessings the fact this is just rain."

"Thank you, Papa, for allowing me to come along for this party. I'm having so much fun," Ginger chimed in.

George reached for his daughter's hand. "After what you've been through the past couple of months, my sweet girl, I wanted to give you a good memory to remember 1855 by."

"Well, you've most certainly done it. This is a train ride I'll never forget."

Ginger watched as her father and Charles Gray took their seats directly across from Ginger and Basil. Then the train with its fourteen cars pulled away from the depot slowly. Ginger glanced out the window at the crowd, which had gathered, despite the weather, to cheer them on their way. She searched the group for the one face that haunted her nightly dreams, but to no avail. She had purposely not asked Basil about Joseph, knowing it would widen the chasm between them. Sighing softly, she bundled up her thoughts of Joseph and put them away, attempting to join in the revelry of the crowd.

The atmosphere inside the train did not match the gloomy, heavy weather outside. People laughed, cheered, and sipped the drinks served to them. A small band had boarded the train, filling the air with lively music and adding to the festivities. The crowd began to sing along to the familiar strains of Stephen Foster's latest tune, "Come Where My Love Lies Dreaming."

Basil managed to snag four drinks from the tray of a waiter making his way slowly through the clogged car. He handed flutes of champagne to Ginger, his father, and Mr. Gray, and then raised his own glass in a toast. "Here's to those of us who were smart enough to invest in the railroad and to be invited along on this inaugural ride."

Many of those around them cheered and raised their glasses along with Basil. He laughed as most of the car joined in the toast with celebratory champagne. Soon, the mood in the car became even livelier, as the drinks kept flowing. The volume of the crowd grew louder as the drinks lessened restraint. More voices joined the chorus of the songs, although most seemed unaware of the melody they were supposed to be following.

The train slowed or stopped at each little town along the way, to the delight of the locals who had gathered along the route to witness this historic event, which was certain to be talked about for years. Basil pointed out several landmarks on the way as they slowly rolled west of St. Louis.

"I've never seen so much open space," Ginger marveled. "New York, or for that matter, the entire East Coast, is so crowded. Why don't more people move here and buy up some of this land?"

"Most of what you're looking at is land the Indians have claim to. The government is systematically forcing them onto reservations so we can civilize the West, but it'll take time."

"Ah, of course, the uncivilized Indians..." She trailed off and glanced at Basil.

"To answer your unspoken question, no, I have not seen Joseph since my return. During the morning at the cabin in the Hamptons, I asked him never to talk to me again, and he's honored my request. I hear his father has been awarded the contract to supply horses to the city when the new trolley cars start up, so I know they're doing well. But Joseph has stayed clear of town, or at least the part I inhabit. For all I know, he may have gone to Canada to join his grandfather and his younger brother."

"Do you miss him? After all, you two were best friends."

"I do miss him. We had some grand times together. And I own up to my part in the debacle in New York. But, despite everything, I can't forgive him for toying with your affections."

"You make it sound like I had no part in what transpired. We weren't just playing with each other, Basil. I fell deeply in love with him."

"But now that you know what his heritage is, surely you've come to your senses?"

Ginger sighed as she patted her brother's hand. "And here I was thinking you had matured since the summer. You're still a very small-minded man, Basil. For the sake of our family, let's just agree to disagree on the matter of Joseph's suitability. Unless you've changed your mind, I don't want to talk about him."

When Basil didn't reply, Ginger said, "All right then, let's put Joseph aside for now. I want to know what would have happened if Annie Schemerhorn had never come up with the idea of a Cotillion and I never would have suffered through the torturous season. You know I was on my way here to help you with the bank. Would you have let me take my rightful place, or would you have continued to be so narrow-minded about a woman working outside the home?"

Basil shifted in his seat, looking uncomfortable. "Ginger, I know you're very talented at picking companies to support, and you've helped the bank's bottom line tremendously. But, still and all, Father has indulged you, giving you an office at the bank and allowing you to leave the house every day and work alongside him. He even wrote and told me he offered to install you as an officer in the bank. I advised him not to be so foolish, and to recant his offer. Such disgraceful behavior is not to be tolerated in a woman of your station. So, although I would have welcomed a visit from you, I would not have allowed you an office space. It's my bank, after all."

Ginger glared at him. "Do you remember what you said when you heard about your actress Rachel's death? You said you had been a self-centered ass all summer. I think the time of year had nothing to do with it. You're *still* a self-centered ass!"

"Let's not fight today, okay? I will never embrace 'women's rights', as you and Amelia Bloomer refer to them. And, I know as long as you think you and Joseph might end up together, there's no hope for us getting along on that score—we are on totally opposite sides. I regret ever bringing him into our lives. I may be an ass, but you're a fool if you think you could ever fit into Joseph's life here. It's best you forget him and move along."

Ginger sighed as she turned her gaze back to the scenery. Her eyes filled with unexpected tears, making the rainy countryside even harder to see. She knew Basil was right. He was an ass, and she was a fool.

Chapter Thirty-One

After several hours, the train reached the town of Hermann, seventy-eight miles west of St. Louis. The train stopped while another railcar was connected to it, bringing the total to fifteen. Basil muttered something about wanting to watch the cars be coupled together, left his seat, and wavered down the aisle.

A company of uniformed soldiers and an additional group of musicians joined in the fun of the ride, filling up the final car. Strains of Johann Strauss's "Radetzky March" filled the air as the band played patriotic tunes in honor of the troops. The commanding officers of the regiment moved through each car, introducing themselves. More champagne was poured, and the festive atmosphere expanded. All the while, rain drenched the surrounding countryside, as the torrential downpour continued.

One of the officers, Lieutenant David Whitman, stopped at the car containing the Fitzpatrick family and Charles Gray. He had been told Mr. Gray was one of the primary backers of the Pacific Railroad and special consideration should be given him. But, in truth, he wanted to talk to the fetching young lady who sat by herself a few feet away. He straightened his spine even more than his regular military stance as he strode down the aisle of the railroad car.

"May I join you?" Lt. Whitman asked, hoping for a nod or some gesture from Ginger.

When she smiled up at him, he introduced himself and dropped into Basil's empty seat. He removed his hat and his dark brown hair curled onto his forehead. His deep blue eyes sparkled as he took in Ginger's comely shape.

"So, do you have some holdings with the railroad as well,

Miss Fitzpatrick?"

Ginger's glance moved over the fine uniform the tall man was wearing before she replied, "I am a huge supporter of the railroads, yes. I hold some stock in them, and I have been advising Mr. Gray with his portfolio. I think railroads are the key to settling the vast American West."

David Whitman's expression revealed his surprise. He had expected a refined East Coast lady, but her intelligence regarding the westward expansion of America was unexpected and welcomed. He grinned at her and made himself comfortable in the seat. He was going to enjoy this ride after all.

"I agree with you. But, until we get the Indian population under control, we won't be able to claim the land as ours. They are fighting us mightily."

Ginger bristled. "And why wouldn't they? This is their land, after all. How can we Europeans just waltz in here and run them off? I'd fight you, too, if I were an Indian!"

David released a small, frustrated sigh. Trying to explain the Indians to an Easterner was like trying to advance the cause of slavery to a Northerner.

"Believe me, if there was any way Indians and whites could coexist, we would be more than willing to try it. But the Indians feel they can roam over any land and slaughter or steal any livestock they come upon. Nor do they like it when land gets fenced in—they don't understand the concept of fences. They think all the land should be free to roam. You can see the problems their attitude would cause for a family trying to scratch out a living in this hard country."

"I do understand the point of view of the families who come west trying to forge a new life for themselves, and I applaud their spirit. But I also can comprehend the Indians' side of things—they have lived here for centuries. Unfortunately, that's my problem in many arenas. I can see both sides of the coin."

David smiled at the small, yet determined woman. "Well, we

don't have to solve all the problems of the world in one day. Why don't you tell me about your life back East? I haven't been there in years, and I long for news of home."

"What part of the East Coast do you hail from?"

"I'm from Savannah, Georgia, and I do miss it."

"Ah, yes, the South."

David studied his seatmate. "Have you spent time in the South, Miss Fitzpatrick?"

"Unfortunately, no. I've never been farther south than Washington, but I've read about the southern lifestyle. Do you think you'll return to the East when your commission expires, or will you settle out here?"

"Good question. I suppose the answer will depend on whether I could find a wife while I'm still on the frontier. I may be forced to go back East, for truly fine, upstanding women are a rate commodity in the West." His gaze appraised her again and he smiled. "Now, tell me everything that's been going on in the civilized part of the country."

Ginger returned his gaze, letting her eyes wander over his face. With a twinkle in her eyes, she asked, "Have you ever heard of Amelia Bloomer?"

♦◊♦

George Fitzpatrick watched Ginger and David, who were deep in conversation. Then he shifted his gaze to Charles. He had a grin on his face.

"It looks like our plan is working," George said. "I haven't seen Ginger this animated in months."

"Yes, she does seem to be enjoying this train ride. Having a dashing young soldier hanging on her every word is an added bonus. I'm so glad she decided to come with us."

"Yes, it was the right thing to do. She's been nearly beside herself with excitement since we began planning this trip. She tried to hide her enthusiasm, but I know her too well."

"Letting me convince her to come was the right call," Charles said. "You do know how to handle the women in your life."

"Well, Ginger is a lot like her mother, and I've had twenty-five years of experience learning Charlotte's habits. With all the daughters in our family, I've been forced to learn how to get along with women. We Fitzpatrick men are outnumbered, aren't we, Basil?"

Basil studied the older gentlemen. "Yes, we are, Father. I wish I had your adroitness and could figure out how to get back into Ginger's good graces like you've done. It seems she's going to be angry with me for the rest of our lives."

"Give her some time. I'm confident you'll work things out, sooner or later. But you have to understand her thinking, if you're ever going to come to a resolution. A woman's place in this country is changing, whether we men like it or not. Some women still enjoy being cared for and coddled by men, but Ginger isn't one of them. I marvel every day at the way her mind works, and she's been a vital reason why our bank is so successful. She needs a strong man beside her, to keep up with her and make her truly happy. And there was no man this past season who fit the bill." He turned to the man seated next to him. "Sorry, Charles, I know your son was one of the men she spent time with."

"Quite all right, George. I know Quentin is not a strong man—not yet, anyway. But with Jane Livingstone telling him what to do, he will have to develop a spine, just to keep her from rolling over him."

George laughed softly as he lit his pipe. "Yes, I expect he will."

Basil pulled a couple of cheroots out of his jacket pocket, and offered one to Mr. Gray. The men sat quietly in the car with the rain sloshing outside, enjoying their tobacco as they watched the countryside roll by slowly.

After several minutes, Basil asked, "It's a shame, is it not, that the railroad provided dashing young officers for the ladies, but no dance hall girls for us gentlemen?"

Charles and George grinned in agreement. "Maybe they just expect the men to marvel at the mechanical construction of this machine," Charles replied. "Would you two care to join me up toward the front of the train so we can look at it firsthand?"

"You and Basil go on ahead," George said. "I'll stay here and keep an eye on Ginger and her young man. Charlotte would have my head if she thought I left our daughter without a chaperone for even a minute of this adventure."

Basil and Charles made their way through the passenger cars to the one nearest the coal car. They peered through the glass as two men atop a huge pile of coal, in the driving rain, shoveled at a rapid pace to keep the huge steam engine fed. Never one to be fascinated by mechanics, Basil quickly lost interest and began to retrace his steps back to the car where his father and Ginger sat. Charles stayed and joined in a discussion with the railroad officials and engineers.

One of the railroad officials said, "We have a scheduled stop coming up. When we were planning this trip, people expressed a desire to climb off the train at this portion of the route to see the massive bridge—it's the reason construction of this leg of the route took so long. However, we're woefully behind schedule, what with all the stops we've made along the way. And there are people waiting for us on the other end, in Jefferson City. What do you think, Mr. Gray? Should we stop for twenty minutes or so and give these fine folks an opportunity to get an up-close look at the 760-foot long bridge over the Gasconade River?"

Charles flicked his gaze over the people in the nearest car. They appeared to be engaged in the types of animated conversations that often happen after sipping too many glasses of champagne. He took in the finely coiffed hair of the ladies in their still-damp clothing, considered the rain outside, and shook his head.

"I don't think you'll have too many takers wanting to exit this warm car and go out into the rain, even if it is to see the latest marvel of technology."

After further consideration—and some animated discussion between the bridge engineer and the railroad officials—the decision was made. They would merely slow the train as it crossed the bridge, giving the passengers ample time to be impressed by the view of the bridge and the river thirty-six feet below.

Chapter Thirty-Two

Ginger, George, and David were in the midst of a lively discussion with one of the railroad engineers about their preference for bridges over tunnels, as they and the other passengers in the car watched the front portion of the train follow the bend in the tracks to the bridge.

The first two cars rolled onto the bridge. Suddenly, a thunderous cracking broke their conversation. The huge wooden piers supporting the bridge structure collapsed. Compromised by the rain and the torrent of water roiling through the riverbed, the piers fell like dominoes under the weight of the train. The hideous sound of breaking timbers was quickly replaced by screams as the passengers in the rear of the train watched the first seven cars, along with the bridge structure, tumble into the water below.

Screams and the repetitive echoes of wood breaking apart and metal grating on metal filled the air.

People in the forward cars moaned. Ginger let out a piercing scream as their own railroad car suddenly lurched and jumped the track, flipping on its side. The car began a long slide down the steep embankment. David pushed Ginger down between the seats as he and George grabbed the rails on the seat backs. Ginger screamed in fright again and again when the railcar picked up speed as it plummeted down the hill.

People were tossed in all directions, and the sounds of bones breaking and bodies being thrown against hard objects filled the air. Ginger's screams were part of a chorus of voices crying out in fright or in agony. After an endless few moments, the car finally lurched to a stop as the heavy clay-like muck from the river bottom halted the car's forward progress.

After the cacophony of cracking timbers and grinding metal, the sudden silence was deafening as each railcar came to a halt, either in the river or in the mud alongside it. Ginger was lodged between two seats and struggled to right herself. Her skirt and petticoats were wrapped around her body. She pulled herself upright, with David's help, and realized she was standing in the river. Glass from the shattered windows lay at her feet. All around her, people were struggling to upright themselves, screaming for their loved ones or lying about the car in pain.

"Papa, where are you?"

"I'm over here, Ginger. My arm is stuck in the railing. Where's the lieutenant?"

"Right here, sir. Let me help you free your arm."

Ginger and David crept slowly over seats, making their way to George's side. They gently removed his arm from the space between the railing and the seat back. Ginger noticed immediately the bones of his lower arm protruded at an odd angle.

"It looks like your arm is broken, Papa."

She wrapped his good arm around her shoulder and helped him to his feet.

"I'll try to find a way out," David said.

Ginger watched David pick his way down the side of the car, which now acted as a floor. The windows were broken, and the railcar was filled with muck from the river bottom. David reached the door at the end of the car, now horizontal instead of vertical, and pushed against it. Another man helped David force the door open. Under their combined weight, the door gave way, and the rain pelted passengers as they began a hasty exit from the car to the relative safety of the riverbank.

Together, George and Ginger made their way through the treacherous broken glass to the open door where David was assisting the other passengers out of the car.

Ginger handed her father off to David, who helped him through the opening. When it was Ginger's turn, he held her arm tightly. "Are you injured?"

"No, just some bumps and bruises. I think all my petticoats buffeted me from the worst of the fall."

"Good, because my men and I are going to need your help. I must apologize for giving orders. Are you sensitive to the sight of blood?"

Ginger shook her head.

"Once we get these people to shore, we'll turn them over to you for medical treatment. Bandage them up as best you can, and apply tourniquets. We'll move on to the other cars and free the rest of the passengers. We'll just keep sending people to you on shore, okay?"

"But I must find Basil and Mr. Gray!"

"My men and I will see to the recovery operations. You're too small to be of much help removing timbers. You're much more valuable on shore, assisting the wounded. Don't worry, Miss Fitzpatrick, I'll get your brother and your friend out of this mess. It just may take some time."

She was tempted to argue with him, but decided the man made sense. There was probably little she could do to free the passengers who were buried under the bridge structure. She could better serve as a nurse. She was fortunate she had met Dr. Elizabeth Blackwell last spring and learned her nursing techniques. Back then, it was just for a lark, something to do to give her mother fits of apoplexy. Ginger never thought she'd have to use any of what she had learned. But she was grateful for even the little bit of knowledge she had gleaned from the female doctor. Now was the time for the survivors to pull together as one. She nodded to the lieutenant and steeled herself for a long afternoon. What had been such a gay time moments before had turned into a nightmare, worse than anything she could ever have imagined.

Shrieks of pain mixed with breaking glass as other survivors worked to free themselves from the wreckage. The soldiers from the last car—the only one still remaining on the track—came streaming down the embankment to carry the dead and wounded to the river's bank. Ginger helped passengers from her car to the edge of the river. Her father was one of the last to leave the water, having helped everyone else from their car first, and she embraced him.

"We need to get your arm in a splint, Papa."

"Yes, I'm pretty bad off, but I'll live, unlike some of the others."

Together they surveyed the wreckage, as the full enormity of the disaster began to sink in. The railroad cars that, mere minutes before, had been rolling onto the bridge now lay on the floor of the riverbed, covered by heavy wooden timbers from the bridge structure. Under the piles of rubble, people screamed for help. Somewhere in the mess were Basil and Charles Gray.

Ginger allowed herself to shed some tears, which went unnoticed as the unrelenting rain pelted her. She led her father to the bank of the river. Her hair, which had been so carefully coiffed just this morning, now fell around her face in a muddy, sodden mess. Shoving it back from her eyes, she searched the riverbank for a few sticks.

"Here, Papa, sit. I'm going to fix you up." She lifted her skirt and yanked on one of her petticoats, ripping it into strips, and fashioned a splint for her father's arm.

George stifled a scream of pain as she repositioned the broken bone, placed a stick of wood on each side of his arm, and wrapped it all together into a crude splint. His face took on an ashen sheen as he sat on the bank, with rain pelting him.

"I know that was painful, Papa. Your face is so pale." She brushed her hand over his forehead, wiping off the beads of sweat.

"I'll be all right now, Daughter, thank you. Go look for Basil and Mr. Gray. They were in one of the front cars that plunged headlong into the river."

"The lieutenant is trying to get to them, Papa. His men are working to free everyone else. He's sending the people to me, as they get clear of the wreckage, so I can take care of their wounds. He will find them."

She tried to put on a brave face in front of her father as she surveyed the damage to the cars that had tumbled from the bridge. They were twisted and distorted, crunched together as if thrown into a blacksmith's hot furnace. Ginger doubted the outcome would be good for either her brother or her father's best friend.

She ran from one dazed person to another as they came to shore, and ripped apart petticoats to use as bandages. Soon, pieces of her expensive undergarments adorned the heads, arms, and legs of the injured, who sat or lay on the bank of the river, moaning in pain or staring blankly in shock and horror.

One of the soldiers handed her a young boy, and she laid him on the slimy muck beside the river. His eyes were glazed in shock. Ginger ran her hands lightly down the boy's frame, checking for fractures. He winced when she touched his ribcage.

"Does your stomach hurt?"

The boy nodded. "Where's my mother?"

"Were you together?"

The boy again nodded. "I tried to wake her up, but her eyes were closed and she wouldn't open them. Will you try to find her?"

"As soon as I take care of you. What's your name?"

"Daniel." He closed his eyes as a wave of pain overtook his little body.

"Well, Daniel. I'll get your cuts bandaged up and you'll be good as new. The soldiers will work on getting your mother to shore."

Ginger could guess Daniel's mother was one of the lifeless bodies being laid out on the riverbank, but she could not bring herself to tell this small boy he had lost her. He was in a bad way himself. She guessed he had internal injuries of some kind, and all the bandages in the world weren't going to help him.

"You know, Daniel, I have a little sister who's about your age. She likes to play with dolls. What toys do you like?" She hoped her idle talk would take the boy's mind from his pain.

Daniel tried to follow her gentle conversation and answered, "I like trains." He grimaced again as the pain rolled over him. His eyes opened suddenly and he looked to the skies, which still pelted rain on his small body. "Mama, wait for me," he cried out and raised his hand in the air. "I'm coming."

Ginger wrapped his little hand in hers. "Your mama has you now, Daniel."

She watched as the light in his eyes faded to nothingness. Gulping back her tears as she put her hand over his face, she closed his eyes and shielded them momentarily from the relentless rain. She kissed his wet cheek.

All afternoon, the rain continued to lash them. The air was filled with the sounds of soldiers barking out orders, mixed with the cries of the injured, and the heart-wrenching sobs of the living whose loved ones had perished in the wreck.

Chapter Thirty-Three

Joseph watched as the horse and rider raced through the torrential rain toward the ranch house, as if they were being chased by a band of soldiers. He suspected the rider was bringing bad news. As the horse drew closer, he recognized his brother, Raoul, who had been in Canada with his grandfather, learning the ways of the Ojibwa. Joseph was surprised to see him.

Raoul tugged on the horse's reins and stopped, then slid off its bare back, landing near Joseph. Raoul clamped his brother on the shoulder, and blurted out, "I am not too late, then. You are still here."

Joseph placed his hand on his brother's shoulder, too, in a manly hug.

"Too late for what? Is Grandfather all right? You have ridden your horse hard. It is not like you to ride an animal to the point of exhaustion."

"Do you know a white woman from the East?"

Joseph flinched at the words. His brother was studying to become the tribe's shaman. He had a gift for seeing into the future, and was trying to harness his God-given talent to help his people navigate in this changing world.

"Let us go inside. You must be hungry," Joseph said. "Then you can tell me of your vision." He called to their younger brother. "Gaston, would you tend to Raoul's horse?"

Raoul accompanied Joseph inside, where he was greeted by his mother and youngest brother, Etienne. As Mary Tall Feather hurried to gather some food for her sons, Joseph sat quietly, waiting. A sense of dread coiled in his insides. He knew Raoul's vision must have been strong for him to leave Canada and hurry home. Finally, he could wait no longer.

"Mother, please leave us. Raoul has had a vision and he needs to tell me about it. He will visit with you later."

After their mother and Etienne left the room, Raoul asked, "So you know this white woman of my vision?"

"Does this woman of which you speak have a small build and brown hair?"

"Yes, except when the sun catches it, then it has a flash of red."

A cold chill ran through Joseph's body, making him shudder. "Yes, I know this woman."

"She is in grave danger."

"Where is she, Raoul?"

"She is riding on one of those steel buggies."

"A train? Are you certain?"

Raoul lifted an eyebrow at his brother. "When have my visions ever been wrong?"

"True enough. But there are train tracks over half of America now, and more are being laid every day, to the West."

"She is with three men, one as young as she is. All of them are injured."

Even though Joseph had honored Basil's request to never see or talk to him again, he was aware of Basil's movements throughout the city. He knew about the Pacific Railroad's celebratory ride and that Basil's father, George Fitzpatrick, and Charles Gray were going to be on that train. Had Ginger decided at the last minute to join them?

"Tell me of the scene."

"It was dark, with much rain. I saw a wide river, and then heard the crack of timbers and the screech of iron against iron as a bridge collapsed. The steel buggy fell into the river below, like it was a toy."

"The bridge over the wide river is on the Gasconade. It is the route the Pacific Railroad is taking right now." Joseph stood up, as his insides turned icy cold. "Come, Raoul, let us gather our brothers and some equipment. I fear something terrible has happened aboard the train. We must go to her."

Although they assembled what they needed quickly, Joseph felt as if centuries had passed before they were on the road to town. Soon they were joined by others who had just gotten word of the disaster. Soldiers had ridden into town with the news, and men were gathering at the railroad platform. One of them called out as the Lafontaine brothers appeared.

"It's good you've come to town, boys. We were just about to send someone out to your ranch to get you to join us. You've saved us some valuable time, and we can use all the extra time we can get. We need your strength to help free the passengers from the train. Climb aboard."

They all boarded a waiting train and headed out on the same rails the celebratory train had taken, toward the catastrophe awaiting them. Raoul and Joseph sat together on the train.

Raoul asked his older brother, "How do you know this woman?"

"She is Basil Fitzpatrick's sister. We met last summer when I went to New York with him."

"And this woman? She is your woman?"

"Yes."

"You lust for a white woman?" Raoul's lip curled in disgust.

"I have no choice in the matter. You are not the only one who has dreams foretelling the future, my little brother. I dreamt of her many years ago, and asked Grandfather what it meant. He told me it was not yet time for the dream to be revealed, and I would know when it happened. She is the woman from my dreams, and I knew it the moment I first saw her."

Raoul dropped his gaze. "Grandfather must have made the connection. This woman from my dream was the same one as from yours. When I told him of my vision, he said I must ride as fast as I could on the back of the wind to tell you of my dream."

They sat in silence for a few more minutes before Raoul asked, "What happened in New York? Why did you leave her there?"

"It is of no consequence. She is here now. I only hope it is not too late."

Chapter Thirty-Four

Soldiers fanned out in either direction, hurrying to the closest farms with news of the train wreck. The farmers dropped their work and came to the aid of the victims. They offered up the shanties close to the river's bank as temporary shelters for the victims. These rough shacks normally stored the harvest, which was then carried downstream to market, but they now became crude solace from the storm. The soldiers carried the most severely injured persons to these shelters. Women went with them, to perform what rudimentary nursing techniques they could. The dead resembled cordwood as they were laid out beside the river. Nothing more could be done for them. Their families, crying in the rain, kept vigil over their bodies.

Late in the day, one of the large hotels in Hermann, the closest town to the tragedy, offered its facility as a temporary hospital. The offer was gratefully accepted, and, using carts, the soldiers and farmers began moving some of the most severely wounded away from the disaster site. Those who were able to walk began the trek back to Hermann on foot.

Ginger was still at the water's edge, helping care for the victims once they were freed from the wreckage. She thought this day, and the barrage of wounded people, would never come to an end. David and his men worked as efficiently as they could to free the many people trapped beneath the rubble of the bridge, but progress was slow without the proper equipment. Ginger and the people who were only slightly wounded helped the others make it to shore. They bound wounds, set splints for the broken appendages, and comforted those who had lost loved ones.

As tired as she was, Ginger was reluctant to have evening come. Neither Basil nor Mr. Gray had been rescued yet. Blood covered her clothing, as she had spent the afternoon stripping off one petticoat after another to bind the wounds of her fellow passengers. Her petticoats were gone now, and she was tearing strips from her beautiful dress when someone shouted, "Here come the men from St. Louis to help us! Thank the Lord."

She glanced up from the woman she had been bandaging to see a group of thirty or so men streaming over the embankment, carrying axes. Ropes coiled around their bodies. For the second time that day, tears joined the rainwater on her face as she watched these men come to their aid. However, this time her tears were not of sadness, but of joy, as she made out the person leading the charge.

Joseph ran toward her, and swooped her up into his arms. He kissed her with all the ferocity and longing the five intervening months had built up in him. Finally, he set her down. He took a step back and drank in the sight of her, running his hands over the lovely face that haunted his nightly dreams, brushing away the wet hair falling into her eyes.

"I knew you would be here. I was aware that Basil and your father were onboard the train, but not until my brother told me of his vision did I realize you were with them—and in danger." His eyes traveled down her body seeing the blood covering her from head to toe. "Where are you injured? We need to get you to the hospital!"

She placed her hands on each side of his face, and kissed him again. "I'm fine. I only suffered a few bruises. I've been helping the others, patching them up as best I can. Papa's on his way to the hospital in Hermann with a broken arm. But you must help us find Basil and Mr. Gray. They were in one of the front cars, and the soldiers have yet to locate all of those people."

"We are here to rescue them." He turned to leave her side,

and then swiveled back and put his arms around her. "I knew we would meet again, *ma petite*. I am glad you are safe."

She had fashioned a hairband out of a piece of her petticoat to hold her disheveled locks out of her eyes, but some had escaped. With no remaining petticoats, her dress hung limply at her sides. She smiled up at him, running her hands down her soiled dress. "I must look a fright."

He gently brushed the stray hair away from her face. "No, I have never seen a more beautiful sight in my life. You look almost like an Indian with your headband."

She smiled, radiantly. "Well, I do know a word or two of Ojibwa."

"Have no fear. I will find your brother and Mr. Gray."

As Joseph began to stride toward the wreckage, Ginger called out to him. "*Gizahgin!*" She was finally able to declare her love for him, which she had not been able to do at the cabin before he had been wrenched away from her. Her eyes filled with tears again as she gazed at the proud man who had won her heart. His eyes blazed as he nodded once in agreement and tapped his heart with his hand, before going to assist in finding the remainder of the victims. For the first time since the disaster struck, Ginger sensed a ray of hope.

Joseph issued instructions to the men with him in a mixture of English and Ojibwa. The group began to walk toward the submerged railcars. Joseph's brothers, Etienne and Gaston, had been close enough to hear Ginger's declaration and to see Joseph's reaction.

"*Gizahgin?* Joseph?" His brothers stared at him with open mouths.

"Raoul and I will tell you all about her when this nightmare is over. Right now, we have work to do."

Chapter Thirty-Five

Joseph, his brothers, and the rest of the St. Louis men combined their strength and equipment to efficiently remove a mound of splintered timbers from the submerged cars. Joseph observed a few people moving about inside each car, frantically trying to escape. Deciding the best approach was to empty one car at a time, Joseph broke a window and lowered one of the St. Louis men down inside a car, which rested on its side.

The man inside the car began to hoist people up, while Joseph and Gaston pulled passengers out through the broken window. They handed the dazed and injured victims to men who waited in the cold water to carry these victims to the river's edge. Most were severely injured, having sustained the full force of the headlong plunge into the icy river. More than once, Joseph was handed a body of someone who had not survived the fall.

He and his men worked systematically through the wreckage, without exchanging many words. They knew what was necessary and applied themselves as a team to accomplish their mission. The soldiers who had been performing the rescue operations since the train fell from the tracks took a much-needed break as the St. Louis men fell into place.

David and his crew sat beside the river, glad to finally rest. The farmers' wives brought baskets of food, and the hungry grateful men made quick work of their offerings. Ginger helped distribute the food among the soldiers. When she got to David, she sat down, as weary as he was.

"Is your father still here?" he asked.

"No, he is walking to the hospital. We thought it best he

leave and get out of this relentless rain."

"A wise decision. You should get out of the rain, too. You've been working nonstop since this nightmare began."

"As have you. But I won't leave until Basil and Mr. Gray are rescued."

They watched the recovery efforts in progress.

"Those men seem to know exactly what they're doing." David pointed. "Look at the man on top of the wreckage. He only needs one hand to lift people out. What strength!"

Ginger's heart swelled with pride as the lieutenant praised Joseph.

"His name is Joseph. He's extremely strong, yet gentle at the same time."

David gazed at Ginger. In this unguarded moment, she made no attempt to mask her feelings. David knew the answer to his question even before he asked.

"You know him, then?"

"Yes, I know Joseph," she replied softly. Her voice lingered over his name.

"But did you not just arrive from New York? Isn't this your first trip west?"

"Yes, you are correct. I haven't been to St. Louis before. But Joseph is, or at least *was*, a friend of my brother's. They came to New York over the summer to spend some time with my family."

"What happened while he and your brother were in New York?"

Ginger's eyes narrowed. "Why would you automatically assume something happened in New York?"

"Because you just said he *was* a friend of Basil's, implying he is not now. It seems odd that he joined your brother on a journey and now they are not friendly."

Ginger considered what to tell this soldier. Her maid, Colleen, had given her some very good advice a few months back. As Colleen's words of wisdom ran through her head, she knew what to say. The minute Joseph had run down the embankment and swept her off her feet, she acknowledged the forces beyond their control that were responsible for bringing them together again. She was not going to deny her destiny a moment longer.

"Joseph and I fell in love during his visit." She turned to feast her eyes on Joseph, standing tall over the crumpled railcar.

"So why would falling in love with your brother's best friend damage the relationship between your brother and him? You'd think your brother would be thrilled with the match."

Ginger smiled impishly at the man sitting beside her. "It's hard for him to approve of the match. He may never. Because, you see, Joseph has mixed blood. His father is French-Canadian. His mother is one of those pesky Indians you've been trying to eradicate from the face of the West."

She turned back to watch Joseph work, knowing David was going to have a difficult time processing what she had just told him. She knew he had been thinking since they met that he had perhaps found his East Coast wife, and she was sorry to disappoint him. He seemed like a nice enough man. But she had decided to honor the path that had been chosen for her and Joseph years ago, long before they met.

♦◊♦

One after another mangled body was lifted out of the railroad car and handed off to the waiting arms of the St. Louis men. As the tenth person was hoisted up from the second car, Joseph reached out to a familiar hand. He lifted Basil from the mass of twisted metal and passed him off to another man, standing in the river. Another man took over pulling people from the wreckage, as Joseph jumped down from the car and rushed to Basil's side. He helped Basil out of the river.

Joseph and Basil grasped each other's shoulders.

"It's good to see you again, Joseph. You seem to always be saving me."

"I am glad you have survived the fall with nothing more than a few scrapes and bruises, from the looks of it. Ginger will be happy to see you. She has been frantic, waiting for you and Mr. Gray to be rescued."

"Are Ginger and Father okay?"

"I understand your father is on his way to the hospital with a broken arm, but Ginger is still here. She is over on the bank." Joseph motioned to the side of the river where Ginger was busy working on her latest patient. "She has been helping the wounded all afternoon. Are you able to stand on your own?"

"Yes, I'll be okay." He called and waved to his sister. She looked up from the gentleman she was tending to, and waved back at him, with a huge smile on her face.

"I fear, though, for Mr. Gray. He was in the car right behind the coal car when the bridge collapsed."

"Are you certain?" Joseph asked. "We have not been able to get to his car yet."

"It will be a miracle if he's still alive. Let's go try to find him."

A few hours later, Charles Gray was finally pulled from the railcar nearest the engine. Of the seven people who were in the car, he was the only survivor.

"It's good to see you men." Charles Gray tried to smile as he was lifted out of the car.

"Take it easy, Mr. Gray," Basil replied. "We've got you now. How are you feeling?"

"My legs are broken, so I guess I won't be walking out of here," he said, grimacing with pain but still retaining some shreds of his sense of humor. "And I am so cold from the hours spent in the water."

"We'll get you out of this rain and warmed up a bit, but it might be a rough time until you get to the hospital in Hermann.

Father's there already."

"And Ginger? Is she okay?"

"She's fine, and has been acting as the head nurse since the wreck happened. You'd be proud of her."

Basil and Joseph cautiously carried the injured man up the embankment. Although they moved as slowly and smoothly as possible, Mr. Gray gasped and moaned in agony as they climbed the steep hill. By the time they finally placed him in the hospital train, about to depart for Hermann, Charles Gray had passed out from the pain.

The rain continued all through the night and the next day, as Ginger, Basil, Joseph, and David worked together to carry the remaining survivors to safety. The soldiers loaded the dead bodies onto the freight cars the railroad sent out from St. Louis. The severely injured were at last in the hospital hotel in Hermann. The survivors and walking wounded were loaded onto passenger cars for the ride back to Hermann, stunned and overwhelmed by the tragedy. The same people who'd celebrated happily on the way out from St. Louis were now a forlorn and shocked group who couldn't wait to leave the site of the disaster.

Finally, there was no one left to help. In little more than twenty-four hours, the passengers onboard the train had seen their lives upended. The event would go down in history as the worst train disaster in the country. The last of the rescuers boarded the passenger cars with the others.

The moment Ginger took a seat next to Joseph she burst into tears. She no longer needed to put on a brave face to help the others, who were worse off than she was. She finally broke down as she allowed exhaustion and shock to take hold.

The crash of the Pacific Railroad was the most dreadful experience she had ever lived through. Ginger shuddered as the image of the little boy who died in her arms flashed before her eyes. She had never before even seen a dead person, much less watched someone die in her arms. Listening to her patients' stories and the misery they were all facing took its toll as well. She was grateful her family and Mr. Gray were safe, if not yet out of danger. She tucked herself under Joseph's protective arm and cried herself out.

When Joseph realized her tears were coming to an end, he reached into the pocket of his shirt and pulled out a piece of fabric. He handed it to her so she could dry her eyes. She looked at the cloth swatch, and then up at him, with a question in her eyes. He smiled at her.

"When I was tracking you through the forest at the Hamptons, I found a torn piece of cloth from your riding habit hanging on a branch. This is how I knew I was on your trail. I tucked it into my shirt and forgot about it until I was headed home."

"And you've kept it all this time?"

"I keep it in my pocket every day, to feel closer to you. It still smells faintly of your lilac scent."

She reached up to him and wound her fingers through his hair. "So you sensed, too, we were not done with our story?"

"My grandfather knew about you, years ago. I used to dream of lilacs, when I was just coming into my manhood, and it frightened me. I asked him to interpret my vision, because I could make no sense of it. He said it was not yet time for the dream to be realized."

"But it is the time now?"

Joseph picked up her other hand and kissed her knuckles. "Yes, my love. Now is the time."

She shivered as a chill run through her body, which had nothing to do with the horrifying experience she had just lived through or the damp clothing on her body. She sighed in contentment, and leaned back against Joseph's hard body.

Chapter Thirty-Six

At the hotel, Ginger was grateful she could finally bathe and remove the caked-on dried blood, along with the muck and silt of the riverbed, from her body and hair. Although she would have liked to don a new frock and fashion her hair into a chignon, she had none of the accouterments of high society at her disposal.

She had done her best to rinse the worst of the filth from her dress when she finished with the bathwater, but she couldn't help but cringe as she climbed back into the damp and dirty dress and gazed at her reflection in the mirror. Her hair hung almost to her waist, straight and unadorned. She used the scrap of her petticoat, which she had tied around her head earlier, and wound it into a ribbon to hold her hair together at the nape of her neck, then draped it over one shoulder. Her face was scrubbed clean, but free of any type of makeup, and the skirt of her dress hung limply at her sides.

She pinched her cheeks to get some color in her face and sighed. This was not how she wanted to look in front of Joseph, but it would have to suffice. After all, her appearance hadn't seemed to matter to him at the river's edge. Her heart stuttered as she remembered how he had raced down the hill to her and swept her off her feet.

Suddenly, she couldn't wait to find her man again. *Her man!* Colleen, her maid, had been right months earlier when she told Ginger true love would find a way. It was just a shame it took a tragedy of this magnitude to once again bring them together. This time, however, she would not let them be wrenched apart, despite her family's wishes. After all, Colleen also said she needed to make her own happiness. She took one final look in the mirror, and left the room to walk into the rest of her life.

♦◊♦

Joseph paced the large reception lobby as he waited for Ginger to come downstairs. Ever since the morning he exited the cabin in the Hamptons, leaving her in her brother's care, he had tried to cage his heart. He pushed all thoughts of her from his mind during the day. He worked himself to exhaustion on a daily basis, allowing no time to daydream. Then, he dropped like a stone into bed each evening.

That was when his torment truly began. He might manage to control his mind during the day, but his nightly dreams were beyond his reach. As he slept, he relived the encounter with her in the small hunter's cabin in the forest. He replayed the vision of her eyes glazing over as her first-ever orgasm cascaded over her body. His mouth remembered the sweetness of her breast. He awoke in a sweat, with the covers twisted around him, and the scent of lilacs in the air—and he knew he would get no more rest that night. The next day, he worked himself even harder, praying for one night of peaceful sleep with no tormented dreams. But it hadn't happened. For five months, his sleep had been fitful.

He traveled to Canada to see his grandfather and to ask the wise elder what his most recent dreams meant. His grandfather told him he was not yet done with the woman or her family. So Joseph knew he would see her again, somehow and some way.

His heart had nearly burst from his chest when he first caught sight of her tending to the wounded at the side of the river. She was even more beautiful than he remembered, and when she called out to him, "*Gizahgin*," the Ojibwa word he'd used in the cabin to tell her of his love for her, his heart leaped out of the cage he had put it in. He knew he wanted to spend the remainder of his life with her. Now, all he had to do was to convince her family.

But first, he wanted to see his woman again.

He looked up the long staircase as Ginger bounded down them and into his arms. He leaned down and kissed her again, reveling in his right to do so. Then, he broke the kiss and held her out at arm's length.

"You are truly beautiful, my beloved."

"No, I'm not. I have no makeup on, my hair is a mess, and my dress is still wet and muddy. All my petticoats are gone."

Joseph turned her gently to observe one side of her, and then the other. "I must say, I prefer you without the petticoats. I can see your lovely hips now." To prove his point, he ran one of his large hands over the swell of her hip.

Ginger's laugh tinkled in the air as she moved closer to him. She wrapped her fingers into his long, dark hair and brought his face down to her level for a long and passionate kiss.

Joseph broke from the kiss long enough to whisper, "When we get back to St. Louis, we will marry."

Ginger broke out in goose bumps at his proposal, her heart doing flip-flops. "As you wish, Joseph. *Gizahgin.*" She stood on her tiptoes and kissed him again. As the kiss ended, she smiled up at him. "Do you suppose we can find anything to eat in this hotel? I'm famished!"

Chapter Thirty-Seven

The following morning, Ginger, Joseph, and Basil boarded the passenger train with the others for the trip back to St. Louis. Charles Gray lay in one of the hospital cars at the front of the train and George Fitzpatrick decided to ride there as well, to keep him company. The railcars were all linked together for the long journey back to St. Louis. However, seventeen miles east of Hermann the train stopped.

"What is it now?" Basil asked, craning his neck out the window.

"It seems we have stopped at the Boeuf Creek overpass. The creek must be flooded from all the rain," Joseph said as they exited the train.

Together, the three of them, along with Joseph's brothers, walked to the bridge to take a look. The creek was no longer a gentle little stream of water, but an angry, roiling rush of water slamming into the wooden trestle bridge. Trees floated in the raging swirl, and were stacked up against the bridge pilings, making the bridge unsafe for the long train to pass over.

With the Gasconade tragedy still fresh in their minds, the railroad engineers weren't taking any chances. They ordered another train to be brought from St. Louis and placed in position on the east side of the bridge over the Boeuf.

The railroad officials went from one car to another with their update. "Okay, folks, it'll be a while longer before we can get you back to the city. We're sorry for the delay, but we have decided it's best to be safe. Sit back and relax. We'll get you out of here as soon as we can. We expect it'll take a couple of hours for the train to arrive."

As Basil again took his seat in the passenger car, he gazed at Ginger and Joseph, who had not left each other since the Gasconade River disaster site. He noticed how gently they touched each other, as if afraid they might be separated again if they didn't hold onto each other.

Ginger caught his look. "Not this time, Basil. I won't listen to you, or obey you."

His gaze flickered from Ginger to Joseph, and he read determination in the tall man's eyes, as well.

"You realize your life with Joseph will not be an easy one, do you not?" Basil reminded his sister.

"I'm well aware, Basil. I may not have grown up on the frontier like Joseph did, but I can tell how hard it is to make a living here. I think I can help the Lafontaines turn a better profit on their ranch. I've been reading everything I can find on raising horses since I met Joseph, and I have some ideas about how to get a bigger profit margin per horse than he's getting now. Plus, I think he can make a lot of money supplying horses to the Cavalry division of the Army. Heaven knows they can use better quality horses than they currently provide their men. I have lots of plans for us."

Basil grinned as he turned to Joseph. "Maybe you're the one I should be warning, not her."

"We will be fine, if we can ever get out of this mess."

"Basil, does this mean you are finally going to accept the fact that Joseph and I belong together? Without a fight or without banishing him from my sight?"

Basil threw his hands into the air. "Certainly, no man wants his sister to pick a hard road for herself. Life and marriage are difficult enough without asking for more hardship. Certain elements of society will ostracize you because you have dared to marry an Indian. Your children will face ridicule and rejection because of their small amount of Indian blood."

Ginger grew pale, but Basil continued. "I've seen it happen, to Joseph, while I've been in his company. But, after watching the two of you together, I can see you are truly in love and not just toying with each other's affections, as I had thought. If anyone can make a go of it when the deck is stacked against them, I'd put my money on you."

"Do you think Papa will approve?"

"I don't know. He was never really comfortable with the ruse Mother perpetuated to explain Joseph's appearance in our midst. I think he breathed a sigh of relief the day Joseph left the Hamptons. But he did say one thing on this trip you might be able to use to help convince him."

"Really? Whatever did Papa say?'

"He told Charles Gray you needed a strong man to walk beside you through life, partially in order to keep up with you. And there is no one stronger, in my mind, than Joseph."

Ginger touched Joseph's face. "He'll be able to keep up with me."

Joseph took her hand in his and grazed her knuckles with his mouth while staring deeply into her eyes, tenderly expressing his love for her.

"So if Father gives this union his blessing, so will I," said Basil.

"He will. I'm sure of it. And thank you, Basil, for finally accepting that Joseph and I belong together."

Basil sighed and looked out the window at the swirling mess of Boeuf Creek, his thoughts resembling the torrent of water. Ginger was choosing a most difficult path for her life, a choice totally foreign to her. It wasn't just the public ridicule he feared. It was the hard life of a frontier woman. He'd seen the women in town, worn and defeated by the harsh reality of daily life, and the worry that comes with having too many mouths to feed. Those women's lives were as rough as their hands.

Ginger's life had been one of indulgence up to this time. He was certain Joseph would do all he could to care for her every need. However, there was only so much a man could do. Childbirth was a woman's lot, and Basil had heard of far too many instances of women dying in labor here on the edge of the wilderness.

The hard, unrelenting tasks of daily life and giving birth to children were the two most prevalent reasons for early death among women on the frontier. He hoped Ginger was up to the life she had chosen for herself. Silently, he hoped their father could still talk some sense into her. *She's always valued what Father had to say before. Maybe he can convince her one more time.*

Chapter Thirty-Eight

Later in the day, the new train arrived from St. Louis. While it was being positioned to take on passengers, Ginger and Basil looked in on Charles Gray and their father in the hospital cars.

George sat next to Charles, whose broken legs were only splinted, because rude bindings were the best that could be done until they returned to St. Louis. They broke off their conversation when the two young people joined them. Ginger caught the moan and the wince of pain crossing Mr. Gray's face, even though he was fighting to hold them back. She noticed how his ashen face resembled his name.

"What's happening with the train, Basil? Charles needs to see a competent doctor as soon as possible."

"The bridge ahead is taking a lot of punishment from the waters below. I think the engineers want to lighten the load as we go across the bridge, so those who can walk across will do so first. The hospital cars will come across afterwards. They'll push one car over at a time, so as not to put undue strain on the bridge, until all the cars are safely on the other side. Then, we'll finally all be able to get back to town."

George smiled. "You know, when this trip began, I thought St. Louis was a rugged border town, with few of the embellishments of New York. Now, I think it's got so much refined luxury I can't wait to get back there!"

"Thinking of moving? Soon enough we'll be there," Basil replied.

George asked, "Where's your young man, Ginger?"

"You mean Joseph?"

"No, I was talking about David, the lieutenant. Is Joseph

here, too?"

"He came yesterday afternoon, with the St. Louis men. He helped to free Basil and Mr. Gray from the wreckage."

"And did a damn fine job of it, I must say," Charles Gray muttered through his clenched teeth. "I watched him leading the men as they discussed the best way to get me out of the car. I've never seen a man with such composure and dignity."

George nodded slightly as he assessed this new situation. "I'll admit he has strength and dignity. But I had hoped never to see him again."

"Isn't this the same man who found Ginger in the woods at the Hamptons and saved her life?" Charles asked. "And who saved Basil from being beaten to death on his first night in St. Louis?"

George, Basil and Ginger nodded.

"So, he's saved Basil, Ginger, and now me, has he?"

Again, they nodded.

"Well, I can see why you'd want to avoid him, then," Charles replied with a heavy dose of irony. "Are you worried you might be next?"

George glared at Charles. "Stay out of this, my friend. You don't know the whole story." He turned his gaze back to Ginger. "So what's happened to your young man, David?"

Ginger sighed. "The lieutenant was never my 'young man,' Papa. We just had a few minutes of pleasant conversation before the nightmare began. But, to answer your question, he has rejoined his regiment and they're doing what they can to help everyone get back to St. Louis. We're all about to walk across the bridge. Then, you'll come over on the railcar. We'll see you on the other side, okay?" Ginger smiled at the two gentlemen and kissed her father.

Once outside, Ginger, Basil, Joseph, and his brothers huddled with the rest of the able-bodied passengers as they listened to the railroad officials. "We need the strongest men to stay behind until we get the hospital cars across. We will push them manually over the bridge one at a time. Women and children will cross the bridge first, then the men. Let's get started."

Ginger looked at Joseph. "Even though I swore we would never be separated again, it seems we will be one last time. You are needed on this side to help the hospital cars get across. I'll walk over by myself."

He smiled at her. "Basil will go across as soon as the women and children are over. My youngest brother, Etienne, will accompany you, though. He is only sixteen, even though he thinks he is a man. I will see to it he takes care of you until I can cross."

The first group of women and children picked their way slowly across the wooden bridge. Joseph watched with some trepidation as huge tree branches, carried downstream by the raging waters, continued to slam into the structure. Timbers creaked above the sound of the rushing water, and Joseph watched as the bridge swayed slightly.

Soon enough, it was Ginger and Etienne's turn to cross. Joseph pulled his brother aside for last-minute instructions.

"I want you to take Ginger's hand and run across the bridge. Get across as fast as you can, but do not leave her side. I think the bridge is about to fall apart."

Etienne studied the structure, and then said to Joseph, "Perhaps we should not cross it at all? I have no desire to fall into the river."

"Just get to the other side as fast as you can. It should take no more than a minute to cross if you run."

He then moved to Ginger's side, and took her into his arms. As they kissed, he whispered in her ear. "My brother is afraid of heights, so I would appreciate it if you would make a game of this and challenge him to see who can get across the bridge the fastest. It will take his mind off the height."

Ginger nodded solemnly. "I will make certain he does not know I'm aware of his fear. I'll be back in your arms soon, my love."

Etienne took Ginger's hand. The two brothers nodded to each other before Etienne led Ginger to the edge of the bridge. After a moment's conversation, they took off, sprinting across the span quickly to the other side. Joseph breathed easier, knowing his beloved and his brother were safe.

Basil crossed soon after Ginger, along with the rest of the passengers. Then, Joseph helped muscle the first hospital car into position on the rails. The front end of the car touched the entrance to the bridge. The railroad engineer was about to give the command to begin pushing when the bridge shuddered mightily as a huge tree slammed into it.

Passengers on both sides of the river gasped and stared in horror as the bridge collapsed in a matter of seconds. The men shoved the hospital car away from the brink, and stood helplessly, watching the timbers from the bridge get swallowed up in the mighty waters below.

Chapter Thirty-Nine

Ginger, Etienne, and Basil stared with dismay and shock at the chasm where the bridge they had just crossed mere minutes earlier had been.

"Good God, we nearly had the Gasconade disaster all over again," Basil declared, shaking his head. "If the hospital train had been a few feet farther out, it would have tumbled into the mess below. And you know the passengers would not have survived a second time."

"But now Joseph, Papa, and Mr. Gray are stranded! However will they ever get across this divide?"

Etienne smiled at the pair of city folks. "I expect they will get across the way my people have for centuries. Long before the railroads, we used the river to get from one place to the next. There is still a ferry running from the town of New Haven. The train will head back there and ferry everyone across to the town of Washington."

"So, should we go to Washington and wait for them?" Ginger asked, anxiously.

Basil replied. "I think what we need to do is head to St. Louis and the telegraph office. You know Mother will be frantic with worry—I'm sure word of this wreck has already filtered back to New York. Let's send her a message and ask her and Mrs. Gray to come here."

"But I want to stay close to Papa and Joseph!"

"Joseph will watch over your father and the other gentleman," Etienne said proudly.

Basil replied, "True enough. It's best we go to St. Louis directly, and send a reassuring telegram to Mother."

Ginger let out a frustrated sigh. "Yes, you do make sense.

Let's get onboard this train and return to town."

The ride back to St. Louis was finally accomplished without further excitement. After they pulled into the station at St. Louis, Ginger and Basil headed to the telegraph office.

"How does this sound? 'Survived the Gasconade wreck STOP George broken arm STOP Charles broken legs pneumonia STOP Ginger Basil fine STOP Please come STOP.' "

"Send it on, Bas. It sounds all right. I wish the news were better, especially for Mrs. Gray, but considering how much worse it could be, I think we should be counting our blessings."

"If Mother and Mrs. Gray can leave on the next train, they should arrive in St. Louis at about the same time the hospital train comes in."

"You think it will take three days for them to finish the trip?"

"Well, they must wait for the waters to recede a bit before attempting to cross the river by ferry. Then, everyone needs to be carried from the train to the ferry, and then carried from the ferry to the new train in Washington, once they get to the other side. I imagine it will take a number of days to bring everyone safely here."

"What a nightmare this trip has become," Ginger said. "The only saving grace is Joseph and I are together again."

♦◊♦

The train, loaded with the seriously injured and dead from the Gasconade disaster, was shuttled back to New Haven for the water crossing. Joseph entered the car containing George and Charles.

"Mr. Fitzpatrick, Mr. Gray," he nodded to them. "It is good to see you again, although I wish the circumstances were different."

"Thank you, Joseph, for all you've done to save the lives of the people who were trapped in those cars under all the bridge timbers. I'll be forever grateful," Mr. Gray said as he shook Joseph's hand.

"Had the situation been reversed, I have no doubt you would have done the same. Mr. Fitzpatrick, may we talk privately?"

Charles and George exchanged a glance, then George stood and followed Joseph to a quiet corner of the car. Both men sat.

"I am grateful to you as well, Joseph," George began the conversation. "Not only did you pull my son and my best friend from the wreckage yesterday, but I never was able to properly thank you for finding Ginger in the woods in the Hamptons. I will be eternally thankful. She is my dear, precious child."

"She is a child no longer, Mr. Fitzpatrick, but a lovely, vibrant woman, and I love her as much as you do."

George fidgeted in his seat. "But you must know it's for the best if you do not have her."

"I do not believe Ginger thinks so. Nor do I. I would like to ask for your blessing on our union."

"You know, I never approved of you being among our family this past summer. After Basil pulled his stunt at the Cotillion, it kind of tipped our hand, and we had to come up with a reasonable explanation for why you were among us. I thought Charlotte came up with a fairly plausible idea on the spur of the moment. But I knew all along we were playing with fire. I just didn't realize how close to my family the blaze would come."

"I am in agreement with you about Basil. I thought from the beginning my being in New York was a bad idea. He compounded the problem by accepting the challenge of the horserace on my behalf. It was a foolish idea, nearly resulting in Ginger's death."

"Basil's crazy idea of bringing you east has had much more serious and long-lasting ramifications than a stupid horserace. Ginger has never really elaborated on the time she spent with you in the hunter's cabin, but I assume something transpired between the two of you. My darling, charming daughter has been a shell of her former self since then."

George stared at the floor for a moment. When he looked back up at Joseph, he had tears in his eyes. "You should have seen the change in her from the minute she was offered this chance to come to St. Louis. She was once again the familiar, lovable Ginger we all adore. Just knowing she was going to be in the town where you lived brought my child back to life."

"And why does that bring tears to your eyes? I should think you would be pleased."

"She's a young woman who has never known anything but New York and the coddled life I've been able to provide her. She has only a rosy picture in her head of what living with you would be like. But you have to know her fantasy does not come anywhere close to the harsh reality of life on the frontier. I'm afraid she's made up her mind, so it is up to you to set her straight."

"You mean, you are asking me to misrepresent my feelings for her? To tell her I no longer love her?"

"If telling her a lie is what it takes, man, please, I'm begging you."

Joseph shifted in his seat as he pondered George's plea. His steely gaze pierced the man. "I am sorry, Mr. Fitzpatrick. I cannot honor your request. Years ago, I had a reoccurring dream, which my grandfather told me I would understand when the time was right. I now realize the dream foretold of meeting Ginger. The gods knew we were meant to be together and I cannot turn my back on our destiny. If we had not met each other in New York, we would have when she claimed her prize of a trip here to St. Louis when the season was done."

"You're trying to tell me this entire charade we put on all summer was *supposed* to happen? Unbelievable."

Joseph locked eyes with George. "However you wish to explain it. But it was not a random act, and my feelings for Ginger were beyond my control from the first moment I saw her. As were hers for me. I know of your objections, which was why I tried to deny our feelings for most of the summer. And why I offered no protest when I was asked to leave."

"But yet, here we are. In the middle of the biggest disaster the Pacific Railroad has ever experienced, and you and Ginger have found each other again."

"Yes."

In the heavy silence that followed, the two men sat for some time, each lost in his own thoughts. Joseph was the first to speak.

"I am well aware of the difficulties Ginger will face when she becomes my wife. I have encountered ridicule my entire life because of my background. But my Indian heritage is something I am very proud of and I will not deny it, as you and your family tried to do all summer. I will teach Ginger and our children, if we are fortunate enough to have them, about the Ojibwa people and their way of life."

"But it's not just your Indian blood, Joseph. Surely, you know Ginger is used to having a maid, a housekeeper, a cook..."

"Yet she is a strong, vital woman, fully capable of taking care of herself and others. Did you not see her at the disaster site? She worked tirelessly, bandaging up people as they came ashore, consoling those whose loved ones had perished, calming the children."

"Yes, I'll admit, she was the reassuring, rational one, from the moment we took our dive down the slope in the car. Thank the Lord she was there."

"Or the gods."

George turned to gaze out the window. After several minutes, he sighed heavily and looked back at Joseph, who was waiting and watching quietly.

"Of all my girls, I think Ginger is the most capable of taking care of herself. There must be something to this 'predestined' idea of which you speak. We could have come into town, taken a little train ride, and gone home without running into you. Instead, we have a disaster of epic proportions, resulting in you and Ginger finding each other again."

"The circumstances are unfortunate, but the outcome would have been the same one way or another. I believed it the day I left New York. Otherwise, I never would have gone."

"So you're here to ask for my blessing on your union?"

"We would like to marry while you are still in St. Louis, so you can be in attendance. But whether you bless the union or not, Ginger will not be returning to New York."

"How can you be so confident in this matter?"

"Because I know we are meant to be together."

George sighed, accepting the inevitable. "I'd like her mother to be here, too, so she can caution Ginger about what to expect of life on the frontier."

"Do you not think my mother is a better person to ask? She has been raising her family out here for thirty years."

George sighed again. "Yes, I expect so. All right then, Joseph. If you'll consent to wait until Charlotte can arrive from New York, I'll give you my blessing to marry my willful daughter. She will not make life easy for you."

"I will endeavor to make life easy for her, though. You need not worry about her safety. I would lay down my life for her."

"If I had any doubts about your ability to take care of her, I would not agree to your union. I was hoping with this trip Ginger would see what St. Louis was like and compare it unfavorably to New York, but she did just the opposite. She loved every moment of her time in town. I think she'll be fine out here, with you by her side."

"Thank you, sir."

"Just make certain to give me a healthy supply of grandchildren, will you?"

"I will try my best. Will nine suffice?"

"Nine is a nice number."

Chapter Forty

It took several days before everyone finally made it back to St. Louis, and they were once again ensconced in the National Hotel. Charles Gray was able to procure a nurse to stay by his side at all times. His legs were properly splinted and wrapped, and his pneumonia seemed to be lessening, but it would be weeks before he would be able to board the train back to New York.

George Fitzpatrick had the hotel room next to Charles, with Ginger across the hall. During the day they each spent time with Charles, although the medicine given him for pain made him extremely sleepy. During one of his many naps, Ginger knocked on her father's door.

"What a pleasant surprise, Ginger," George said as he opened the door to see his young daughter. He kissed her cheek, and stepped aside so she could enter the room.

"I've been so worried about Mr. Gray I have been forgetting to ask about your broken arm! How are you feeling, Papa?"

He took a seat in the room's only chair, and slumped, cradling his arm. "In comparison to what Charles is dealing with, it's nothing. I'll admit it aches, but I'll be fine, thanks to your ministrations early on. Wherever did you learn to set a broken bone?"

Ginger smiled. "Elizabeth Blackwell taught me last spring. Remember, I took her introductory class in nursing? Of course, I never would have met her if I hadn't been a friend of Amelia Bloomer's. So, you see, there is a real benefit to having me campaign for women's rights."

"Well, you certainly were in the right place at the right time.

You undoubtedly saved some lives, and lessened the pain and suffering of many others."

"But the ones who died while I was trying to help them will haunt my dreams for a long time." She shuddered. "It was most definitely the worst thing I've ever lived through."

"I feel just terrible about all of this. It was my brilliant idea to bring you along on this trip."

Ginger looked at her father in surprise. "But Mr. Gray was the one who suggested it."

"He was doing me a favor. I knew you couldn't say no to a client, but you could say no to your own father."

"But why did you want me to come? You have been so opposed to Joseph from the beginning. Surely, you must have known there was the risk of seeing him again."

"I wasn't really counting on seeing him. After all, Basil said he'd not seen Joseph since he returned. We thought he was in Canada, so I figured it would be safe for you to visit. I thought we could just come to town, you'd see St. Louis was not the ideal town you had built it up to be in your mind, we'd take a little train ride, and leave for home. I just wanted to give you something to look forward to, to cheer you up a little. But because of my harebrained idea, I placed you in danger. Your mother and I could have easily lost you forever. Instead, we are merely losing you to St. Louis."

"What are you getting at, Papa?"

"Did Joseph not ask for your hand in marriage?'

Ginger smiled as she remembered. "It was not so much 'asked' as 'told' but yes, Joseph and I are planning to marry. When did you two find the time to talk?" She reflexively held her breath while waiting for his answer.

"Well, we did have a few days together before we could cross the creek and get back to civilization. He mentioned something about a dream he'd had long ago, about lilacs or some such nonsense, and how it meant he was predestined to meet you and fall in love. I'm not saying I buy into any of it, but it does seem odd that we are all here, and this disaster brought us all back together again, just like last summer."

"Does this mean you approve of the marriage?"

"It's going to be a much harder life for you than you imagine. I'd be lying if I said Joseph was my first choice for you. I'd much rather you marry someone who can provide you with the lifestyle you've enjoyed up until now. You'll end up with hands as rough and callused as his are, and the life here will be brutal at times. But, if anyone is capable of standing by his side and helping to carve out a decent life on this frontier, you can. Of all my daughters, you are the only one I'd consider capable of leaving a life of privilege behind."

Ginger went to her father's side and knelt by his chair. He ran his hand lightly over her hair as tears filled her upturned eyes. "He is a good man, Papa."

"Yes, daughter, I know. And he's got the strength of character you need, for you are one strong lady yourself. Please talk to his mother, though, about what will be expected of you as a frontier wife before the marriage takes place. I want you to know firsthand what you're getting yourself into. And, it's most selfish of me, but I will miss having you beside me every day at the bank."

"I think I will miss our time together at the bank most of all, too."

"Now you know what you have to do, don't you?"

"You mean, convince Mother to accept Joseph as the only man for me?"

George smiled. "It will be no easy task. She's decided nothing less than a military man will suffice."

"Will you not help me at all?"

"I'll step in if needed, but this is something I'd rather the two of you discuss between yourselves. All I've ever wanted is peace and harmony in the family. And I told Joseph I expect no less than nine grandchildren from the pair of you, so the sooner you marry the better, as far as I'm concerned."

Ginger glanced up in amazement at her father. *Well, bless my bloomers.*

◆◇◆

Mary Tall Feather opened the cedar trunk in the bedroom of her family's home and reverently took her wedding dress from storage. It had been carefully wrapped in a piece of cloth. As she removed the cloth from the gown, Ginger's breath escaped in a long sigh.

"It's exquisite, Mary!"

She ran her fingers over the fine beadwork on the white deerskin, and the long fringe on the bottom edge of the skirt. Feathers were attached to the sleeves.

"Here, Ginger. Hold it up to you and let us see if it fits. We are about the same size."

Ginger eagerly held the dress up and let her hands fondle the feathers. "Will I look good in this, Mary? It's so different from anything I've ever worn before."

Mary watched this white woman whom her eldest son had chosen for a wife. It was hoped, when her own father arranged her marriage, that she and her children would assimilate themselves into the white man's culture. *So, this is to be the way,* she guessed. Her father was a wise man, and her son had chosen wisely. Ginger would be a most welcomed daughter.

"You would look lovely in anything you chose to wear on your wedding day. Try this on, and let me see if it needs any adjustment."

As Ginger went behind a screen to change into the dress, she ventured a question. "Were you anxious on the night of your wedding?"

Mary laughed. "I was more frightened than anything. I was just a young woman, only fifteen years old."

"But were you madly in love with Emile?"

Mary remembered the circumstances that led up to her hasty wedding. "No, I had not even met him. My father knew the Indian ways were soon to die out and the best way for his daughter to survive and prosper was to marry into white society. He waited for a capable man to come into his camp, one he thought could provide a decent life for me and give me many fine sons. When he met Emile, he asked if I could accompany him when he left."

Ginger shivered as she stood in the same dress Mary had worn that day, imagining Mary's emotions her first evening as a bride. Her heart went out to the frightened young girl, and was glad she now was a happy woman, with many strong sons and a lovely young daughter.

Ginger came out from behind the screen and the two women looked at each other.

Mary nodded before she declared, "It will do nicely."

Ginger grasped Mary's hands in her own. "Thank you, Mary, for allowing me to wear your gown. I think it is most fitting, because I'm about to begin a new life. Can you share with me some of what your daily life is like here? What challenges will I face? My father is also a wise man, and he told me you are the perfect person to tell me exactly what my new life will be like."

"It will be much hard work. I will help you learn what is expected of you. But, at the end of each day, if you can climb into bed with the man you love, even life on the frontier can be rewarding." Mary smiled at her, and kissed her cheek. "You are a good match for my Joseph."

♦◊♦

An hour later, when they emerged from the room, Ginger was surprised to find Joseph waiting for her. She thought he was out with the horses. But he had been pacing in the living room while she and Mary talked. She went to him and wrapped her arms around him.

"Are you pacing because your mother and I took so long? And that she was telling me all your secrets?"

He smiled at her. "No, *ma petite*. Does my mother's dress fit you?"

"Joseph, it's the most gorgeous dress! I can't wait for the ceremony." She lowered her voice, "For more reasons than being able to wear the dress."

He captured her lips in a light kiss. "Do you remember what I told you the night in the Hamptons cabin?"

"You told me many wonderful things that evening. Which are you referring to?"

"My reply when you asked if I planned to keep you barefoot and pregnant."

Ginger smiled up at him as she remembered his response. "You said you would let me wear moccasins, as I recall."

He released her and retrieved a box from under a chair. "Open it, please."

Inside the box was the most exquisite pair of moccasins she had ever seen. They were light tan in color, highly beaded, and about mid-calf in height. There was a row of fringe around the cuff. She ran her fingers over them, luxuriating in the buttery-soft feel of the hide. Tears filled her eyes.

"Did you make these?"

He nodded. "I started them the day I got home from New York. I knew we would meet again. I remembered how your feet felt when I held them in my hands that night, after I took off your muddy boots, and was able to gauge the size of these moccasins from that memory."

She reached up her hand and lowered his face to meet hers. As they kissed softly, she whispered, "*Gizahgin*, Joseph."

Chapter Forty-One

The next day, Ginger and Basil went to the train station to meet Charlotte Fitzpatrick and Eleanor Gray. As Charlotte alighted from the train, she grabbed both of her children in a bear hug and began to wail.

"You have no idea the torment we went through until we got your telegram. I thought for certain my husband and two of my dear children had met the Grim Reaper, in an icy cold, watery grave. And Eleanor was certain Charles was a dead man."

She pulled a linen handkerchief from her lacy reticule, which hung from her wrist on a drawstring, and began dabbing her eyes.

Ginger grinned at her mother. "Such melodrama, Mother. Although far too many people did lose their lives in an icy, watery grave, and we could easily have been among those less fortunate. Mr. Gray got the worst of it, but he's mending nicely now. Come, I'll take you to see Papa and Mr. Gray." She hugged both Mrs. Gray and her mother.

The two ladies smoothed their modest silk traveling dresses and positioned their bonnets on their curls. Despite the fact they had been traveling for days on the train, they looked like the high society ladies they indeed were in their fashionable dresses of navy and brown. They pulled their matching velvet mantillas around their shoulders to ward off the late November chill and hurried away from the wooden station platform to the luxurious hotel across the street. Basil stayed behind to collect their bags.

Ginger showed Eleanor to her husband's room. Charles was finally able to reduce the amount of pain medicine he was taking, and he remained lucid for longer amounts of time, so Ginger was almost certain Mrs. Gray would find him awake. Charlotte and Ginger continued on to the next room, and George.

Charlotte again burst into tears when she glimpsed her husband with his arm in a sling. George smiled, wrapped his good arm around her, and then kissed her.

"There, there. It's all right now. Everything's all right, now that you're here."

"But you must have been in such pain. It hurts me just to look at your arm now. I can't imagine."

"Well, thanks to Ginger, I received excellent emergency treatment on site. I was her first patient."

Charlotte's head swiveled from George to Ginger. "Whatever are you talking about? Ginger has no medical training."

"It may have gone unnoticed by you, Mother, in all the flurry of the season, but I met Dr. Elizabeth Blackwell in the spring. Remember, I told you Amelia Bloomer and I got to spend time with her?"

"Elizabeth whom, dear?"

"Elizabeth Blackwell, the first female doctor in the United States. I met her when she came to the city last spring. She and her sister plan to set up an infirmary where women can learn medicine, and she tested her theories on a group of us. I never thought I'd be using her techniques quite as much as I did, but it was fortunate I had the training. It certainly came in handy. I'll have to send her a letter when all the dust from this trip settles."

"You mean you worked as a nurse at the site of the crash? You bandaged up people? You saw blood?"

Ginger grinned, remembering how her mother always fainted at the sight of blood. "Yes, Mother. I used up all my petticoats and some of my skirt to bandage people's wounds.

There was rather a lot of blood, and muck and cold and rain. It was a truly awful ordeal and something I prefer not to talk about now. For the time being, could we not relive the terrible ride and go to visit the Grays instead?"

The Fitzpatricks trooped over to Charles's room, because he was still fairly immobile. His eyes were clearer, and the color was returning to his face. Ginger went to him and took his hand.

"Mr. Gray, Mrs. Gray, I'm so sorry I ever got you involved with the railroads," Ginger apologized. "After all, if I hadn't pushed you to invest heavily with them, none of us would have been on the train. And I can only imagine what this accident has done to the price of the Pacific Railroad's stock. Your poor portfolio has probably taken a beating, and it's all my fault."

Charles squeezed her hand slightly, and a ghost of a smile flickered across his face. "Whatever are you talking about, my dear? None of this was your fault. We are all alive, which is a good thing. And while it is an event that we and our offspring will always remember, I don't think anything will dampen the enthusiasm for the railroads for long. They are too vital to the settlement of this grand country. This is the most excitement any of us has ever had. So let us rejoice in our not-so-small accomplishment of getting out of the disaster with our lives, and look forward to returning to New York, where we can tell the tale over and over again at dinner parties."

George's eyes danced as he looked at his best friend. "Well said, Charles. We should begin to plan our return to New York soon."

Ginger kept hold of Mr. Gray's hand as she turned to face her mother. "I'm afraid the dinner parties in New York will have to be held without my presence. I won't be returning with you. I'm staying here in St. Louis."

Ginger registered Charlotte's sharp intake of breath even from where she was standing. She stared at her mother and their eyes flashed.

"Has Basil relented then and allowed you into the bank? Please, dear, tell me a new position at the bank is the only reason why you're going to stay here."

"No, Mother. There's another, and much more important, reason for me to stay behind."

"Have you seen that half...that, uh...Joseph since you've been here?"

"*That Joseph*, as you call him, saved Basil and Mr. Gray from the wreckage of the railcars. You should be bowing before him in thanks and admiration, instead of speaking his name as if it was manure on your shoes!"

"Perhaps we should discuss this in private, rather than in front of the Grays," Charlotte said uncomfortably.

"As you wish, Mother." Ginger turned to Charles and Eleanor Gray. "I hope you have a pleasant evening. I'll see you both tomorrow."

Ginger left the room with a graceful step, her head held high. George and Charlotte hurried after her. In the Fitzpatricks' room, Ginger looked imploringly at her father, who suddenly seemed very interested in his fingernails. Then she turned to face her mother. Charlotte lowered her eyes and fluffed the ruffles of her dress.

"Of course I'm grateful, Ginger, for what Joseph did to help save Basil and Charles. And for finding you in the woods at the Hamptons last July, for that matter. But, being thankful doesn't overcome the fact he is totally unsuitable for you. He's a heathen, you're a Christian; he's a rancher, you're a fashionable socialite, he's a..."

"Enough, Mother! I'm well aware of what you think Joseph is and isn't, and I don't care! I love him. I will never fit into the social circles of New York, as you are well aware. Lord knows you've tried your best to make it happen, but my views of what life should be like for all of us, not just men, are diametrically opposed to society's notion of what duties a woman should have." Her eyes flashed at her mother.

"You also know, if it weren't for Papa's indulgence, I would never have been allowed to work in the bank, or anywhere outside the home. Working is the only way I've been able to tolerate my life these past few years. I am nineteen, and capable of making my own decisions, so this is what I'm going to do. Joseph and I are getting married tomorrow or the next day, at his father's ranch. I'd like you and Papa to stay for the wedding, but only if you could at least pretend to be happy for me during the celebration."

Ginger watched as her mother swallowed hard at the announcement. Charlotte glanced at her defiant daughter, and sighed. "I was so afraid something like this would happen if you came on this trip. This is not what I planned for you."

"My mind is made up, Mother. Can you try to be pleased for me?"

Charlotte brushed the tears from her eyes as she took in Ginger's raised chin and straight posture. She walked over to her and took her daughter's hand, letting out a deep breath. "I know what the look on your face means, and I know there will be no changing your mind. You have been a willful child since you came out of the womb, so I suppose your desire to marry an Indian should not be so surprising. And your father and I can't ever seem to say no to you. I must insist, though, that this union be legal in the eyes of the state. You will need to find, at the very least, a justice of the peace, if not a minister from the Church of England. So, if you can meet my small request and you'd like us to stay for the wedding, we'd be delighted. But first things first. Whatever will you wear for a bridal gown?"

Ginger laughed as her tears began to fall, and she hugged her mother. "Thank you, Mother. Wait until you see my gown. Joseph's mother is letting me use her wedding dress! It's white deerskin with beautiful beading on the front, and the most glorious long fringe everywhere! And I have a new pair of moccasins Joseph made for me. I have so much to go over with you about the ceremony. Let's leave Papa to his pipe and go somewhere where we can talk."

"Oh, dear," Charlotte replied as she was hustled from the room. "My daughter's wedding dress is made from deerskin instead of taffeta and lace. Can you at least pin a piece of lace on your head, in deference to your own culture?"

"We'll see, Mother, we'll see."

George grinned to himself as he filled his pipe with tobacco. He had seen no need to jump into the conversation at all. Ginger had handled Charlotte with great aplomb. He wondered if Eleanor Gray had been listening to their conversation with a water glass held up to the wall between the two rooms. He grinned again. Convention be hanged. His Ginger was getting married!

Chapter Forty-Two

Basil and Joseph watched the wedding guests assemble in the modest front room of Emile Lafontaine's ranch house. It was a small gathering made up of Joseph's parents, three brothers and a sister, Ginger's father, Eleanor Gray, and a handful of friends and family acquaintances. They were awaiting the arrival of Ginger and her mother so the wedding ceremony could commence.

Joseph wore a new shirt made from a deer hide, which had been carefully cured and felt as silky-smooth as butter against his skin. It was heavily fringed and beaded with bright turquoise and red beads creating a mosaic of a bird in flight. It stretched tautly over Joseph's wide shoulders and chest, and was extremely festive in appearance. His leggings were buckskin, too, as were his calf-high moccasins. His long, straight black hair was tied in a queue at the nape of his neck. He looked polished and strong.

Basil looked his friend over from head to toe. "Any nerves, Joseph?"

"None."

"So you are willing to tie yourself down with one woman?"

"When the woman is Ginger, yes, I am."

"How can you be so positive she is the right woman for you? What about your fine speech a few months back when you said you'd have nothing to do with a woman who wanted to make her own way?"

"We have both been guilty of saying stupid things in the past. As I recall the conversation, we were talking about women who wanted no men in their lives. Ginger cannot be included as one of those women, because she is in full agreement that we belong together."

Basil smiled. "I guess you're going to have to build a house now, for the two of you. Will you need a loan from the bank for it?"

"You mean, your bank is again willing to do business with the Lafontaines?"

Basil slapped his old friend on the shoulder. "Hey, the Lafontaines are now family! I've missed you, these last months."

"It was a bad time. I am sorry it took a disaster to bring us back together, but so be it. I am about to marry the only woman I ever could see a future with, so regardless of the circumstances, I am pleased with the outcome."

"You will take good care of her, won't you? She may be headstrong, but she is unschooled in the ways of the West."

Joseph fixed Basil in a hard stare. "You will never need to worry about Ginger. I will protect her with my life, if need be, from any harm, as will my father and brothers. She has charmed them all by now, you know. I think Gaston is considering coming east to New York to look for his bride soon."

Basil groaned in response. "Just make certain he doesn't come for next year's season. Jasmine and Heather are going to be on the loose next spring, trying to find husbands, and I wash my hands of any responsibility for the two of them. If he values his sanity, he won't come anywhere near New York City."

At that moment, the door opened, and Charlotte entered the room, with a hankie already held to her eyes. She had donned a day dress of light green silk with five wide bands of dark-green ribbon layered in graduated steps around the hem. The top of her dress had the same green ribbon set side by side in vertical bands forming a V, and it accentuated the smallness of her waistline, even after giving birth so many times. The sleeves were narrow, constructed of the finest lace over the green silk and cut to encircle her wrists. She had pinned a heavy emerald brooch at the neckline and completed her ensemble by placing a lace bonnet on her head. Its long emerald-green ribbons dangled on either side of her face. To commemorate the occasion and the joining of the two cultures, she had affixed both flowers and a feather on the top of the bonnet.

She walked up to Joseph and patted his heavily embellished deerskin shirt. "You are being given one of my most precious children today, and all I ask is that you look after her well-being as much as her father and I have during her first nineteen years."

Joseph took Charlotte's hand and kissed it. "She will be safe, and treasured, with me."

Charlotte's tears came harder. "Actually, I know we are not giving her to you today. Ginger's heart has been yours since the first night you two danced together, at my suggestion. So I guess I'm responsible for this pairing. Well, me along with your gods who gave you the vision dream those many years ago. It just took me some time to know and accept it."

She stood on her tiptoes and kissed Joseph's cheek. "Welcome to our family."

"*Merci, migwetch*, and thank you, Mrs. Fitzpatrick. And welcome to mine."

Charlotte took her seat beside Basil, and continued to cry as Ginger made her appearance in the doorway, holding her father's good arm. The dress of deerskin fit close to her body, clinging to her supple curves. Its bodice with its modest scooped neckline was embellished with beads of every color. Feathers were attached at the sleeves, which stopped at her elbows. The heavy fringe at the bottom of the dress swayed when she walked. Unencumbered by layers of petticoats, her step was lively and her feet, encased in moccasins, made no sound as she entered the hushed room. Adorning her ginger-colored locks was a handkerchief of the finest lace. She kissed her father's cheek before they began their walk down the short aisle between the chairs.

She gazed at Joseph, who stood at the end of the modest room with his brother Gaston and the justice of the peace. When his eyes locked on hers, it was as if they were the only two people in the room. She tried to slow her pace to keep in time with her father's step, but she practically ran the last few steps, eliciting chuckles from the gathered audience.

She went through the ceremony as if in a dream. Her only real memory of the short service was Joseph's hand firmly holding her own as she answered questions from the justice and repeated her vows to Joseph, while Raoul beat a steady rhythm on a ceremonial tribal drum. When asked if she took this man to be her husband, she declared, "Most definitely, I do!" Then, she kissed him exuberantly and opened her eyes to see his inviting chocolate eyes blaze with desire at her touch. She couldn't wait for their wedding night to begin!

The wedding dinner was an odd mix of traditional Ojibwa and French food, including corn bread and rice, along with a sage-stuffed fried bread, a roasted turkey with an orange-and-maple-syrup glaze, making the skin crispy and savory, glazed beets, and winter squash. Instead of a traditional wedding cake, crepes filled with sweet whipped cream and drizzled with maple syrup were served. Sparkling wine was poured, and glasses were held high, as each father toasted the newlyweds, followed by Basil's and Gaston's tributes.

Joseph and Ginger finally exited the house, amid cheers and laughter. Midnight was tied up and waiting at the porch railing. Joseph's brothers had decked out the horse with colorful ribbons woven into the mane and tail to commemorate the wedding. Joseph untied the horse, picked up his bride, and vaulted onto the horse's bare back. Then he turned Midnight toward the woods surrounding the ranch house, and rode toward a small hunting cabin his mother had decorated for the wedding night.

◆◇◆

As the horse trotted away from the house, Ginger settled into Joseph's arms. Her stomach twitched in anticipation of their upcoming evening. She sighed contentedly and burrowed herself against his strong, broad chest as she rode sidesaddle in front of him. She had been to the ranch in the previous days, but only to meet his parents and family, and to see the immediate grounds of the impressive spread. She spent time in the pens where the horses were kept, petting them and anointing each with a name.

She had already met the brothers, who had helped in the rescue. Gaston was quiet, Raoul was brooding. But Etienne, who had raced with her across the bridge shortly before its collapse, had been a constant companion during the past several days. Ginger was the first cultured woman he had met, and he was constantly showing off his strength and power. Joseph's sister, Elise, was a precious child and everyone's favorite. Mary Tall Feather was soft-spoken and knowledgeable, and his father was an entertaining man who had many of the same traits as her father. She knew Emile and Mary would become her fast friends.

Ginger and Joseph were headed to a part of the ranch she had not seen before, and her eyes widened as she began to realize the entire scope of the Lafontaine family business. She observed field after field being cultivated with food for the many horses they kept, as well as produce for the large family to consume.

"How many acres does your father own?"

"Several hundred now, but we have plans to add more next year. We are talking to the farmer whose property adjoins ours about buying his land, which would enable us to have more crops for our horses. With St. Louis expanding as it is, fairly soon our land will be at the town's doorstep."

"Making it even more valuable." Ginger's analytical mind

began to whirl with possibilities.

"You are not to have any ideas tonight about how to help the family business. Tonight, you are to think only of how to please your husband." As Ginger turned her head, he captured her full lips in a gentle kiss.

"I have been thinking of little else for the past five months, Joseph. I may not know everything about lovemaking yet, but I know there is more to it than what we experienced in the cabin months ago. Where are we headed?"

"We are going to our hunter's cabin in the middle of the woods. My family uses it every fall, when we need to lay in a store of meat for winter."

"We were in a hunter's cabin the night of the horserace, too!"

"Which is why I chose it. I want to finish what we started, without the intrusion of Basil this time."

A shiver of excitement ran down her spine as she thought back to the night five months earlier, when Joseph had declared his love for her—only to be wrenched from her grasp immediately afterwards.

She smiled up at him. "I can't wait. *Gizahgin*, Joseph." She kissed him passionately.

"*Gizahgin, ma petite.* My heart, my *odayin*, is yours and has been since the night of the Cotillion. The minute I touched you as we walked to the dance floor, I knew my life would never be the same."

"You certainly hid your feelings well!" she teased him.

"Not well enough. I could not keep from thinking about you, and wanting you."

She wrapped her arms tightly around his neck. "I want you, too. In every way possible. Are we almost there?"

"It is a bit of a ways into the woods. My mother and Elise were there earlier, getting the cabin ready for us."

Ginger's body hummed in anticipation of the upcoming evening. "Your mother told me about how she and your father got together. Your grandfather sounds like a very wise man. It takes a man with great vision to have known thirty years ago that the Indian ways were changing. But doesn't your grandfather still live in an Ojibwa camp?"

"Yes, but he is on a reservation and cannot stray from the designated 'Indian' area. If my mother had taken another Indian as a partner and had children, we would all be confined to the reservation and would not be free to walk the streets of town or earn a living. It is not like the old days. Grandfather was right, as he is about many things. I will have to tell him I now understand the dream I had many years ago."

"What dream?"

"My dream of lilacs. When I was still a young man, I asked him to interpret the dream for me, and he said it was not time for me to know the answer. But you are the answer, I now know. Ever since I first took your hand to lead you to the dance floor and smelled your lilac scent, I knew meeting you was what the dream was about. And today, our wedding, is the culmination of the dream."

Ginger thought her love for Joseph could not grow any more, but she was wrong. Her heart expanded in her chest as he revealed this part of his past to her. *Let no one say again we were not meant to meet each other.* She was stunned to realize Joseph had dreamed of her years before their actual first encounter. It was as if some force beyond their control had moved them into position so they could find each other.

She turned her face up for another kiss before she snuggled even deeper against his chest. "Isn't your brother, Raoul, living most of the year on the reservation? Why would he turn his back on his white roots? Why would your grandfather allow it, if he knows the Indian way is dying out?"

"Raoul is a very angry young man. He hates it when white people taunt him about his Indian blood, when he is so proud of it. He asked my mother why it was only the Indian blood people found so offensive—he considers his white blood tainted. My father and Raoul had a bitter battle, and Raoul packed up and went to Grandfather's. I imagine he will return to Canada shortly. If anyone can survive being a traditional Indian, it will be Raoul."

"I hope someday Raoul finds what he's searching for. But as for us, any sign of the cabin yet?"

Joseph laughed and urged the horse into a canter.

Chapter Forty-Three

By the time they got to the little cabin, both Joseph and Ginger were in a high state of arousal. Joseph quickly took care of Midnight. His mother and sister had lit and banked a fire earlier to remove the chill from the air. Joseph added wood and the small blaze soon began to crackle as it filled the air with warmth. He wrapped his arms around Ginger and pulled her into an embrace.

His maleness had bumped up against her during the ride from the house, but, as she rubbed against him, he got even harder. She was heady with excitement, and with the knowledge that she was, in her own way, as strong as he was, and able to make his body quiver just as he did hers. She kissed him with all the passion she had stored up for months. Tears began to make their way down her cheeks.

"Why are you crying, *ma petite*? Are you now regretting your decision to turn your back on your old life?"

"No, never. I'm just so happy, I can't contain myself. I love you more than life itself. I never thought this day would come."

He laughed, a deep rumbling sound rising up from his chest. He stood an arm's length away from her. "Let me see if I can remember the sequence of events correctly. The night we were in the cabin, you were unconscious and soaking wet. I wrapped you in a blanket and then I disrobed you."

At his words, a chill of excitement shivered down her body. "Yes, I believe you are correct, although I was not conscious at the time, so my memory could be a bit faulty."

He swooped her into his arms again, and laid her on the bed, pulling a quilt over her. "I should like to disrobe you again, this time while you are awake."

Ginger's body began to shake as his lips caught hers. He pulled her lower lip into his mouth and began teasing it with a gentle rhythm she remembered from their first night.

"Close your eyes, my *oyadin*."

Ginger obeyed, shutting her eyes, while every nerve ending in her body sang in excitement. She shivered again, in anticipation. Joseph slowly removed her moccasins. As he uncovered each foot, he stopped to caress it, rolling his knuckles into the arch of her foot gently. She sighed, and her breath caught in her throat.

His hands moved slowly up her body underneath the covers. He slid the deerskin dress out of his way as he worked his way up, caressing her legs, running a large rough hand lightly over each hip. He gently tugged on her drawers and removed them. His hand moved lightly over the mound of hair between her legs and she shuddered. A moan escaped her lips. Her body flamed with desire, expanding from the core of her being all the way out to her fingertips.

She moved her hands to stroke his body.

"No, *ma petite*," Joseph whispered as he pulled her hands away. "You first."

His hands went back to her body, and he lifted the dress over her head. He kissed her passionately as he unpinned the lace from her hair, and then removed the blanket.

Ginger stared up at him, seeing the ardor in his eyes as he raked his gaze down her body. She boldly looked back at him as his eyes sought hers. "You are beautiful, Joseph."

"As are you, *ma petite*."

Ginger watched his face as his fingers traced the landscape of her cheekbones and fluttered over her eyes. She sensed the tenderness coupled with the fierceness of his need, and her heart filled yet again. He ran his thumb across her generous lower lip and her body quaked in response.

Joseph took her face in his hands and began a leisurely exploration of her mouth with his. She eagerly opened herself to him, and their tongues entwined and rolled against each other. In her nightly dreams of their short time in the cabin in the Hamptons, she'd relived the memory of his mouth on hers. Now, she could truly drink him in for as long as she wanted. She delved her tongue deeper into his mouth, wanting to touch all of him, and knowing they had all the time in the world.

She wove her fingers into his long, silky black hair and lost herself in the sensations he was creating in her. She tilted his head ever so slightly and kissed the beating pulse point she discovered on his neck. His low groan was her reward.

She ran her hands down his chest, still covered with the deerskin shirt. Like at the cabin in the Hamptons, he was still completely clothed and she lay naked in his arms. Vowing silently not to let it happen again, Ginger began to slowly raise his shirt and touched an inch of his dark skin at a time. He lay beside her, his breath catching each time she exposed more of his body to her scrutiny. He put up little resistance, and Ginger smiled as she tugged the shirt over his head.

She sat up and looked at his bare chest. "I've never seen such a fine chest in all my life," she whispered as she ran her hands up and down Joseph's upper body.

"And have you seen many a man's chest, *ma petite*?"

She cast a disapproving eye at him. "You know the answer to the question already. But I have lived with three brothers and my father, all of whom I've had the occasion to see bare-chested at one time or another."

"And you are now qualified as an expert, then?"

"I didn't say I was an expert, for goodness sake. Can't you just accept the compliment and say thank you?"

Joseph's laugh rumbled up from his well-muscled chest. He caught one of her small hands in his and raised it to his lips. "*Merci*, my *oyadin*. So I have a fine chest. Do you see anything else you might like to explore?"

Ginger smiled saucily back at him. "I want to see all of you, sir."

"I think you will tonight."

Joseph growled as he pulled her to him, and the sensation of his naked chest pressing up against her bosom nearly took her breath away. He cupped the silky sides of her breasts in his hands and she closed her eyes. He ran his thumbs across her nipples and her body quivered involuntarily. As he captured the tip of her breast in his mouth, she did quit breathing for a moment. The gentle tug of his lips on her nipple sent waves of desire coursing through her body to the core of her being. She lost herself in the sensation as her need swelled. When he removed his mouth, she let out a whimper of dismay. She opened her eyes and watched as he drank in the sight of her.

She noticed his body quivering in anticipation, too, and she realized his need for her was making his body quake. The powerful thought made her even bolder.

He lay at her side, running his hands up and down her body, raising her temperature to an almost unbearable point. Ginger thought every inch of skin his hands caressed was now branded with his touch. He raised one of her hands to his mouth and kissed the palm. Then, he led the hand to his leggings and breechcloth.

Excited at the invitation, she dipped her hand under the cloth to find Joseph's hard erection. She reached out tentatively and encircled the pulsing shaft. Joseph groaned and pitched on the bed.

"Are you all right? Am I hurting you?"

"No. You are doing just fine." His groans became louder.

He reached for her hand after a few more seconds. "Perhaps you are too good. Let us save that for later. I would like you to undress me fully now."

Ginger got on her knees, shivering with anticipation. She

untied his breechcloth and removed it, watching in wonder as his hard maleness lurched when she freed it. She next removed his moccasins and leggings. When she had divested him of the last of his clothing, she continued to sit on her knees and greedily look at him.

"Have I told you lately you are a beautiful man?"

Joseph's eyes locked on hers, desire burning brightly in them, as he pulled her toward him. He reached between her legs and caressed the soft skin of her inner thighs. She caught her breath as his unexpected touch heated her yet again. She had been so enthralled at looking at him that Joseph had surprised her. She sensed the moisture gathering between her thighs as his hand drew nearer to her core. His hand grazed lightly over her mound of ginger-colored hair, and her body clenched at the brush, knowing somehow there was so much more to come yet tonight. Waves of sensation built in her body, and she wanted the release he had given her in the cabin many months ago. She pushed herself into his hand, begging for fulfillment.

Joseph laughed low in his throat, and his fingers did her bidding. His touch turned from gentle to indulging as he began to glide his fingers over her sweet spot. He nestled the pulsing nub between his fingers and caressed it back and forth. Ginger's ragged breath gave way to gasps as rays of delight shot through her body to all her nerve endings. She moaned, and bit Joseph's shoulder lightly. The feel of her teeth on his skin inflamed his desire. His gentle rhythm became more insistent.

Ginger's eyes glazed over with emotion as she watched Joseph's face. He kept his thumb on her nub as he pressed a long finger to her opening. She gasped as he slid his finger inside her. Her body bucked, and she strained to give more of herself to him. He inserted yet another finger, all the while massaging her sweet spot. She threw her head from one side to the other as she fisted the covers in her lust.

"Open your eyes to me, Ginger, my love. I want to watch you."

As Ginger crested in orgasm, she kept her eyes on Joseph and knew she was finally where she was always meant to be.

They lay beside each other as Ginger's breathing slowly came back to a normal range. Her hands ran over Joseph's body, exploring at leisure all the places previously hidden from her. He kissed her, beginning at her hairline, and left a trail of scorching feather-light kisses down her face and neck. Her blood surged through her veins again as he teased the pulse at her neck into full awareness.

"It is my turn now, *ma petite.*"

"You must show me what to do. You have made me feel wonderful, and I want to know how to make you have these same feelings."

He laughed gently as he turned his attention to her breasts, first cupping each in a large hand and gently kneading them with his knuckles, much like he had her feet. Then, he lowered his mouth and took a nipple into it. She gasped in delight as he began to suckle her tip. So quickly after cresting in orgasm, her body was ready for more of his touch. She rose to meet his eager mouth, and again her heart was seared by this intimate gesture of his lips on her breast.

When he removed his mouth from her breasts, she cried out in dismay. But Joseph lowered himself and kissed the sweet spot between her legs, teasing her into a fitful state of higher arousal than she had ever dreamed. She gasped with shock, then wonder, as he toyed with her and made her tear at the blanket in excitement. She ran her fingers through his long locks as she let herself drift into her arousal.

Joseph moved his hand from her hip to her center and ran a finger around the cleft between her legs. She thought she had experienced all the feelings lovemaking had to offer, and was thrilled by the shockwaves of lust his touch sent coursing through her body. This, *this* was beyond words. She writhed on the bed, unable to do more than moan. Then, he plunged his finger inside her again, and her body lurched in anticipation.

He swung his body on top of hers, and she was surprised to note his erection was still very hard. She looked up at him in wonder.

He smiled at her, and replied to her unanswered question. "Yes, my love, there is more, and this is what lovemaking is all about. He began to tease her to full arousal yet again by rubbing his pulsing erection up through the cleft between her legs. She shivered and reached to touch him as her knees fell open to invite him in.

She ran her hands up his hard, muscular thighs, reveling at the touch of skin against skin. She raised her body to him and kissed him slowly. His hand moved to caress her breast, but she brushed it away.

"No, my love. As you said, this time, it's your pleasure."

She ran her hand slowly up and down his hard shaft as he continued to tease her opening, which was now slick with desire. In spite of the fact she was trying to see to his satisfaction, each time he ran his erection over her nub, she groaned in need, as well.

Ginger listened in delight as her fondling made Joseph's breath become as ragged as hers had been moments ago. She lowered her mouth to his chest and suckled one of his nipples, teasing it to a dark brown pucker. She mimicked what he had done to her a few minutes earlier, and was pleased to hear his quick intake of breath. She moved her hands over his broad chest, marveling in his dark smooth skin.

She returned her attention to his hard erection and smiled as Joseph's breathing quickened as she tightened her hold on him. She began to stroke it up and down, matching the movement Joseph had used on her earlier. His body bucked as her fingers stroked him. She looked into his eyes and witnessed the smoldering embers there. He placed himself over her and slowly immersed the tip of his erection into her. She gasped as this new sensation overtook her.

Joseph moved slowly, embedding himself into her a bit at a time, until he reached her maidenhead. He kissed her face as he whispered, "This may hurt a bit, but just this once, I promise."

"I know. Mother and I talked about it last night. It means I am yours completely once you breach my threshold."

Joseph grinned. "You know you have been mine completely ever since the first night we met. This merely makes it official." He pushed through the small tissue barrier and filled her fully. Their moans and cries of lust filled the cabin and the night air, as they finally became husband and wife.

Chapter Forty-Four

Shards of sunlight streamed into Joseph's eyes, waking him from the soundest sleep he'd had in months. Admittedly, he had not slept long, for he and Ginger could not keep their hands off each other during the night, and their first evening of lovemaking continued well into the early morning hours. They finally fell into an exhausted sleep only when they could no longer keep their eyes open.

He turned on his side to get a better look at the woman who had held his heart for the past seven months, ever since he first spied her in the streets of New York, her hair aflutter around her and her eyes shining with excitement. She was curled up against his body, one arm flung across his broad chest. Even asleep, she looked enchanting. There was no denying the fact his Ginger was a strikingly lovely woman, but her outward beauty was not what had drawn him to her. Rather, it was her wonderful intelligence that he had found irresistible. He was drawn to her playful spirit and her dedication to her causes, too. And her inquisitiveness in the bedroom. She had become quite an accomplished lover last night, and he knew if he lived to be a hundred years old, he could not possibly ever get enough of her.

Joseph was getting hard again, just thinking about her. He wondered how much more quickly he would become fully engorged if he merely touched her. He gently ran his fingers through her hair, brushing it away from her face. She stirred softly, making a small noise, and his shaft responded as he thought it would. He let his hand slip down her body and cup one breast. For a moment, he simply held it in his palm, feeling its weight and softness. Her skin resembled the finest satin in texture. He ran his thumb over her nipple, and was surprised when, even in her sleep, the nipple responded to his touch by peaking and growing hard. He continued to fondle her breast and tease her nipple. Soon enough, he watched Ginger's entire body begin to respond to his touch. She moved languidly under his hand, moaning softly in her sleep, and her torso pushed forward of its own accord to offer him more of her. She opened her eyes and gazed into his dark, stormy ones.

"What a delightful way to wake up," Ginger said with a smile and placed a kiss on his lips. She then kissed each eyelid and each finely chiseled cheek.

"I plan to wake you every morning in this same manner, so get used to it. After all, I did promise your father we would provide him with nine grandchildren. It will be a lot of work to plant my seed in you so many times, but I believe I am up to the task."

Ginger squirmed under his gaze. "Papa told me you and he talked, but gave me none of the details. I'm so glad I was not in the room during that conversation. It's mortifying to think that Papa and Mother know what we are doing."

"My love, they *do* have nine children of their own, you know."

"Well, yes, I know. But to think..." Her skin flushed. "I can only imagine the conversation you had with Papa."

Joseph decided to take her mind off the talk with her father.

"I have two challenges for you this morning, my love." He ran his hand over her hair.

"Only two? I thought life on the frontier was full of challenges," she teased.

"Well, because it is our honeymoon, today there will be only two. Are you ready? First, we need to decide where we will build our home. So I will take you to several places I think are suitable and let you decide."

Ginger's eyes began to sparkle. "I like the sound of this particular challenge. Can we go now?"

She began to rise from the bed, but Joseph reached for her arm and brought her back by his side.

"I have not yet revealed the second challenge. I have four spots on my body which, I have discovered, are very sensitive to your touch, and I challenge you to find them all."

Her eyes took on a gleam. "I like the sound of this challenge even more. It's like a scavenger hunt, almost. Let's see, four areas..."

She eagerly began to explore his body. She moved her hand over his torso and down to his hard shaft, which was pulsing in readiness. She wrapped one hand around it and raised an eyebrow at him.

"Obviously," he choked out a response.

Ginger continued to explore the planes and valleys of his body. She ran her hands down his muscular legs, noting how those muscles twitched in response to her touch. She ran a band of kisses down the front of each leg. When she worked her way around to the back of one knee, Joseph let out an involuntary gasp as his leg jumped. She smiled and glanced up from her ministrations.

"Number Two," she purred.

The back of his other knee didn't elicit the same response, so she continued her explorations, working her way up his body, over his chest. She stopped there to tease his nipples. Although his nipples hardened under her mouth, her touch didn't elicit the strong shudder of delight the first two areas had. She moved up the landscape of his body, exploring his strong jaw line and neck. She watched as his pulse jumped in his neck and ran her tongue over it.

As his body quivered, she whispered, "And we have Number Three."

Joseph was about to explode from her touch. He did have

four locations on his body he wanted her to find, but every place where Ginger placed her hand or her mouth was blazing with desire now. He kept his hands curled at his side, knowing if he touched her he'd have to plow into her immediately—and she did seem to be enjoying the game. He decided to give her a hint of the location of the fourth spot, to hurry things along. He rolled over onto his stomach.

"Ah, the back. Of course," was Ginger's delighted response.

She ran her hands over his massive shoulders, thrilling at the feel of his muscles as they moved under her fingers. She traced every inch of skin, searching for the elusive fourth hot spot. She ran her hands over each hip, noting his well-rounded backside. She ran a finger down the crack between his butt cheeks. She placed a kiss in the hollow between his hips at the base of his spine and was rewarded when his body jolted under her, as his cry of delight filled the air.

"Aha, Number Four!" she cried as Joseph moved suddenly and pinned her underneath him.

"Yes, *ma petite*. Very good. You have found all four locations." He kissed her with all the stored up passion her movements had aroused in him.

She looked up at him with a saucy expression on her face. "So what's my prize for finding all the items on your list?"

"This," Joseph growled, as his hand found its way to her sweet spot and began to torment her nub.

He laced his other hand through her hair and explored her mouth, moving his tongue in and out with the same rhythm he was setting in her lower region. Keeping his thumb pulsing on her nub, he inserted one finger into her, reveling in the soft slickness. He inserted another finger, and a third, and began a gentle in and out motion. He watched as her body bucked under him and she grabbed hold of the bedclothes to hang on. As her orgasm overtook her, he positioned himself over her body and rapidly sought his own release.

Chapter Forty-Five

They mounted Midnight and took off through the woods to the first area Joseph was considering for their house. As they came upon the clearing in the middle of the woods, Ginger gazed delightedly at the small stream at the edge of the opening. She imagined sitting on the porch on a summer's evening and listening to the gurgling sounds as the stream rolled along.

They dismounted, and Joseph held Ginger's hand as they walked along the stream. Her mind pictured wildflowers growing along its banks in the spring, and she could imagine herself with a bucket, getting water for her evening bath before she lay in Joseph's arms. She sighed contentedly.

"This is a picture-perfect spot."

"Do not be so quick to decide, my love. I have two more spots for you to look at."

"But this one is wonderful. Can we not spread out our meal and stay here? Maybe we could even make love by the bank of the creek?"

She pulled his head down for a kiss, which became a long, languorous melding of one body with another. Minutes later, Joseph came up for air and raised his head.

"As tempting as it sounds, it is late November in Missouri. Making love outdoors is probably not the best idea. Plus, I do want you to see all the possibilities before making a final decision. Let us mount up."

Sighing, Ginger wrapped her arms around Joseph's neck as he cradled her in one arm as he leaped onto the horse's back. She grazed his chin with her lips. "Somehow, even getting on a horse's back with you is a sensual experience. Lead on."

She sat astride Midnight, in front of Joseph. Her skirt was pulled up, revealing an ample amount of ankle, but she didn't care. This wasn't New York, and she could not create a scandal today. But she would have to consider different clothing for her life on the frontier. Conventional New York street clothing would no longer suffice. Her mind buzzed with thoughts of how to realign her wardrobe to include more comfortable attire.

As she leaned back against Joseph, a feeling of true contentment came over her. It really mattered little where they placed their home on his father's land, or what she wore. As long as Joseph was with her, she would be happy anywhere and in any type of clothing. She placed her hand on the strong arm encircling her, and luxuriated in the feel of him.

All too quickly, they came to the second spot Joseph had picked. It was also near a creek, but on the wide prairie. Ginger surveyed it from her perch on the horse.

"Don't you think it would get too hot here in summer, with no trees around to shelter it?"

"You are a quick learner, *ma petite*. The advantage to this piece of land is the closeness of the river. But it does get very hot here in the long summer."

They rode to the next location in silence, both of them wrapped in their own thoughts. Ginger closed her eyes, relaxing in the warmth from the sun on her face and the gentle gait of the horse. She was nearly lulled to sleep in Joseph's arms.

"We are home," he said, quietly.

Ginger opened her eyes and her breath left her. She gazed out from their mountaintop location and drank in the view, which extended for miles in each direction. Emile and Mary's house could be seen in the distance, the woods came right to the edge of the clearing, and a gentle breeze blew in from the west across her cheeks.

She looked up at Joseph and asked, "How did you know I would love this place?"

He helped her down from the horse and took her into his arms. "Because our hearts beat as one. This is my favorite spot on the ranch, so I knew it would be yours, as well. There is a water source on the backside of the mountain, and many trees close by from which we can build a home."

"I can picture a big front porch right here." Ginger ran lightly from one edge of the clearing to the other, fanning her arms out to show the dimensions of the porch she was envisioning. "When can we start building?"

"Not until spring, most likely. I can smell snow in the air today. The first of many snows."

"But the sun is out! How can there be snow?" She stopped to sniff the air. "I don't smell a thing."

Joseph laughed as he took her into his arms. "Soon enough, *ma petite*, you will learn the ways of the West. Right now, though, I think I should give you your first kiss on the site of our new home."

He wrapped his arms around Ginger and picked her up off her feet. She wound her legs around his middle as he gave in to the passion he had been feeling all afternoon.

"I have changed my mind, *ma petite*. I think making love out of doors in the end of November is a fine idea."

He untangled her skirt and moved his hand up the inside of her leg, pleased she had not bothered with putting on her infamous bloomers today, and only wore her drawers, which were open to her cleft. His hand grazed over her patch of hair and he growled in delight as her breath became ragged. He moved his breechcloth aside and positioned his ready manhood at her opening. As his mouth sought hers, he cupped her bottom and pulled her onto his hard shaft. Ginger threw her head back as she matched the up and down motion his hands were coaxing from her, and their mutual orgasms surfaced as one.

Chapter Forty-Six

The following day, Ginger, Joseph, Basil, and Eleanor Gray stood on the railroad platform to see Charlotte and George off to New York. The snow Joseph had predicted fell lightly around them, making the streets of St. Louis look clean and crisp. Mrs. Gray was staying on for a few more weeks, until Charles could safely be transported back to the city, but she wanted to be on hand to say goodbye to her friends.

"You'll have to come back once we get our house built, Papa," Ginger declared as they waited for the train to come into the station. "We're going to put it up on top of the mountain overlooking Joseph's parents' home. It's a wonderful site."

Her gaze shifted from her father to Joseph. They shared a smile, each remembering the lovemaking at their new homestead the previous afternoon.

"I hope by next spring we'll have word my second grandchild is on the way, too," Charlotte responded. "After all, Pepper dawdled for three years before she thought to provide me with a grandchild to fawn over. I hope you won't take quite so long, Ginger."

Ginger's color rose and she buried herself in Joseph's chest. As he wrapped a protective arm around her, Ginger said, "Please, Mother."

Charlotte patted her daughter's arm. "I'm just teasing, you know. Take all the time you need. However, I understand Joseph promised your father nine grandchildren, and I know it is no easy task to produce that many."

Ginger was grateful when the platform began to fill with other people waiting to board the train, so her mother would stop this incessant line of conversation. Certain things, she felt, were better left unsaid.

"Miss Fitzpatrick, Mr. Fitzpatrick, how nice to see you again!"

Ginger looked up in confusion. Then she spotted Lieutenant David Whitman approaching them. David shook her father's hand. He looked at the assembled group and smiled at Charlotte.

"Am I to assume this is your lovely wife, Mr. Fitzpatrick?"

Charlotte beamed at the young officer, as George introduced her to David.

Ginger smiled up at him. "What a pleasure to see you again, too, Lieutenant. However, I'm no longer Miss Fitzpatrick, but Mrs. Lafontaine."

David's face flashed momentary disappointment before he took Joseph's hand in his. "Ah, yes, the strong man from St. Louis who helped rescue the train wreck victims. You were quite impressive out there in the river. Congratulations to the both of you. I had a sense this was coming."

Ginger introduced David to Basil and Mrs. Gray before asking, "Are you traveling today, Lieutenant, or seeing someone off?"

"I am traveling back to my post, near Hermann, along with the rest of my men. We have done all we can for everyone who had the misfortune to be on the Pacific train."

Charlotte had caught the look of disappointment on David's face and knew something had transpired between her daughter and this fine young man while they were on the train.

"Oh, you were on the train as well?" Charlotte asked innocently.

"Yes, ma'am. I was in the same car as your husband and daughter when the accident happened. Because we weren't on the bridge when it collapsed, our car rolled down the embankment, and we were fortunate enough to sustain only light injuries."

"So you were able to help everyone else, then?"

"Yes, your daughter and I made a good team. I freed people from the wreckage and she took care of them on the shore."

"I see." Charlotte replied, her mind whirling. Then, she smiled at David.

"Such a pity you won't be joining us as we head east," Charlotte laid her hand on David's arm. "But you must plan to visit New York next spring. I have two daughters coming out then, and I just know they'd love to meet you."

Ginger and Joseph glanced at each other, and smiled.

"That's my mother," Ginger laughed. "She made me go through the season last spring, in the hopes I'd end up married. Now, she's already moving on to the next season and to finding suitable husbands for my sisters, Jasmine and Heather. Watch out, Lieutenant, or you'll become part of the family before you know what's happened."

David tapped his thigh with his fingers as he digested this information. If the next two Fitzpatrick daughters looked anything like Ginger, he would not be opposed to joining their family.

"Issue me an invitation, Mrs. Fitzpatrick, and I'll be there."

Charlotte clapped her hands in delight. Now, she'd have something to occupy her thoughts during the long train ride home.

About the Author

Amazon best-selling author Becky Lower has traveled the United States in search of great settings for her novels. She loves to write about two people finding each other and falling in love amid the backdrop of a great setting, be it in America on a covered wagon headed west or in Regency England. Her Cotillion Ball Series features the nine children from an upscale New York family prior to and during the Civil War. Her first Regency, A Regency Yuletide, received the Crowned Heart and has been nominated for the prestigious RONE award from InD'Tale Magazine. A regular contributor to USA Today's Happy Ever After section, her books have been featured in the column on nine separate occasions. Becky loves to hear from her readers at beckyloweauthor@gmail.com. Visit her website at www.beckyloweauthor.com.

GAMBLING ON FOREVER BY BECKY LOWER

When Elise Lafontaine spies her father's missing saddlebag with its all-important papers slung over the shoulder of a man boarding a riverboat, she follows him, hoping to retrieve the contents. Her plans come to an abrupt halt when she is declined entry to the boat, since she is an unaccompanied female.

From his perch on the top deck, handsome riverboat gambler James Garnett witnesses her denied entry. When she shoots him a look of desperation, how can he resist those deep blue eyes and beautiful face? Of course, he comes to her rescue.

COMING SOON

THE ABOLITIONIST'S SECRET By Becky Lower
Book Two of the Cotillion Ball Series

When shy Heather Fitzpatrick befriends a young slave woman and her child, she stumbles into a world of the Underground Railroad she'd never known existed in New York City.

Made in the USA
Columbia, SC
16 August 2018